Praise for *A Boy's Guide to Outer Space*

"At turns poignant, zany, always fresh and exuberant, *A Boy's Guide to Outer Space* is a bittersweet coming of age story, beautifully told in exquisite prose."

—Linda Lappin, author of *Loving Modigliani: The Afterlife of Jeanne Hébuterne*

"A kaleidoscopic and astronomic depiction of boyhood's metamorphosis into manhood. Selgin's bildungsroman celebrates the mysteries of teenage years from the vantage point of Half, a curious lad who inadvertently befriends a German POW in Connecticut in 1963 while wrestling with the guilt of his disabled brother's tragic fate. Wrought with bottle rockets and rocket ships, *A Boy's Guide to Outer Space* is a dazzling explosion of stars, innocence, and transcendence."

—Nathan Elias, author of *Coil Quake Rift*

"Leopold Napoli IV, known to his friends as 'Half,' is one of the most compelling narrators in modern literature. His narrative of that one extraordinary year of his life has everything: heart, wit, sly humor, tragedy, and a significant if unusual friendship. Selgin is a magnificent storyteller, and he has gifted us a confident, audacious novel delivered in beautiful, miraculous prose."

—Chika Unigwe, author of *The Middle Daughter*

"In his finely crafted novel, Peter Selgin presents a lost world of 1960's small town life with all its constrictions and aspirations. On the threshold of childhood's end, 'Half' Napoli and his coarse pals, the Back Shop Boys, create adventures and myths for themselves in their dying hat factory town. When a foreign-born stranger, 'the Man in Blue,' arrives, Half finds his life and beliefs upended. Selgin skillfully balances the warmth of nostalgia with the disquieting blaze of youthful doubt and guilt. It's a poignant tale, with its share of loss and betrayal, but also a boisterous and humorous one—and, at its core, a meditation on the survival of the spirit."

—Michael Nethercott, author of *The Séance Society* and *The Haunting Ballad*

"In *A Boy's Guide to Outer Space*, Peter Selgin has crafted the touching philosophical tale of a boy's coming of age with masterful eloquence. A world of fading prosperity, the complexities of adolescence, the pain of horrific loss, and the beauty of forbidden friendship—all are woven into a mesmerizing page turner. Selgin's insights into the human condition along with his beautifully drawn characters make him the rival of our literary icons."

—Morgan Howell, author of *The Moon Won't Talk*

"Reminiscent of Alain Fournier's 1913 classic, *Le Grand Meaulnes*, this is a novel for readers who love the drama of mysterious worlds and the spell of enchanting words."

—Alta Ifland, author of *The Wife Who Wasn't*

"'Like all good stories this one starts with an exploding star.' So begins Peter Selgin's terrific new novel *A Boy's Guide to Outer Space*, and this charming, wise book is proof enough of that. The kid living the story daydreams of adventures on the moon and beyond, and lives by his late father's advice to follow his fears. Little does Half know that following his fears will lead to life-changing encounters and irreversible decisions; it's his own world where he finds the unexpected, adventure, and real danger. Ultimately, this insightful book reminds us that inner space is where we need guidance most."

—David Ebenbach, author of *How to Mars*

"*A Boy's Guide to Outer Space* is unlike any novel I have ever read. It is so many things at once—a story of fathers and sons, a story about friendship, a war story (two war stories!), a UFO story (not an inclusive list, I hasten to say) and by turns zany, heartbreaking, exuberant, tragic, and witty—that I found myself holding my breath for entire portions of it. I never once knew what was going to happen next—where I would be taken, what new turns were coming. I'm still breathless, hours after finishing it."

—Michelle Herman, author of *Close-Up*

"Peter Selgin's novel about an unlikely friendship between two solitary people—a man with a secret past and a boy who lost his father—is a tender, wise, and deeply moving coming of age story. Read it. You are in for a very great pleasure."

—Megan Staffel, author of *The Exit Coach*

A Boy's Guide to Outer Space

Peter Selgin

Regal House Publishing

Published by
Regal House Publishing, LLC
Raleigh, NC 27605

ISBN -13 (paperback): 9781646035113
ISBN -13 (epub): 9781646035120
Library of Congress Control Number: 2023950842

Cover images and design by © Peter Selgin

Regal House Publishing, LLC
https://regalhousepublishing.com

Printed in the United States of America

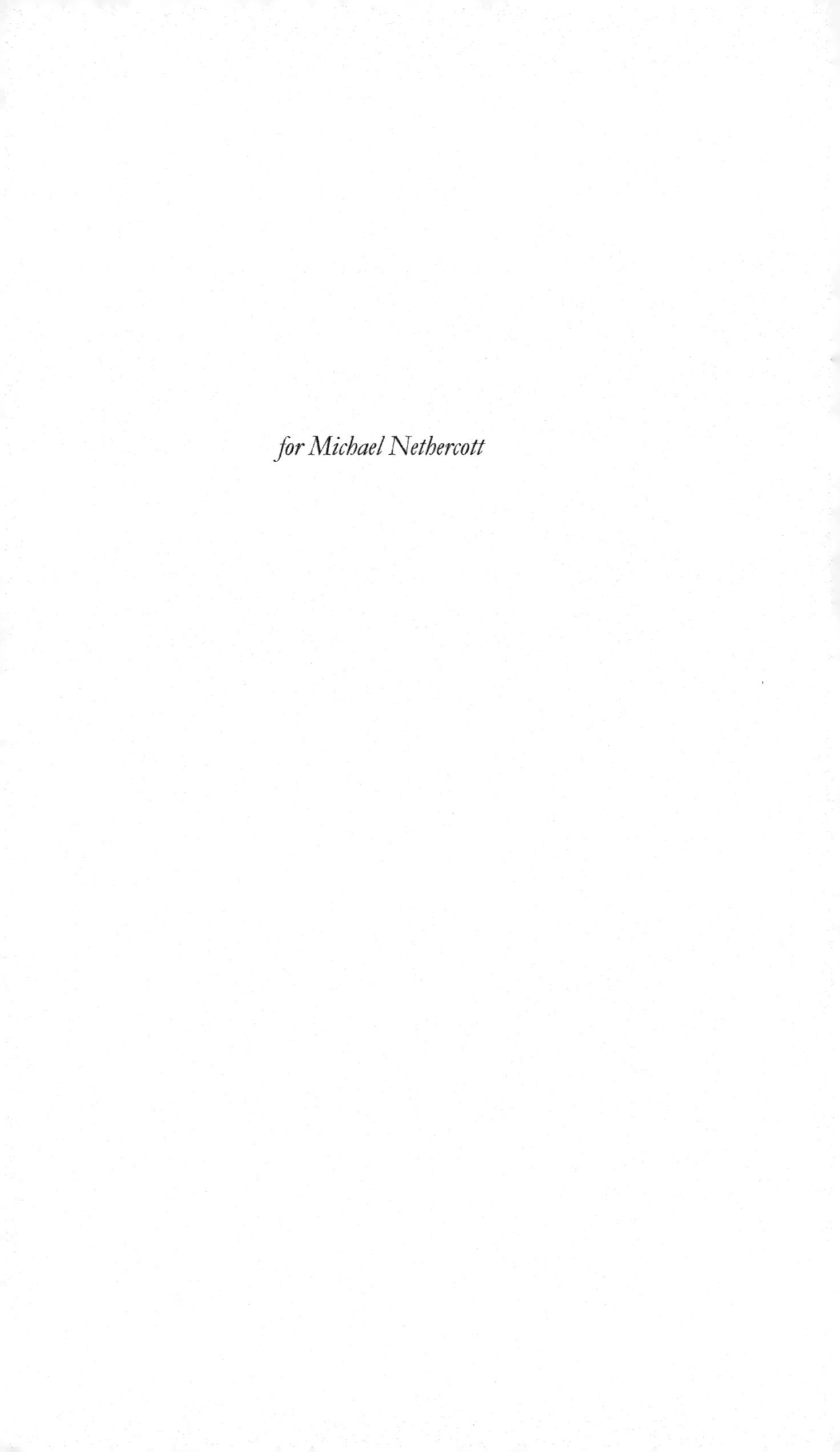

for Michael Nethercott

Plato in Timaeus, Plotinus in Enneads, elaborate the idea that the soul is a stranger on earth, that it has descended from the spaceless and timeless universe, or that it has 'fallen' on account of sin into matter.

—J. E. Cirlot, *A Dictionary of Symbols*

Come to know what is in front of you, and that which is hidden from you will become clear to you. For there is nothing hidden that will not become manifest.

—Gospel of Thomas

Prologue:

Cape Canaveral, Florida
June, 2020

Like all good stories this one starts with an exploding star.

It happened three weeks ago, around two o'clock in the morning. Unable to sleep, I had wandered into my son's bedroom—he's in his second year of graduate school now—and sat there gazing through the telescope I bought him for his sixteenth birthday, when I noticed a sapphire-blue dot high in the eastern sky where there should have been nothing but a black void. At first I thought it might be an airplane or a satellite. But the way the dot just sat there, motionless, alone in its isolated corner of space, rendered those possibilities impossible.

Suddenly the blue dot burst apart, splitting into a dozen bright pale orbs of different pastel colors. The smaller stars danced around a central bright blue nucleus before shooting off in various directions, with one especially brilliant blue star shooting straight down to earth, where it appeared to explode, lighting up the eastern horizon with an ice-blue camera-bulb-like flash.

The next morning I was out walking Mr. McDog, our black Lab (so named for his love of a popular fast-food chain's golden french fries). It was the third month of the Covid epidemic. One does lots of walking during a pandemic (this was before Governor DeSantis ordered all the beaches closed). McDog and I were taking our usual route along a stretch of shore here known as the "Space Coast" when we chanced upon an exceptional bit of flotsam: pale-blue, cone-shaped, metallic, about the size of a two-person tent and shaped like a giant hat. From underneath its scorched brim a tangle of wires, cords, and cables of various colors slithered spaghetti-like.

McDog and I are dedicated beachcombers, ever on the lookout for the Atlantic tide's noteworthier offerings. You'd be surprised by what washes up on these shores. Last year, the ocean's generous but capricious currents delivered a sperm whale—eighty-six feet long and categorically dead—to our sandy front doorstep. Despite repeated dustings with truckloads of quicklime, for over a week the whale's putrefying corpse claimed the beach with its apocalyptic stench. The county had to hire a tugboat to drag the thing out to sea.

Not all of the sea's curious offerings have been organic. Since Mr. McDog and I began walking here four years ago, rarely has a month gone by without our encountering some surf-scoured, wrack-robed, salt-bleached testament to human ingenuity or folly. And I don't mean your typical maritime rubble: waterlogged hatch-covers, beached bell-buoys, and so forth. I'm talking space junk: charred heat-deflector shields, spent rocket boosters, the occasional GEM (that's Graphite Epoxy Motor to you earthlings)... They don't call it the Space Coast for nothing.

But what made that hat-shaped object truly uncanny is this: one morning fifty-seven years ago, in 1963, I came upon the very same object, or one exactly like it, on a horsetail fern-lined trail in Hattertown, Connecticut, the town in which I supposedly grew up. That exploding blue star? It too had its equivalent one May morning in Hattertown, an extraordinary morning heralding the extraordinary year that followed: the year Jack Thomas entered my life. The year my stepbrother Gordon lost his.

What follow are my memories of that year and of those days. They're the memories of a seventy-year-old pensioner living on Cape Canaveral, Florida, an old guy who just happens to share his young subject's DNA along with his name: Leopold Napoli IV, though to his friends back then for reasons to be explained he was known simply as "Half."

This is Half's story more than it's mine, the story of an ordinary American boy who, like most ordinary American boys, longed for things out of this world.

In Half's case he just happened to find them.

Part 1

The Back Shop Boys

When I was ten years old my father gave me some advice, or tried to.

"Son," he said, bobbing a marshmallow over a campfire that we had built, "I've got three pieces of advice to give you." He swigged from his ever-handy bottle of Rock & Rye. "The first piece of advice is: Never stick anything in your ears. The second is: If you're going to build a rope swing, use a thick rope. The third bit of advice..."

My father paused. "The third bit..." he repeated.

As the campfire's glow glazed my father's gaunt, stubbled, sweaty face, the focus of his gaze turned inexorably inward. His slate-blue pupils lost their luster. He chewed his lower lip, pulled at his nose, sniffed several times, furrowed his brow, nibbled his tongue, scratched the short stiff hairs on the back of his neck.

"...the third bit..."

We were watching the Crofus & Corbet Hat Manufacturing Company's main building go up in flames. One of the chief forms of entertainment in Hattertown back then was watching hat factories burn down—something they did, or seemed to do, obligingly, on a regular basis, as if burning down were the primary purpose for which they'd been constructed to begin with. Dad would seek out a vantage point high on a hill in that town of many hills. On cold nights he would sometimes build us a campfire, a miniature blaze to mirror the one raging down in the gulley below us. While roasting marshmallows we'd take in smoke, flames, and the whirling red lights and puling sirens of fire engines. If the view was accessible by car we'd sit side-by-side in my father's banana-yellow Studebaker Champion, the bones of his sunken cheeks burnished copper by flames. He would swig from his pint bottle of Rock & Rye while I munched Cracker Jack from a box, just like at the drive-in theater.

The hat factories burned gloriously, the orange flames

licking utility lines, shooting up star-like sparks that joined the constellations, or formed their own. If the wind blew our way we'd cover our mouths with damp rags Dad provided for the occasion, aware that the smoke carried toxic fumes from the chemicals used to turn the raw pelts of rabbits and beavers into high-quality felt. One evening, while we watched the Sutton-Dexter hat factory burn down, a flurry of burning half-finished hats swirled into the twilight, miniature flying saucers of flaming triple-X felt. One came within inches of landing on my head.

"Now *that's* something!" my father said, slapping his knee first, then mine, his outburst as singular as the event itself. My father was a man of very few words. Winks, chucks on the chin, pats on the back, and slaps on the knee were his main forms of communication.

Dad conveyed his feelings otherwise, too. The summer of my seventh year he spent building a trolley car in our backyard. Powered by twin Briggs & Stratton lawn mower engines, it had caned seats and a bell Dad rang as it clacked along tracks made from plumbing pipes. Dad wore his striped pajamas (the closest thing he had to a conductor's uniform). Though the trolley car's route extended only as far as the clothesline pole and back, I imagined us rolling across America, over hills and across meadows, through sleepy towns and noisy cities. Over the twin engines' roars my father sang:

A ride on the trolley is jolly
Whatever you pay for the fare…

Some wondered how it was that my father always seemed to know when a hat factory was about to burn down. A few even insinuated that he himself set the blazes, a suggestion that I refused to accept. My father was a crude man: uneducated, inarticulate, reeking of Rock & Rye and hat-factory fumes. He loved hot dogs, fireworks, Gene Kelly, baseball, bourbon, and me, his son. In one of her less-sober moments my mother admitted to me that the only reasons she married him were because he was a good dancer and he knew how to make her laugh.

"Your father was the price I paid," she explained, "for having a sense of humor."

But Dad was no arsonist.

However he came by it, when it came to predicting hat-factory fires my father, Leopold Joseph Napoli III, was possessed of a Promethean foresight.

At last—with a bony arm around my neck and a heavy sigh (his breath a rye whisky blowtorch)—my father said:

"Sorry, son, but I forget what the third bit of advice was."

He burst out laughing then, his head thrown back, his laughter echoing out across the flame-lit distance, until a coughing fit seized him and his laughter turned to viscous hacks. So ended the longest conversation he and I would ever have.

We went back to watching the hat factory fire, letting its tongues do the talking for us.

That night I dreamed that I was drowning, a recurrent dream. I'd fallen into a lake or a stream or some other body of water, or maybe I'd been pushed. In the dream I gasped and groped and thrashed toward the pale green light of salvation but couldn't reach it. Awakened by and still gasping from my nightmare, I opened my eyes to see my father standing there, in the bedroom doorway, his oblong silhouette framed by moonlight.

"Dad?" I said, propped up on one elbow, catching my breath.

The silhouette swigged from a bottle.

"What gives?"

"I remembered the third bit of advice, son," my father said.

I waited.

"Follow your fears."

"Huh?"

"Your fears. Follow your fears."

As suddenly as it appeared my father's silhouette was gone. A patch of dawn filled the space where it stood.

My father died on a Wednesday. Mom was working in town that day, at Mr. Stevens'—the town optometrist's—office. I found Dad sitting on the toilet, his mouth agape, head thrown back, gazing up at the bathroom ceiling as if waiting for a hole to form there. A bluebird tapped at the windowpane. Dad smoked like a burning hat factory all his life. But long before his lungs gave out, he suffered from headaches, fatigue, depression, irascibility, vertigo, sore throats, and tremors so violent at times he couldn't hold a screwdriver or tie his own shoelaces: all classic symptoms of mercury poisoning, also known as "Mad Hatter's Disease"—or, locally, as "The Hattertown Shakes."

Everyone who worked in the hat factories was exposed to some mercury, but none more than the Back Shop workers, those who processed the raw pelts of rabbits and beavers into felt. Though they stopped using mercury soon after World War II, by then my father had breathed in twenty years' worth of the stuff, having worked in hat factories ever since he was old enough to reach the foot pedal of a hat blocking machine, as had his father, Leopoldi di Napoli II, and his father's father, Leopoldi di Napoli. Like them, and though the official cause of death was entered by the coroner as "lung infection," my father died of "the shakes."

And though he knew he had been poisoned, my father never said a word about it to anyone. To have done so would have broken a tacit agreement among the Back Shop workers, and anyway it would only have gotten him fired. So my father kept his illness a secret—until the shakes got so bad they forced him first into an early retirement, then into an early grave.

Hats killed my father.

I had just turned eleven.

The trolley car went up on cinderblocks. For a while I tried taking care of it. I varnished the cane seats and polished the bell with a mixture of toothpaste and Worcestershire sauce as my father had taught me. I smeared moving parts with marine grease, wire-brushed iron wheels, freshened yellow paint and pinstripes. Still the bell tarnished; rust froze the drive shafts in their bearings. Vines crept over the seats, strangling them first before splitting them apart. Eventually Mr. Dingy, our landlord, had the thing carted away.

With Dad's death all the colors seemed to drain out of my world. Trees didn't talk to me; birds didn't sing or fly for me. The sky was a cement wall over my head. A taste of ashes filled my mouth and embittered my days. I felt the vague restless yearning experienced by many kids my age, but with a sour, disconsolate twist.

What little consolation I found wasn't on earth but among the stars. By then Sputnik had spun around the world, launching us into the space age. I gave myself over to daydreams of outer space and took comfort in amassing astonishingly useless trivia from encyclopedias: *the sun is 330,330 times larger than Earth; Venus is the only planet in the solar system that rotates clockwise; in Nakhla, Egypt, on June 28, 1911, a dog was killed by a meteor*...flights of mental frippery designed to propel me, as sure as any rocket, out of the dull atmosphere of my freshly fatherless world.

I longed for something, what, exactly, I couldn't say. Something out of this world: a spark, a flame, a gleam or glimmer or glitter of hope or transcendence or redemption, a heavenly hat factory fire to brighten up my gloom-filled days. To touch or be touched by the uncanny, the mysterious, by something unfathomable. I longed to partake of something of the infinite.

So things stood till the summer of my thirteenth year. The summer I followed my fears.

The summer I met the Man in Blue.

We called him the Man in Blue, though of course he had a name. He had more than one, as a matter of fact, though none of us knew that back then. All we knew then was that he walked around town in blue coveralls gathering things in a rucksack he wore on his back. How long he had been in our town was a mystery, too. It seemed as if he'd been there forever, a permanent feature of the landscape, as much a part of it as its ruddy brick hat factory chimneys.

Otherwise we knew nothing about him: a good thing, since it freed us to believe anything we wanted.

"I bet he's a spy," Victor offered.

"I bet he's queer," Skunky submitted, peering through dime-store binoculars. "You can tell by how he walks. See how he shuffles? Only queers walk like that!"

"It's a limp," Victor surmised. "He's limping. Something's wrong with his left leg. I bet he broke it parachuting out of his spy plane!"

"I bet he's got VD," Skunky conjectured, his nickname owing to a white streak in his otherwise jet-black hair. "I bet he's got a whole bunch of diseases, including a few that haven't even been discovered yet."

Zag, our short, muscular leader, said nothing. He chewed the end of a horsetail fern and clenched his fists.

"I bet he escaped from Silver Hills," Victor postulated, referring to the state psychiatric hospital a dozen miles away in Newbury.

"I bet he's a serial killer," Skunky speculated. "I bet he's got a cave in the woods. That's where he drags his victims before he cuts them up into pieces and eats them."

Zag spit over the cliffside.

"Uhn haah dah," said Gordon, my stepbrother.

"I bet he practices black magic," said Victor. "That stick of his? Wherever he taps it on the ground poisonous mushrooms sprout!"

"If he pees on a tree the bark will turn black!" said Skunky.

"Don't ever look him straight in the eyes," Victor advised. "It could permanently stunt your growth!"

"Don't let him spit on you either," Skunky said. "His spit will burn clear through your clothes and skin down to bone!"

A deaf dumb diseased Commie queer spy lunatic escaped mass murderer. The Man in Blue was all those things and anything else we wanted him to be.

As other kids believed in Santa Claus, Bigfoot, and the boogeyman, we believed in the Man in Blue, if only to pity, fear, and despise him.

We (who had nicknames for everything) called ourselves the Back Shop Boys, since before they got too sick or retired or died or the factories they worked for went out of business our fathers all worked in the Back Shops of hat factories. There were four of us: Wade "Skunky" Bledsoe, Victor Szentgyorgyi (pronounced: "Saint George"), and Larry "Zag" Lengyl, our leader and my best friend. And me, Leo Napoli—or Half, as they called me, since I had only half a middle finger on my right hand, the other half blown off during a Fourth of July mishap.

Then there was Gordon, my stepbrother. Gordon who, though a year older than me, was still in the second grade. Gordon whose Coke-bottle-thick glasses and red Boy's Club cap failed to conceal his bug-eyes. Gordon whose nose ran perpetually, whose shirtsleeves (when no one rolled them for him) were invariably encrusted with layers of dried snot, whose forearms (when someone did) were glazed with the stuff as if by a coat of shellac. Gordon who, back in those barbarous pre-PC days, wasn't "intellectually challenged" or "developmentally disabled," but subject to far cruder labels that we Back Shop Boys dispensed liberally.

Gordon didn't care what we called him as long as we let him tag along with us, and as long as nothing came between him and his magical hot dog, the illusion of a floating bullet of flesh formed when he touched the tips of his index fingers together and stared cross-eyed at them—easy for Gordy to do, his eyes being permanently crossed.

The three words Gordy spoke were "a hot dog"—or, more precisely, since he couldn't enunciate his consonants: *uhn haah dah.* He spoke them always in the same tone of amazement, as if witnessing the phenomenon for the very first time. Sometimes he'd try to eat the thing, earning a pair of bitten fingertips and bursting into tears for his trouble. At first we found this amusing, but like most of Gordon's quirks it got old pretty fast.

And though my stepbrother's vocabulary was limited to three words, he could extract more eloquence from a fifty-cent yo-yo than anyone I knew. Walk the Dog, Rock the Baby, Time Warp, Gravity Pull… Like the planets that circle our sun, around that toy consisting of two thick disks connected by a wooden dowel with a string wound around it, all his powers of acuity and agility coalesced and revolved.

Gordon: my cross, my curse. My constant compulsory companion.

We sat there, on top of Cheese Hill, watching as the Man in Blue limped across the Caxton-Dumont hat factory parking lot, headed our way. "Cheese Hill" was our name for the limestone cliff jutting over the factory like the prow of a clipper ship. We called it that since the limestone broke off in crumbly pale-yellow, cheese-like chunks that we'd hurl onto the hat factory reject shed's corrugated metal roof, enticing the old security guard out of his little shack to shake his fist at us, which gesture we Back Shop Boys met with palms outthrust and shouts of *Sieg Heil!* and *Heil Hitler!*

From Cheese Hill we could see most of the town. To the left side of the view were the train tracks, with the fuel oil storage tanks arrayed next to them in increasing size like the cannisters my mother kept coffee, tea, flour, and sugar in; to the right of the view was the middle school, its copper cupola crowned by a fierce-looking lightning rod. Slithering like a brown snake through the center of the view was the aptly named Brim River, since every ten years or so it breached its banks, flooding much of the town.

Lording over this landscape: a dozen tall smokestacks, twelve brick middle fingers poking up into the dingy Connecticut sky. From the top of Cheese Hill we could read the faded names of the hat factories they stood for: MALLORY, HOYT, CROFUS & CORBET, LEE, KNOX, DOBBS, DALTON, DUNLAP, SUTTON-DEXTER, BENTON, MERRIMAC, HOWES VON-GAL. Once, those twelve chimneys darkened the sky with soot and prosperity, but by the summer of 1963 all but one had gone extinct.

As for the other eleven, only their shadows still darkened things: long black shadows creeping through parking lots, sliding past playgrounds, slithering onto front porches and across back yards, gliding past the hours, minutes, and seconds of each day like the hands of a colossal gloomy clock.

The Man in Blue approached, limping across the oil-stained parking lot. It was Sunday morning. Church bells tolled. We kicked the backs of our PF Flyers ("... *make you run faster and jump higher!*") against the cliff. A breeze ran its fingers through my hair. The buds on the trees along Felt Street were just starting to bloom.

As the Man in Blue stepped into range we snapped off cheese bombs. Gripping them, we cast each other defiant looks. Skunky spit over the cliff. Victor wiped sweat from his pimply forehead. Zag clenched and unclenched his fists. Zippo, Zag's mutt dog, barked his snout off as usual. We sat there, mouths dry, breaths held, coiled like springs (except Gordy, who stared at his fingers).

"Uhn haah dah."

The Man in Blue drew closer. His rucksack bulged. Whatever filled it made clanking sounds. We gripped our cheese bombs tighter.

"Somebody throw!"

"Darers first!"

"I know: let's all throw at once!"

"Good idea. You first!"

"On a count of three!" Zag ordered. "One, two—"

A solitary cheese bomb—mine—arced through the atmosphere, its color shifting in flight: dark against bright blue sky, neutral against drab factory bricks, pale where it burst apart inches from the tip of the Man in Blue's walking stick. The skittered fragments painted a chalky star on the pavement.

The Man in Blue stopped walking. He gazed up at us, his round glasses mirroring the blue sky. His face was the brown of hat-factory bricks. He didn't yell or look angry. He might even have smiled; it was hard to say with that scruffy beard. He stood there for a while. Then he hoisted up his rucksack and kept walking across the parking lot and out of sight.

"We've got to get the goods on him," Zag concluded after he'd gone. From the sleeve of his T-shirt he unrolled a pack of cigarettes. "It's our civic duty," he said, lighting one.

"Why don't we all follow him and find out where he lives?" Skunky suggested.

Zag shook his head. "Too conspicuous. This is a one-person job. Any volunteers?"

We all looked at each other.

"Uhn haah dah," Gordy said.

"Guess we'll have to draw for it," said Zag.

We followed Zag down to Bum's Trail, a long-abandoned dirt road through the woods bristling with horsetail ferns. Zag picked four and held them so we couldn't tell which was the longest. "Whoever draws the short fern investigates and reports back to the rest of us," he explained.

We drew one horsetail fern apiece. By the feel of it I knew I hadn't drawn the shortest. At first I felt relieved, then I felt disappointed. We were about to show each other when, behind my back, I snapped my horsetail fern in half.

Follow your fears.

The next afternoon I returned to Cheese Hill. Gordon was with me. Gordon was always with me. Wherever I went, whatever I did, he was there, always, clinging to me like my shadow.

Together we waited for the Man in Blue.

To kill time while waiting Gordy played with my Duncan Midnight Special yo-yo. As for me, I had my knapsack full of diversions: the jackknife my father had given me, my *Boy's Guide to Outer Space,* and my Space Orb Kaleidoscope. The Space Orb was my favorite. It turned my unremittingly drab world into alien realms of crystalline brilliance.

If the contents of my knapsack weren't enough to distract me, I could always fall back on trivia. My brain was a rucksack stuffed with useless facts. Count on me to inform you that an ordinary sheet of paper folded in half fifty times will attain a thickness sufficient to arrive at the sun. *On an earth the size of a basketball, Mount Everest would be so flat you wouldn't be able to feel it. The # sign on a typewriter is called an "octothorpe"* ...

A quarter to three. We'd come straight from school. Since my father died, I'd completely lost interest in my education. In classes, on my shopping-bag book covers, I doodled rocket ships blasting off, orbiting space stations, astronauts in bubble helmets, the NASA logo with its blue halo and slashed red chevron. The only thing that interested me at school was Belinda Dalton, who sat at the desk in front of mine in third-period biology and to my left in fifth-period English. Belinda was the great-great-great-great-granddaughter of Barclay Moses Dalton, the man single-handedly responsible for turning a sleepy farm community known then as Hastings Junction into "The Town that Crowned America." Belinda's hair, which she wore in twin pigtails, was the same color as the flames that spouted from hat factories when they burned down. For over a year I'd had a crush on her—a hopeless one, since there was no chance that she, a Highlander, would have anything to do with me, a Lowlander by birth; worse: a Back Shop Boy.

Belinda's father died the same week as mine. During recess one day she described the pale blue light she saw beyond her bedroom door the night the ambulance came for him. Awakened by fevered whisperings, she opened the door and stood there, bathed in the blue light, her cries sounding to her like those of someone screaming under water. Along with the blue light, an inexplicable breeze blew up the staircase. It lifted her gown as she made her way down it, one hand holding the railing, the other shielding her eyes from the blue glare. When she reached the bottom the light and the wind both suddenly stopped. Belinda stood alone in her empty house. Later that morning, having gone back to bed, she awoke to gentle knocking and the certainty that her mother had come to tell her that her father was dead.

Belinda told me all this while hanging upside-down on the jungle gym, her bright orange pigtails dangling like lengths of burning rope. I wanted to console her, to utter some soothingly profound words. What do you say to comfort to someone whose father has just died? Had I known, I'd have spoken those same magical words to myself.

Instead I offered up the following sugary gumdrop of trivia:

"Did you know," I submitted with burning authority, "that the volume of the moon is almost exactly the same as the volume of the Pacific Ocean?"

Belinda stared at me. I repeated myself.

She kept staring, her eyes as sullen and remote as Pluto.

"No kidding, they're the same volume!" I explained with unalloyed glee. "Imagine: the whole Pacific Ocean fitting in the moon! You wouldn't think it possible, would you?"

Belinda kept staring, her eyes hard, jaw set.

I changed the subject. "Did you know hydrogen is the least dense substance on earth? I bet you can't guess what the most dense substance is?"

"Your *brain*?" Belinda ventured.

"Nope. *Frozen* hydrogen! The same element!"

The bell rang. Belinda jumped off the jungle gym and hurried off, her fiery pigtails bouncing. I shouted after her:

"Don't you want to hear about Saturn's rings?"

Having failed to win Belinda's heart through science, I fell back on daydreams and doodles. I sketched Project Mercury capsules flaming through Earth's atmosphere, splash-landing and bobbing alongside aircraft carriers in choppy seas. I could draw Colonel John Glenn from memory, all freckles and heroic grin.

To be John Glenn, to ride a series of explosions to the moon and back, to come home to headlines and my very own ticker-tape parade, to pack this gloomy existence of mine into an Atlas LV-3B rocket and send it hurtling through 238,900 miles of frozen, empty space.

To touch something of the infinite. That was my dream.

As I peered through the Space Orb Kaleidoscope, amid brick-colored swirls suddenly a blue flower flourished. The Man in Blue limped across the Caxton-Dumont factory parking lot. I snatched Gordon's red Boy's Club cap off his head and swatted him with it.

"Come on!"

We scrambled down the path to where we'd stashed our bikes. Leaving Gordon's tomato-red Schwinn Tornado (cantilevered frame, whitewall tires, chrome-plated fenders and horn tank, streamlined Fenderlight seat springs: a fabulous machine thoroughly wasted on its owner) behind, we climbed onto my piece-o-crap Royce Union and rode off. With Gordon holding on from behind and me pedaling furiously I tailed the Man in Blue. Soon we were crossing the green iron bridge across the Brim River.

The sky hung heavy and gray as a wet wool blanket. On the far side of the bridge the Doughboy Diner's onion-shaped ventilator spewed french fry grease into the afternoon air. A sudden gust blew Gordy's red Boy's Club cap off. I stopped to fetch it for him.

At Pelt Road the Man in Blue took a left and started up the hill there. He'd reached the crest when he stopped and turned. We were passing the hobby shop. I pulled us into the vestibule where, for a few minutes, I faked a deep interest in model airplanes, paint boxes, and chemistry sets. When I looked back up the road the Man in Blue was gone.

With Gordon riding with me I knew I'd never catch up with him. So I did something I wasn't supposed to do. I dropped him off at the Congregational church, where all the other so-called "special" kids gathered every day after school. The red door to the social hall was locked. The other parents hadn't arrived yet.

"Wait here," I told Gordy. "The other kids will be here soon."

Though he spoke only three words, my stepbrother's face had its own wide vocabulary and could be extremely eloquent. It passed through no fewer than a dozen different emotions before arriving at tears.

"Aw, come off it," I said, wiping them and snot off his face with my handkerchief. "It'll just be a couple minutes."

He looked up so the whites showed under his eyes. The look said, *Promise?*

I smiled and nodded. "Here," I said, taking the yo-yo from my sack and handing it to him. He stopped crying. A smile crept over his snotty face. I wiped more tears away. Then I threw a mock jab at his shoulder—Gordon loved that—gave him the thumbs-up (he loved that, too), and took off.

By the time I caught up with him again the Man in Blue was headed down Blocker Avenue, carrying what looked like a bag of groceries. From Blocker he took a right onto Fuller Lane, then a left on Bumping Hill Road, which climbed a steep grade for a quarter mile before falling as steeply to where it stretched out flat through acres of marsh.

I heard a rumble of thunder and saw the first shy drops of

rain strike the road in front of me. Soon drizzle turned into downpour. The rain bounced like hairpins off the pavement. It slid under the collar of my windbreaker as I pedaled, keeping the Man in Blue in sight, watching the shoulders of his blue coveralls darken with rain. Maybe it was the way he walked, or the brown sunburned skin on the back of his neck, but suddenly I felt like I was following my father, letting him take me to the place where people go when they die.

Beyond the swamp the road climbed steeply again. I knew that stretch of road well, having pedaled up it dozens of times with the Back Shop Boys. A thousand feet beyond the crest of the next hill an unpaved road veered to the left around the trunk of a big old dead oak tree, the road to Lost Lake and what was left of the Dalton estate, established there a hundred and seventy-one years ago by Barclay Moses Dalton, Belinda's great-great (etc.) grandfather, the man who brought the hatting industry to what would become Hattertown.

According to local lore Barclay Dalton had been a struggling Yankee fur trapper when, one freezing winter morning, he plugged a hole in his boot using a scrap of rabbit fur. Later that night when he took off his boots he realized that the pressure and sweat from his foot had transformed the blob of fur into a soft, stiff, malleable substance. Over the next few weeks he experimented with it, pounding, bending, and twisting it into various forms, until he realized the substance was ideally suited for making men's hats. A year later, in 1785, Barclay opened the first hat factory in Hastings Junction. Inspired by its success, other hat factories sprouted up like mushrooms after a spring rain. By 1885 Hattertown's dozen hat factories were pounding out over two million hats per year—among them, it was said, the famous stovepipe hat worn by President Abraham Lincoln himself.

The Man in Blue turned down the road to the former Dalton estate, which lay hidden behind a rusted chain-link fence spangled with ivy and NO TRESPASSING signs. Since the mansion burned down eight years earlier the estate had been all but deserted. All but, I say, since whoever put up those NO TRESSPASSING signs failed to take into account us Back Shop Boys, for whom such warnings were as enticing as honey to flies. Though six feet tall and topped with coiled barbed wire, the fence likewise failed to discourage us.

The Man in Blue didn't climb over the fence. He kept on walking past it, headed for Lost Lake. What for? I wondered. To swim? In early *May*? In the *rain*?

Then I remembered the caretaker's cottage, the one that lay in ruins at the end of that gravel road. I knew it lay in ruins, since we Back Shop Boys ruined it. A few months after my father's funeral, when I was twelve, we broke into and ransacked the place, tipping over a pot-bellied stove, gouging holes in walls with a fire poker. Zag found a box of apothecary jars with glass stoppers. Skunky found an enamelware colander. Victor discovered a crate of Mason jars filled with strawberry preserves (we pried one jar open and sampled its contents, brown but still sweet). Though my mother hadn't yet married my stepfather, Gordy had already been put in my charge. He found a pair of gardening gloves, their fingers glued together by mildew. In a dusty armoire we found a small wooden chest full of travel brochures bristling with pictures of multi-funneled passenger steamships. The whole cottage floor was carpeted with mildewy magazines and newspapers. From their sodden pages something like seaweed sprouted.

In the yard behind the cottage all sorts of junk lay in piles around a closet-sized wooden shed. A few yards from the shed there was a large rectangular box with a hinged top. Gordon stood looking down at it.

"What's the matter, Gordy?" Skunky teased him. "Afraid the boogeyman's gonna jump out and bite your face off?"

"Never know, there may be a rotting dead body in there," Victor speculated.

"Knock it off," I said.

Gordon turned to me. I nodded. When he raised the box's lid, the hinges squeaked. With a yelp he fell back-first into a patch of ferns. As Skunky and I helped him to his feet, he gasped and spluttered like someone drowning.

It was Victor's turn next to peer into the wooden box.

"Holy Christ!" he said, reeling back.

Skunky and Zag took their turns with similar results.

It was my turn. I took a deep breath, raised the lid, and glimpsed a lumpy white mass like the shortening my mother used for baking pies. It hit me then—a smell unlike anything I'd ever smelled before. The smell singed my nostrils. It scorched my eyeballs. I reeled, coughed, spluttered, retched.

Days later, applying his cursory knowledge of chemistry, Skunky identified the white compound as caked ammonium chloride, used as a disinfectant in outhouses. But for me at that moment it was the Smell of Evil itself.

We got the hell out of there, but not before taking turns shooting out every last one of the cottage's dozens of windowpanes with Skunky's pump-action BB gun.

It would never have occurred to me that someone might actually live in that cottage again, not after what we did to it. So imagine my surprise when, walking my bike on the gravel road, as I rounded the bend, there, gleaming white, with every one of its little windowpanes replaced, stood the caretaker's cottage, looking like it had been built the day before.

A queasy feeling came over me then: a seasick, hollow, dizzy feeling, as if I'd passed through one of those swirling time tunnels in cheesy science fiction movies.

The rain had stopped. Patches of blue broke through the clouds. I watched as the Man in Blue opened the green door and entered the cottage. To the left of the door was a small sign, green painted letters carved into varnished wood:

FERN COTTAGE

I looked around. Sure enough the grounds surrounding the cottage were strewn with green ferns, their complicated fronds dazzled with raindrops. The ferns lapped at the cottage's shingles, nipped at them with sharp green teeth, licked them with pointy tongues of emerald, malachite, and jade. As far as my eyes could see, the woods were thickly carpeted with ferns.

I straddled my bike, staring at the cottage's front door, wondering what to do next, waiting for a light to go on inside, a sound, something. The windows remained dark. I heard silence and the sound of leftover rain. I leaned my bike against a tree and took a step closer, thinking, What if he sees me through one of those windowpanes, standing here with a dumb look on my face? This is dumb, I said to myself. Really dumb.

You should leave, now. *Leave, now. Leave, now…*

The green door opened. The Man in Blue stood there. He wore a plaid robe. He looked at me but said nothing. I reminded myself that he couldn't talk, that he was dumb—not dumb as in ignorant, dumb as in deaf and dumb. He kept staring, his mouth a straight line under the scruffy beard.

"Hello," I said.

"…"

"I think I'm lost. I was trying to get back to the road. Can you tell me how to get back to the road?"

"…"

"Never mind, I'll figure it out. Thanks!"

I took a step back, then another.

Then I turned, grabbed my bike, hopped on, and took off.

By the time I got to the church it was a quarter past four. Gordon was gone. One of the other parents must have given him a ride home.

As fast as I could I rode to what I still thought of as my stepfather's house, one with too many gables and turrets, to find Gordon and my mother watching *Make Room for Daddy* in the downstairs parlor. My mother lay stretched out on the sofa in her rose-colored rayon robe. My stepbrother lay there on the sofa with her, stretched out in the hollow V formed by her slightly parted legs, his crew-cut head resting on her *mons veneris,* where she massaged it gently with her right hand while her left hand alternately conveyed sips of Taylor's Cream Sherry and Planters peanuts from a jar to her mouth.

"You left Gordon," she said, nibbling a peanut, not taking her eyes off the television screen on which Danny Thomas gave one of his TV kids a bath. "You're never supposed to leave your stepbrother. Not ever. Never."

"I know," I conceded.

"It's the one thing that we ask of you," my mother said without taking her eyes off Danny Thomas, "the one and only thing. Thank God Mrs. Gustafson brought him home."

I watched her massage my stepbrother's head. To think that there'd been a time not that long ago when I had occupied that same hallowed position, when it had been my head, not my stepbrother's, that my mother massaged lovingly if absently, when I had been her innocent little angel. Now that position was firmly filled by the only child of Husband #2, a child whose advantages over his predecessor could not, in my mother's eyes, be overestimated. Unlike me—and provided that he understood them correctly—my stepbrother honored my mother's wishes. He obeyed her commands. He wasn't sour or sullen. Nor did he tend to engage in lies, secrecy, contrariness, and amorphous existential despair.

"Hey, Gordy," I said, tousling—or trying to tousle—my stepbrother's too-short crew-cut. He didn't turn or acknowledge my presence in any way. His eyes remained glued to the TV screen, his slack features bathed in its icy emissions, his striped T-shirt bunched under his belly where it had slid away from my mother's consoling crotch. Though he pretended to be deeply engrossed in Danny Thomas' problems, it didn't take a genius to see that my stepbrother was pissed off at me.

"If I've told you once," my mother said, "I've told you a thousand times not to leave your brother alone, ever. It's the one thing that I ask of you, Leo. The one and only thing."

I was tempted to say, *He's not my brother, he's my stepbrother*, but thought better of it. By then my mother had already consumed a fair amount of cream sherry and showed no signs of abatement. Every evening after dinner she was in the habit of drinking at least one glass of cream sherry—not a little glass, either, but a Christmas-themed tumbler decorated with holly leaves and red berries. She nibbled another peanut (she dispatched her legumes meticulously, one-by-one), her eyes intent on Mr. Thomas, who by then had been caught by his kids trying on his wife's underwear over his pajamas. The laugh track sounded like bacon frying.

"*...the one and only thing...*" my mother repeated.

Her quilted, rose-colored, rayon robe had slipped off, exposing the legs of the chorus-line dancer she once dreamed of becoming. When she was sixteen my mother ran away to join the Radio City Rockettes. With fifty dollars and—as she put it—"a suitcase full of dreams," she walked five miles to the Danville train station, got on a New York City-bound train, and watched the only world she had ever known slip by through the dirt-tinted window. No sooner did she arrive in Grand Central Station than a stranger approached her, a handsome, silver-haired, goateed businessman dressed in a double-breasted suit. He asked her if he could be of any help, then offered her lunch at a nearby coffee shop. Within an hour my mother found herself fending off his gropes and kisses in a nearby hotel suite. How she managed to escape the businessman's clutches my mother didn't elaborate, but the ordeal left her so discomposed she never went to the audition. Instead she boarded the next train back to Danville, where, from the station, with tears in her eyes, she phoned the man whose banana-yellow Studebaker Champion soon arrived to take her home, her knight in yellow armor. A month later she married my father. So went the story as told by my mother under the influence of several tumblers of cheap cream sherry.

"I'm hungry," I said. "Is there anything to eat?"

"Will you get a load of this kid of mine," my mother said, shaking her head. "Shows up whenever the heck he feels like it and then expects to be waited on like royalty. There's Polish sausage on the stove."

"Elephant dong?" I exclaimed enthusiastically. This was my term of endearment for Polish kielbasa sausage, what my father had always called it.

"I wish you wouldn't call it that," my mother said with a frown. "It's disgusting. Thank goodness your stepfather isn't here to hear you say it."

True enough. Had he been there, my stepfather's normally pale cheeks would have turned the same dark pink as the Polish comestible itself. Walter J. Waple was as intolerant of references to the reproductive organs of male pachyderms as he was of unpolished shoes, untrimmed fingernails, belching, Bolsheviks, beanies, and beatniks.

"Where's Mr. Waple, anyway?"

"At his store. Where else? Would it break your heart to refer to him for once as your *stepfather?* Is that asking too much? If I called you 'Mr. Napoli,' how would that suit you?"

"I prefer Your Eminence."

"Wise guy."

"Why is he working so late?"

"Who knows? He's got some project he's working on. Go on

and grab yourself some kielbasa. *Lassie* will be on soon. Your Eminence."

As the theme music to *Lassie* swelled and the Hollywood collie leapt onto a rock in front of a snow-capped rear-screen projected mountain, with my tray of lukewarm sausage I stretched out on the carpet next to Gordon. Superimposed over the title sequence, my mother's reflection sipped more sherry from her tumbler. Some people should never drink, and my mother was one of them. Liquor did something to the corners of her mouth that gave her features a grim aspect and made her look a decade older than her thirty-six years. The nutty sweet aroma of bargain-basement sherry sickened my stomach. Mom drank to dull her depression, to soften its edges. By the third glass she tended to leak regrets: how she had wasted her life, how if only she had done this, if only she had done that, if only, if only, if only… *Why, with my talent and good looks I could have been something. I could've been a movie star! I could have married into nobility and wealth! I could have been the wife of a world-class brain or heart surgeon or a diplomat or the prime minister of some country. Instead I had to marry that good-for-nothing-hat-factory-back-shop-worker father of yours and end up spending the rest of my days stuck here in Hattertown…*

My mother's squandered potential was a scratchy old record that she played over and over again. (Am I being unfair? Probably, but only the way that caricaturists are unfair to their subjects, by accentuating qualities that are incontrovertibly there.) When she drank, Mom drank too much, and for the first eighteen years of my life, she drank just about every night that I can remember. I can't blame her entirely. Her own mother was a lush and her father a tyrant who made her quit school and go to work in a hat factory (as a hat band seamstress) at sixteen. He belittled her every chance he got while relishing her every failure as though it were the fruit of a tree planted by himself and watered with her haplessness. My mother's story is that of a woman who, faced with only bad choices, made them.

She lit a Chesterfield King. "So where on earth did His Royal Highness disappear to all day today?" she asked, blowing the question out in a series of smoke puffs. "I suppose you were hanging around with that no-good gang of yours as usual?"

"You suppose wrong."

"Uhn haah dah," said Gordon.

"Don't lie to me, Leo. I can always tell when you're lying."

"Whatever you say, Mom."

Timmy and Lassie rescued a bald eagle shot by a hunter. While the eagle recovered from its wound, Timmy and Lassie found her nest full of eggs and returned the eagle to it. Timmy was virtuous. He never lied to his mother.

"I sure wish that you would find yourself a better class of friends to hang around with," my mother said. "You're a Highlander now, Leo. You've no reason to fraternize with such riff-raff when you could be making friends with people of your own social class. Grant Clarke, for instance." Grant was one of the smarter kids in school, bound for Princeton via private school. He wore Hushpuppies and tennis sweaters. No one liked him. "He's the sort of good influence you should be cultivating instead of those delinquents of yours."

"Sure, Mom."

"I tell you those boys are nothing but trouble. Zag's a hot-headed bully. As for the other two… I swear, one of these days they're going to get you in deep water."

Mom was right. The Back Shop Boys were nothing but trouble. We were bored. We lacked social skills. Zag punched his way through life; Victor lied his way through; via crude chemistry Skunky tried to stink and blast his way. I sketched astronauts and looked through my telescope.

When a commercial came on I took my tray, went back into the kitchen, and slid the kielbasa of which I'd eaten only a few bites into the trash pail. I was still shaken up from my encounter with the Man in Blue. I watched a bit more of *Lassie*, then got up to go to bed.

"It's not even seven-thirty," my mother said.

"I'm going to look through my telescope."

"You and that telescope of yours! What do you expect to see through that thing that you haven't seen a thousand times before? There are only so many stars, Leo."

I kissed her cheek. "'Night, Mom."

"I swear I might as well not have a son anymore. Leo *who*? Oh, you mean that kid who's always looking through his telescope?"

"Goodnight, Gordy." I stepped through the beaded curtain into the hallway.

"...except when he's off doing heaven knows what with his shady friends and lying through his teeth to his mother about it..."

As I climbed the stairs to my room my mother yelled:

"You'll miss *Denise the Menace*. And *The Wonderful World of Color*!"

Part 2

Outer Space

The telescope was a gift from my stepfather, one of many gifts with which he tried to buy his way into my good graces, including but not limited to a twelve-foot toboggan, a globe that lit up from inside, and a traveling chess set with magnetized pieces and imitation alligator-skin carrying case.

The toboggan gathered dust in the garage. The rest of my stepfather's gifts I stashed in their original boxes in the dark depths of my bedroom closet.

It drove my mother crazy. "How is it possible," she wondered, "that I, who am nothing if not a paragon of graciousness, could have brought such an ungrateful specimen into this world? Can't you see your stepfather's just trying to be *nice* to you? Is that so *terrible*? What has that poor man ever done to earn such contempt from you?"

Had I answered, my answer would have been short but not sweet. *He killed my father.* The equation went something like this:

a: Hats killed my father
b: Walter Waple = hats
∴ *W. W. killed my father*

So I refused my stepfather's gifts. I treated them with the contempt an honest judge shows for a bribe. Still, and notwithstanding my bottomless supply of righteous indignation, I couldn't bring myself to refuse that telescope, having spent the better part of a year lobbying for it, showing my mother ads for it in *Popular Mechanics*:

See the stars, moons, and planets up close!

According to those ads the telescope came with a "free" Star Chart and a 272-page, full-color *Handbook of the Heavens.* Though its useful magnification was only 180X—barely powerful enough to resolve Jupiter's moons—still, at $29.95 it was a bargain.

I remember the day the telescope arrived. It was a Saturday morning. Gordon and I were bellied up to the Zenith, waiting for *Fireball XL-5,* our favorite show, to come on. The series employed a novel technology known as SUPERMARIONATION: the characters were marionettes. You could see the strings when they caught the lights. Three thunderous bassoon chords—as ominous in their way as the notes that open Beethoven's Fifth—heralded the show's title sequence, wherein World Space Patrol Colonel Steve Zodiac and his Slavic sidekick Venus board their unambiguously phallic spaceship, off to rescue some part of the universe from a colorful assortment of intergalactic monsters and evil masterminds.

We were deep into *Fireball XL-5* when the doorbell rang. Mom was sleeping off her latest sherry hangover. My stepfather had gone to his store. I answered the door. The UPS man stood there, in his sewage-colored uniform, holding a four-foot-long cardboard box. I spent the rest of that morning wrestling with parts and instructions, and the afternoon peering through the result at clouds, impatient for darkness, intent on the planets, moons, and stars.

Total darkness didn't fall until seven-thirty. Before aiming my telescope at the night sky I watched that evening's episode of *The Twilight Zone,* in which a pair of astronauts, one male, one female, traveling in separate spaceships from different planets destroyed by nuclear wars, crash-land on an uninhabited planet. His name is Adam; hers: Eve. You can work the rest out for yourself.

For the next three months I spent every spare minute gazing through that telescope. I developed a squint from peering into the thing. I couldn't get enough of stargazing. The planets and stars were all there—just where the star chart said they would be. There were Saturn's rings; there were Jupiter's (then) sixteen moons; there were the Sunflower, the Tadpole, the Whirlpool galaxies; there were brown dwarfs, quasars, pulsars, gamma ray bursts, trans-Neptunian objects, protoplanetary nebulae, and the remnants of supernovae.

But after three months the novelty of stargazing had begun to wear thin. The galaxies all started to look pretty much alike. It wasn't long before the entire universe left me nearly as cold as Planet Earth.

How, I wondered, can something as vast, infinite, and mysterious as the universe leave me feeling so cold, so empty? There must be something more. There *has to be!*

My bedroom's gabled walls featured a tromp l'oeil sky with puffy white clouds, painted there by my stepfather. Against this cloudy backdrop a trio of P51 Mustangs, a gull-winged Stuka, two Messerschmitts, and a P47 Thunderbolt banked and soared, suspended by lengths of fishing line no less invisible than the wires that controlled the marionettes on *Fireball XL-5.* Whirling propeller blades were simulated by discs of clear acetate. Painted bullet holes strafed one of the Messerschmitt's fuselages. From out of one of the Stuka's engines a gouge of smoke-gray cotton curved toward the ceiling. Hoping they would distract him from his fingertips, my stepfather built the model planes for his son (he'd harbored similar hopes for the twenty-gallon ant farm and the 1,000-piece *Queen Mary* jigsaw puzzle). Having failed at their original purpose, the model planes went into Mr. Waple's attic where they gathered dust until my mother agreed to marry him, whereupon my stepfather-to-be hit upon the clever notion of adorning my future bedroom with them.

On learning of his plan my mother was less than enthusiastic. "How do you expect the poor kid to sleep," she wondered, "with the Battle of Britain going on over his head?"

"Nonsense!" my future stepfather replied, puffing one of his many pipes. "Boys love airplanes! Airplanes and war! It's in their blood, if you will. Why at his age I'd have given my right eye for such a display!"

"He'll give his right eye, all right," my mother countered, "when he pokes it out on a propeller blade!"

Thus, to the roars and splutters and *ratttatttattats* of a World

War II dogfight, I'd fall asleep in my new bedroom, only to bail out of a spinning, sweat-soaked bed somewhere around two o'clock in the morning, night after night.

Soon, though, I'd have a good reason to be grateful for those rude wee hour awakenings. If not for them I'd have slept through the one celestial event that would distinguish my up-to-then humdrum career as an astronomer.

The night of my encounter with the Man in Blue, awakened as usual by the dogfighting nightmare, I did what I always did: I gazed through my telescope. By then I had constructed a platform out on the roof outside my window. Except where the limbs of a neighbor's Japanese maple across the street obscured it, the roof offered a clear view of the night sky.

It was a cloudless night, perfect for stargazing. I peered through the aperture, intent on discovering some unknown galaxy or planet. Any fool with a $29.95 telescope can ogle Jupiter's red eye or count Saturn's rings. I longed for something greater, to touch an existence far beyond my own, to be carried light years away from my mundane world, a world gone as cold and gray as the ashes of a hat factory fire.

I set my sights on the empty spaces between stars, those hellish voids punctuated by flecks of divinity, empty spaces that my imagination populated with galaxies inconceivably vast and mysterious. *Astronomy is the science by which men learn how small they are.* Within those dismal voids I searched for a sign, any sign, that the mystery known as "life" was aware of *my* mystery, that the universe gave enough of a damn about me, Leo Napoli IV, to throw him the equivalent of a cosmic wink. Though I was every inch my atheist father's son and believed in a personal God no more than he had, still, I wanted Him to notice me.

Ergo I peered through my $29.95 telescope, wanting as much to be discovered by something out there as to discover it.

Suddenly, in the far upper right corner of the telescope's field, above and to the left of Canis Minoris, in what according to the star chart should have been absolute emptiness, I saw an unusual star. No sooner did I see it than the star burst into an asterism *("a pattern or group of stars typically smaller than a constellation")* of smaller stars of different pastel shades: blue, green, yellow, pink. Like atoms around a nucleus, the colored stars spun frenziedly around a central brighter star before shooting off in different directions, with one star—a pale blue one—shooting straight down to the earth, where it exploded, lighting the horizon with a camera bulb-like flash. Then everything went dark.

For the next hour or so I went on looking through the telescope, expecting something more to happen. When nothing did I got back into bed and lay there, my hands folded over my pajama-clad chest, my eyes wide open, gazing through the web of model fighter planes, wondering if I'd ever gotten out of bed, if that exploding star had been nothing but a dream.

I awoke to bright sunshine. Ten past nine. I'd slept through the alarm. The Back Shop Boys were waiting for us at Cheese Hill. I shook Gordon awake.

"Come on! We're late!"

We took Bum's Trail, the shortcut named for the hobos who once camped along it back in the days of steam locomotives. During winter they warmed themselves on stoves improvised from discarded oil drums and slept on sprung Pullman seats that had somehow found their way into the woods.

As we hurried down the trail more church bells tolled, reminding me that Gordy and I had to be at church later that morning for ten-thirty worship, something I didn't look forward to. When he was alive, on Sundays my father always took us to the Congregational Church for the morning service. We went for the same reason we murmured our prayers at the supper table and before bed: because my mother insisted on it. I didn't mind the charade. But after my father died all bets were off. I was damned if I'd believe in a god who stole fathers from their eleven-year-old sons and left their yellow trolley cars to rot on cinderblocks.

If I believed in a higher power, it was only to doubt and defy him, her, or it. I recall spending part of an afternoon one day staring at one of our town's hat factory chimneys, daring its weathered bricks to move or change color or do anything at all to demonstrate to me God's omnipotence. "Come on, now, Mr. All-Powerful God," I sneered. "Pull off this one puny little miracle for me. I dare you!" No bricks moved.

So much for God's omnipotence.

We were halfway down Bum's Trail when we came upon the

Mysterious Object. It was as big as the furnace in my stepfather's house, and shaped like a giant hat, round on top, with a narrow, scorched brim underneath. It was more than half-buried in the ground, a mound of earth pushed up at its rounded top, a trail of flattened horsetail ferns behind it, their segmented shafts pointing every which way like the short hairs jutting out from the back of Gordy's red Boys Club cap. The thing's outer casing was made of a pale-blue translucent metal, its bottom singed black. What it was or where it had come from I had no idea. Then I remembered the dream I'd had of a blue star plummeting to earth earlier that same morning.

I slapped Gordy's back and hurried to tell the others. Minutes later the Back Shop Boys converged around the thing to ogle it with a mixture of astonishment and skepticism.

"It looks to me like part of a submarine," said Victor, whose dad, according to him, had commanded the World War II submarine that torpedoed the *Bismarck*.

"Maybe it's an A-bomb, one that the Ruskies dropped but for some reason didn't blow up!" Skunky submitted.

Zag spit onto a skunk cabbage plant. "Most definitely a UPJ," he proclaimed, lighting a cigarette.

"What's a UPJ?" Victor inquired.

"An Unidentified Piece of Junk."

I took a step closer.

"Watch out!" Skunky warned. "It could be booby-trapped!"

"Or radioactive!" said Victor. "Look—it's *glowing*!"

I peered under the scorched brim to see a tangle of singed, partially melted colored cables. In places the cables had fused into multicolored blobs. I took the pocketknife that my father had given me from my knapsack, and, using the saw blade the Swiss Army equipped it with, sawed away at the Mysterious Object's guts. Zag asked what I was doing.

"Getting a specimen," I said.

"What for?"

"For an expert opinion." A motley heart-sized blob broke off into my fist.

"Virgil?" said Victor.

"Why not? He's an expert, isn't he?"

"An expert nut-job!" said Skunky.

I plopped the chunk into my knapsack.

"I'm telling you it's just a hunk of junk," said Zag. "An old boiler or part of some old hat factory machine."

"Anyone want to come with me?" I turned to Victor and Skunky who both looked down at their shoes. Neither of them cared to defy Zag.

"Fine. I'll go by myself." Meaning with Gordon.

Virgil Zeno was Hattertown's flying saucer expert, and had been since the morning of March 3, 1954, when he sighted his first UFO in the night skies over Hattertown. Though some failed to recognize the need for such an authority in our town, while others considered him insane, most of Hattertown's then 6,000 inhabitants were happy to give Virgil what they felt was his due. After all, if he was a lunatic, he was a good-natured lunatic as well as a source of local color and amusement. He was also Hattertown's finest mill worker. If granting Virgil authority over the town's extraterrestrial tourists gratified him, why deny him that small, dubious privilege?

But the main reason for the town's indulgence was the terrible accident that, a year to the day before he saw his first UFO, took the lives of his identical brothers.

The Zeno triplets were taking their maiden voyage down Felt Street, headed south in their brand-new green and white DeSoto Firedome convertible, one they had bought for themselves for their thirty-eighth birthday, which happened to fall on Easter Sunday. Verso was behind the wheel; Vito rode shotgun; Virgil sat behind them in the backseat. Though the DeSoto came with a full set of them, back then seat belts were not required. None of the brothers wore his. However they did wear their freshly laundered, spanking-white carpentry overalls. According to my father, who witnessed the events of that terrible morning, had there been no tragedy the Zeno triplets would have left a lasting impression all the same.

The car was approaching the railroad crossing when suddenly the signals flashed and clanged. The train was a freight train carrying spools of raw brass to Waterbury, to be made into screws, grommets, shoe eyelets, and other widgets. Freight trains were especially dangerous. They barreled through the town at odd intervals. You never knew when one was coming.

Instead of braking, in what witnesses described as an attempt to beat the train, Verso gunned the DeSoto's engine. He cleared the first gate, but by then the other gate had trapped them. According to Lester Kirby, the hardware store owner, none of the brothers made any attempt to abandon their new vehicle. As the locomotive bore down on them they sat calmly talking, until—like a cat carrying one of her brood—the engine picked up the DeSoto and carried it several hundred feet before dropping it, in a crumpled mass, at the base of a fuel oil storage tank. Vito and Verso Zeno were killed instantly. Thrown free of the car by the impact, Virgil landed feet-first in a stack of peat moss bales in the feed and supply store lot. Though he survived, his legs didn't.

Virgil Zeno's carpentry shed was located by the railroad tracks, next to the lumberyard. On its rooftop Virgil had erected an enormous cross, twenty-six feet tall by fifteen feet wide, fringed with 500-watt flood lamps. By night the cross glowed like those luminous fish that prowl ocean depths. On the same roof not far from the cross was a large billboard bearing a greeting, black letters on white:

WELCOME VISITORS
FROM OUTER SPACE

In case the visitors didn't happen to speak English, in smaller letters underneath it the greeting was translated into Latin:

AVE HOSPES ARCANO AB
COELO DESCENDENS

Virgil's carpentry shed was painted battleship gray. Through its first-story windows I saw only a squeak of lamplight, so begrimed were they with sawdust. Still, I knew Virgil was in there. He worked every day of the week. When not spinning table or chair legs or milling dovetail joints for a chest of drawers or caressing coats of varnish over tabletops and cabinet doors, he'd be working on his flying saucer in his secret back room. No one was supposed to know about the flying saucer, but every kid in Hattertown did, Virgil having taken each of us, individually, into his confidence and shown us the thing, peeling back the sawdust-covered tarp to offer us a tantalizing glimpse of smooth, polished wood. Yes, you heard right: *wood.* A blend of Spanish cedar, Malaysian teak, bamboo, and elderberry.

"Terrific wood, elderberry," Virgil explained the day he offered me my own personal glimpse. "Dense but lightweight and flexible. Steams easily. The Indians used to make slings and arrow shafts from it. A sling for support, an arrow for thrust and speed. Lots of good uses, elderberry has."

I waited for the rotary saw to stop screaming before knocking. When the door opened, a strong smell of pine resin hit me. Virgil sat in his wheelchair, his white coveralls golden with sawdust. Even sitting he looked gangly, the knobby knees of his useless legs spread and poking up into the air. He lifted his visor, revealing a face as bony and long as the rest of him, lantern jawed, with a hawk nose, its nostrils caked with sawdust. Virgil's froggy eyes were set deep into his elongated skull. Seeing me and Gordy, he smiled. His teeth were long, too, and yellow to match the sawdust coating everything. He shook our hands, clasping one hand in both of his.

"What's up, fellas?" he asked. "Come to learn more about our distant neighbors?"

I took off my knapsack, opened it, extracted the lump of matter I'd sliced from the Mysterious Object, and handed it to Virgil. He studied it, turning it over in his big, callused, sawdust-coated hand, its knuckles like the knots in a rope. After turning it over a few times he looked up seriously and said:

"Where'd you find this?"

I explained.

"Anyone else know about it?" Virgil cast furtive looks over mine and Gordy's shoulders.

I shook my head.

"Sure?"

The question rankled. We Back Shop Boys were nothing if not discreet.

"Better come in," Virgil said.

I followed him in his wheelchair, its wheels drawing dark tracks on the sawdust-covered floor. Every inch of the place was furry with sawdust, including the benches, which were wheelchair height and crowded with augers, adzes, vices, chisels, clamps, mallets, scribes, saws, jigs, drills, and other instruments for torturing lumber. A mule-sized lathe straddled a pile of fresh turnings. I breathed in the smell of ravished wood.

Virgil led us into his back room and told me to shut the door. There, in his secret command post, Virgil Zeno acquainted privileged visitors with electromagnetic propulsion, the Roswell Files, ionized air, 'G' forces, and coronas of bluish-purple flame. The room's cork walls were plastered with photographs, newspaper clippings, and other evidence of extraterrestrial activity sent to Virgil by enthusiasts from all over the country. Virgil lit one of two burners on a stove in the corner and put a kettle on. Even on the muggiest days Virgil always offered his guests Ovaltine ("*The food drink for rocket power*," according to the Secret Squadron in the television commercials). While waiting for the kettle to whistle he put a heaping tablespoon of Ovaltine into two mugs. Having filled the mugs with boiling water, into each—along with an inadvertent dash of sawdust—he plopped two marshmallows from a plastic bag.

"I take it you saw that star explode this morning?" Virgil said, handing me mine.

"You saw it too?"

"How could I miss it? It lit up the whole sky!"

"Weren't you sleeping?"

"I never sleep, not if I can help it!"

He gestured for us to take a seat. The flying saucer having left no room for other furnishings, Gordon and I sat on it. It made a surprisingly comfortable bench. It was where we always sat to hear Virgil's stories, none of which were more thrilling than that of his first UFO sighting, which happened on the night of April 18, 1954.

A year to the day after the accident that killed both of Virgil's brothers, to celebrate his birthday a group of Hattertown citizens chipped in to buy another DeSoto, identical to the first, but green where the other had been red, and fitted with a hand-operated throttle so Virgil could drive it without his legs. That night he drove it up to the new football field that had been built behind the high school and parked it near the fifty-yard line. There, with the top down and the driver's seat reclined, Virgil gazed at the stars that were scattered across the night sky like jewels at the bottom of an inverted ocean.

Until that night Virgil had shown little interest in the night sky. He rarely bothered looking at it, so concerned had he been with things earthbound. Now as he gazed up this awareness filled him with regret—and awe, for suddenly the stars were objects of wonder to him, as though he were seeing them for the first time: which, in a way, he was. Like a poor man raking in diamonds he gathered them in.

Suddenly a shooting star zipped across the eastern sky. It was followed by another, and another. For the next half hour a barrage of shooting stars crisscrossed the heavens. At around two o'clock in the morning (Virgil had switched off the ignition, so he couldn't read the dash clock) the shooting star display ended.

Virgil had started the DeSoto's engine and was about to drive back into town when in the northwestern sky he saw what he later described as a revolving circle of pulsating lights of various colors a quarter mile above the earth's surface. The object appeared to hover directly over the section of town known as Bumping Hill (275° azimuth; elevation 1.5°). As it hovered a group of patchy clouds swept over it, enhancing the impression of luminosity. After hovering there for a minute or so the circle of lights dispersed, flinging off in all different directions, leaving no doubt in Virgil's mind that he had borne witness to a completely novel event.

Two mornings later, under the headline HATTERTOWN RESIDENT SEES UFO, Virgil's testimony appeared in the *Hattertown Gazette.* Showing it to us over breakfast, my father slapped his knee first, then my mother's knee, then my three-year-old knee. That was his full commentary on the subject.

"So," said Virgil, rolling his wheelchair so close his knees touched mine. "Are you positive you're the only other person who saw that star explode?"

"As far as I know I am."

Virgil nodded. "That simplifies matters."

He leaned closer then, propping his elbows on his thighs and his chin on the interlaced fingers of his long, bony hands. His next words were uttered in a voice as smooth as fine-sanded wood and scented with Ovaltine, Black Jack gum, and sawdust:

"Sometime between now and the end of summer you will make contact with an entity from outer space."

Virgil let this bit of news sink in, fixing his froggy eyes on me, their whites stained brown as if his pupils had melted.

"*Me?*" I said.

"This leaves little doubt." Virgil hefted the specimen.

Like many boys of a certain age in Hattertown, Connecticut, I had a tacit understanding with Virgil. The understanding was this: that Virgil would tell me incredible things, and I would believe them. This arrangement was reciprocal. That hunk of fused metal and wire he held in his hand? It could have been a scrap of hat manufacturing machinery, as Zag had suggested, or part of an oddly shaped furnace boiler, or the forsaken prototype of a secret weapon contracted by the Pentagon and manufactured by some exponent of the Military Industrial Complex that President Eisenhower warned us about. It might have fallen from heaven or it might have fallen out of the back of a garbage truck. Whatever its source, its purpose couldn't have been clearer. It existed for the same reason all miracles exist: to make believers out of us.

I asked: "Why me?"

Virgil smiled. When he did his rubbery face looked like a funny page comic lifted and stretched on Silly Putty. "I have no idea. But as sure as eggs is eggs, they picked *you*."

"What am I supposed to do?"

Virgil pursed his lips. "I'm not sure there's much you *can* do, other than stay vigilant."

"Vigilant?"

"Be on your guard."

"Be on my guard for *what*?"

Virgil shook his head. "I wish I could tell you. Don't roll your eyes at me, I'm just the messenger here! All I know is that whatever form this visiting entity takes, it won't be alien in any obvious way. It won't be some little green man like in the movies. Odds are it'll blend in with the surroundings to better escape your notice."

"So how will I know when I see him—or it?"

Virgil shook his head again. "That's just it. You won't. You may have already made contact. It could be someone you know but would never suspect. Or it may be someone you *do* suspect. That's why you need to be vigilant. One thing's for certain: unless you keep that third eye of yours open, you'll never know if you've made contact or not."

"Third eye?"

"Your intuitive eye, the one that sees without seeing. This one here." He twisted a sawdusty thumb into my forehead.

I asked: "Has everyone got a third eye?"

"Sure, but in most people it's permanently sealed shut. For all we know yours is sealed shut too."

As Gordon and I left Virgil's carpentry shed that morning,

the gray shroud that had covered everything since my father's death was suddenly lifted. Like the NBC peacock that graced the living rooms of those lucky enough to afford a color TV, suddenly the world spread its bright, beautiful plumage. With Gordy gripping me from behind, as I pedaled us home to get ready for church, I wondered: what message, urgent and divine, has the universe got in store for me?

The Man in Blue walks. On roads and highways, along the railroad tracks, past homes and stores and abandoned hat factories. He walks in a cathedral of silence, its ceiling vaulted with sky. Vehicles swerve past him, stirring up eddies of dust that soak into the fibers of his blue coveralls. And though he never breaks his stride, he must sense the supreme effort by which the vehicles' drivers resist the urge to run him over.

While walking, he collects things: discarded bottles, burnt-out bulbs, and railroad insulators: thick, jellyfish-like blobs of glass in assorted watery blue and green shades fallen from utility poles along the railroad tracks. He holds them up to the sky to inspect them for defects before putting them in his rucksack or tossing them—like too-small-fish—back into the weeds.

In filling his rucksack he fills his days...

Though I kept spying on him I didn't learn much more about the Man in Blue. What I did learn I kept mostly to myself. If secrets are a form of currency, I hoarded mine like a miser. Asked to report on my reconnaissance, I lived up to my name and told half the truth: that the Man in Blue spent his days wandering the town gathering things in his canvas rucksack.

"What does he collect?" asked Zag.

"Insulators. The ones you find along the railroad tracks."

"What does he do with them?"

"Beats me."

Meanwhile I took Virgil's advice and kept my invisible third eye peeled, suspecting everyone of being an alien from outer space, even friends and family. I lived in a perpetually heightened state of alertness, convinced that my encounter was imminent, that at long last I would partake of something of the infinite.

But as April turned to May and May to June I grew weary

of my vigil. Conviction soured into doubt, doubt curdled into skepticism, and skepticism moldered into scorn. Virgil Zeno, that crazy crippled carpenter, had played me for a fool! I'd never partake of anything of the infinite! By July I'd cast his kooky prophecy out of my mind entirely and reverted to my customary state of gloom.

When Gordon and I next cut through Bum's Trail the Mysterious Object was gone. Someone must have hauled the thing away. All that remained was a weedy ditch.

The days grew hot and muggy. Muggy: how I hated that word, like getting mugged by the heat. Sticky sweat poured down our faces. Sidewalks fried the soles of our sneakers.

When it got so hot that neither the Town Hall water fountain nor the frosty gusts emanating from the ice cream case in McMullen's Five and Dime store cooled us down sufficiently, we pedaled our bikes to Lost Lake, so named since you couldn't see it from the road. While the others took turns jumping off a big rock leaning over the water, Gordon and I sat with our shirts off, enjoying the cool breezes that swept in off the water.

I never learned to swim. Had I known under no circumstances would I have jumped off that rock. Dreams of splash-landing space capsules notwithstanding, I had a morbid fear of water and drowning. I couldn't walk past a body of water without shivering, as if the lake or pond or river would reach out and hurl me into itself. It was my father's fault. When I was four he tried to teach me to swim by throwing me off a dock at Lake Candlewood. It never occurred to him that this method could fail and that he might have to rescue me, as he was ill-equipped to do, being unable to swim himself. It was Dick Stefansky—husband of Mom's friend Eve—who jumped fully clothed off the same dock to rescue me. As he breathed life back into me, Dad looked on through a Rock & Rye-infused haze, his gaunt features slack with astonishment, as if somebody else had thrown his kid into the drink. From then on except to hydrate and shower (I never took baths) I had as little to do with water as possible.

Still, I went to Lost Lake. I had no choice, really, if I wanted to be with my friends. And though it was made of water, the lake was pretty, and I enjoyed the breezes that found us there on that rock.

We dubbed the patch of water beneath the rock "Fool's Hole," and I never tired of pointing out to the others what fools they were for jumping into it. They in turn dubbed me and Gordon the "Rock Squad," since we were in charge of looking out for interlopers, and because they knew if *we* jumped we'd both sink like rocks.

After jumping a few times the others swam out to a small island at the lake's center with the remains of a miniature decorative stone lighthouse on it. Skunky did a sidestroke, Victor swam on his back, Zag zipped far ahead. Their six legs kicked up ragged white paired plumes. While they swam Gordy played with my yo-yo and I perused the latest *Space Man* comic ("Captives of a Mad Race of Space Creatures!") until boredom found me up there on that rock. With my rolled-up comic book I slapped Gordon's shoulder.

"Let's take a walk," I said.

Of the Dalton mansion all that remained was a rectangle of weed-and-moss-covered stones. To one side of it in what had been an estimable pool only vines and creepers swam. The ruins of the estate's outlying structures, its barns, sheds, chicken coops, conservatories, and picnic houses, were so overgrown only the keenest eye could distinguish them from the rest of the woods. Scattered throughout the grounds, hidden there like Easter eggs, were relics of its past: a bronze sundial, a granite birdbath, a marble bench with scrolled armrests, a fountain presided over by a headless, lichen-covered angel, its waters supplanted by weeds.

Having circled the estate once, Gordon and I arrived at the

concrete dam at the lake's far end. At the center of the dam was a sluiceway controlled by a rusted iron valve. When the lake was high, the water slid in a clear Saran Wrap-like sheet over the sluiceway and into a gully, where rocks gnashed it into foam. But the lake was low; no water slid over the sluiceway. I picked a stone up and sidearmed it over the dam.

I could say it was sheer coincidence that brought my stepbrother and me to Fern Cottage, but it wouldn't be true. Since I'd seen it, Fern Cottage and its mysterious occupant hadn't been far from my mind. Approaching it now, I tried to convince myself that I wasn't consumed with curiosity. In a burlesque of aimlessness I scuffed my sneakers on the gravel road and whistled tunelessly to myself. When the cottage veered into view I pretended it wasn't there. Caretaker's cottage? *What* caretaker's cottage?

This dumb show had a very brief run. As we arrived within a dozen yards of it I heard a sound and turned to see the cottage's green door swing open. With my hand clasped over Gordy's mouth, I pulled us into a mound of ferns. Through their fronds we watched as, in his plaid robe with his walking stick, the Man in Blue walked down the slate path leading to the gravel road. There he turned right, heading the way we'd come, toward Fool's Hole. We waited a few more seconds until, with a gesture borrowed from Vic Morrow in *Combat,* I signaled for us to follow him.

From the gravel road the Man in Blue took a shortcut through a tangle of bayberry bushes to the swimming rock, where he stood, leaning on his stick, his head bent forward, peering down over the rock's face. I turned to Gordon, signaling silence with a finger to my lips. Together we crab-scuttled under the low shrubs, mountain laurel mixed with thorny bayberry, toward the edge of exposed granite. There, from behind, with a sprig of laurel camouflaging us, I had a close-up view of my subject. I tried hard not to breathe, to stay calm, stuck there in the thicket with nowhere to turn or run, excited but at the same time saying to myself, *What if he turns and catches us, so close and obviously spying on him? What then?*

The Man in Blue took something from his face—his glasses?—and folded them into a pocket of his robe. He dropped the stick with a clatter. As he spread out his arms the plaid robe fell from his shoulders, exposing a wide, V-shaped back. Kids are notoriously bad at guessing the ages of adults, but if pressed I'd have said between twenty-five and fifty. His legs were lean and taut, doubtless from all that walking, their calves as big and boxy as toasters. A jagged scar ran down the left leg from the hip to the knee.

He lifted one leg from the plaid mound, then the other, then hopped about, freeing his feet. Terrified and in awe, I watched as—naked—he stretched both arms against the blue sky. Then he tipped forward, crouched, put air between his feet and the rock, curved over the edge, and was gone.

Suicide, I said to myself, easing out of the thicket. No one had ever dived head-first into Fool's Hole and lived to tell about it. Over patches of pale lichen I crept forward onto a section of bare granite, avoiding the green plaid robe, and looked over the edge, sure I'd see him lying there in a crumpled heap, but the rock's parabolic curve blocked my view. I leaned out further, one hand braced against a trembling knee. Still I couldn't see directly below me. I edged closer, sitting with the palms of both hands flat on the rock, using them as brakes, peeking through my spread knees, inching forward.

All this time my stepbrother stood behind me, kept there by his dread of heights and the certainty that I'd box his ear if he dared to disobey me. Meanwhile I stretched my neck out bird-like and slid forward another few inches. Still I saw nothing.

Suddenly I felt my hind parts slipping and knew I'd gone too far. I tried to back up, putting all my weight into the balls of my hands, my sneaker bottoms skidding on the boulder's surface. Bits of granite rolled ball bearing-like under my palms, chewing them up. I tried flattening myself against the rock, feeling the fabric of my shirt creep up to my neck as I sought to grip something, anything, with hands, feet, fingers…whatever nature had given me to grip with. I felt the skin peeling off my back.

Then my body turned weightless, floating off the rock face, arms spinning free, sneakers pumping air. I heard a cry—my own. My lips pulled back across my top teeth as the lake rushed up a full house-story under me. The same lake swallowed me, thundering as I pierced its skin to enter a pandemonium of bubbles and darkness.

The world moved upside-down. Sunlight speared topsy-turvy trees. Alongside a pair of hairy legs my eyeballs swung. Through a picket fence of wet hair the ground lurched. My wet T-shirt clung to my back, my thighs tight in sopping denim, my sneakers up there somewhere. As I touched ground a wall of bitterness rose down my inverted throat. I rolled over to puke lake water and breakfast, my hands flat under my elbows.

I looked up to see the man towering over me, his sunburned shoulders hunched as if ready to leap, his ribcage gleaming wet. His eyes bored into mine, looking at but not seeing me, blinded by fear. His penis hung less than a foot away from my nose, a sausage link with a loose, floppy casing. The man bent down to touch me. I screamed:

"*Get away from me, homo!*"

Pursued by my echoes he limped off into the woods.

Remembering Gordon, I ran back to the rock to find him gone. I looked down into the Fool's Hole. *Please God, no.* I called: *Gordon! Gordy!* I looked down at the lake again.

Oh, please, no, no, please no, no, no…

I heard sniffles and turned to see the white tip of a sneaker poking out from behind a bayberry bush. Attached to it, Gordy sat with his arms wrapped around his knees, rocking back and forth, bawling.

"It's okay," I said, stroking him. "It's okay, Gordy; it's okay."

❧

Back at the rock I hid the man's plaid robe and walking stick. The others came back to find me soaking wet.

"I fell in," I explained.

"And all this time we thought your stepbrother was the retard!" Skunky quipped and naturally they all laughed.

One advantage of having half a middle finger: I could flip people the bird in plain sight with impunity. My "Phantom Finger," I called it and put it to good use then and there.

Part 3

The Comformator

On Saturdays I helped my stepfather at his store. I washed windows, dusted shelves, polished display cases, and steam-cleaned hats that, despite frequent encounters with the feather duster, accrued furry mantles of dust.

When not doing any of those things I sat in the tufted red leather chair in the middle of the store, where customers' wives sat (when there were customers), flipping through the trade magazines my stepfather subscribed to—*Hats Off!*, *Hats Galore*, *The Sophisticated Hatter*—magazines packed with stimulating articles, to wit:

> **WHAT'S WRONG WITH MY HAT DISPLAYS?**
> Many stores fail to light their wall cases adequately. Most hat cases have no direct light on the hats; and those which have illumination behind a valance at the top succeed in lighting only the top one or two shelves, such that…
>
> **THE ART OF FITTING FACES**
> When a man's ears stick out from the sides of his head, the wrong hat makes them even more conspicuous. The crown should be proportioned to the face, but an extreme taper should be avoided, while the brim should be flat-set at the back and sides, and snapped full across the…
>
> **HATS FOR THE BIG FELLOW**
> Never sell a big man a hat with a narrow brim and a tapered crown. A narrow brim adds emphasis to a man's weight and to the width of his face and gives the hat an old-fashioned, stodgy air. A too high crown, on the other hand, makes such a man look like a giant, so his height becomes a liability rather than…

WHAT COLOR HAT SHALL I SELL HIM?

Brown hats are best with brown or greenish suits or coats. They rarely look good with gray clothing. Some brown or tan hats may be worn with blue or blue-gray clothing, but the salesman or the customer must have a real color-sense to be sure of these harmonies…

HOW TO SELL QUALITY

First, point out to the customer that in a hat of fine materials and conscientious workmanship the felt is much firmer, smoother, springier, and tighter. Next, get the customer's old hat off his head; this gives you your cue on sizing and price. If it's a $7.50, show him a $10.00. If he makes no objection, try a $12.50, and if that fails to secure his…

HOW TO SHAPE THE HAT

The crease must be centered. For this the bow tie on the leather is your guide. Never shape a hat against the chest as shown in the next picture, a common habit with inexperienced salesmen, but a bad one. It is almost impossible to center a crease this way, or to judge how deep the crease is being made. In short, it's the job of a butcher, not an artist…

Waple Hats was located ("conveniently," according to the ads my stepfather ran on WHAT, the local radio station) on Felt Street, between Top Hat Tailors and The Velvet Box Jewelers. That Saturday morning it rained. I parked my bike in the alley. Holding an umbrella over both mine and Gordy's heads, I led us around to the store's main entrance.

The front door set off a string of bells. Seeing us my stepfather smiled. He wore his double-breasted gray suit and puffed his Calabash pipe. I smelled his cologne—aftershave?—a calm, clean, dignified smell that, combined with the smell of his pipe tobacco, conveyed a sense of masculine order and grace.

Like everything else about my stepfather I held that smell in contempt.

He tousled Gordon's hair and gave my hand a hearty shake. Walter J. Waple was an inveterate hand-shaker.

"What's up, sport?" he said per our routine.

"I dunno," I said, rolling my eyes. "What's up with you?"

"Gas prices are up, taxes are up, unemployment is up, and hats are up!" From a nearby display stand my stepfather took a red-feathered porkpie and plopped it onto my head while rabbit-punching my shoulder, making me wish myself dead.

By then Gordon and my Dunkin' Midnight Special yo-yo had taken their usual seat on a folding metal chair by the cash register. My stepfather put my umbrella into a stand by the door, then helped me off with my raincoat, exposing the suit he'd bought along with a pair of brown wingtips for me to wear exclusively at his store, the latter hidden under galoshes.

"You've come on a red-letter day, as it were, sport," my stepfather said as I pried the galoshes off. "Wait till you see what I've got in store for you—get it, in *store*? It'll knock your socks—or rather, your *hat* off! Ha-ha!"

He indicated the tufted red leather chair. "Sit down. Take a load off your feet. I'll be back in a jiff!"

So saying he disappeared into his office.

The other reason for my helping my stepfather at his store: to "cheer him up," in my mother's words. Not that my stepfather needed cheering. The world could have gone "to hell in a handbasket, if you will," and along with his cologne, Walter J. Waple would have worn his eternally chipper smile.

Not that Walter Waple lacked cause for gloom. His hat business was failing and had been for some time. All across America sales of men's hats were in decline, the steepest downturn having occurred after World War II. Some claimed the war itself was to blame. Having come to equate headgear with military subjugation, returning vets wanted nothing to do with hats. Others pointed to changes in the designs of automobiles, with their low-slung roofs that made hat-tipping invisible if not altogether impossible. Still others blamed air travel, which put luggage space at a premium, forcing hat-wearers to choose between keeping their hats in their laps or having them crushed under suitcases. It didn't help that bars and restaurants had taken to charging patrons for checking hats. Finally, there were those scientific studies suggesting that the wearing of hats promoted baldness in men, studies whose validity Walter J. Waple denied vociferously.

"Upon my word," he argued, "why everyone knows wearing a hat is good for the scalp! It protects the follicles from humidity, dust, dirt, excess heat and cold, not to mention sunburn, soot, rain, hail, bird droppings, and other undesirable elements! The worst thing a fellow can do to his scalp is expose it to the fickle winds of fate, if you will!"

Someone had left a copy of *Life* magazine on the tufted chair. I sat flipping its pages while gazing through the store's large display windows. Since it was summer Panama hats dominated the left-hand window display. Under a yellow construction-paper sun a streamer announced:

Straws to Cover Every Head Type in Town!

The right-hand display, to which I'd contributed, featured nine fedoras of different colors revolving around another sun, this one of papier-mâché. Behind them a dozen road maps were pinned to a sky-blue chintz curtain. By the same fishing line he'd used in my bedroom, model cars, buses, trains, passenger planes, and other forms of transportation dangled. This window's banner said:

See the World in a Caxton-Dumont

It was an impressive display, or would have been, had it not been upstaged by the recently installed neon sign:

Waple & Son Hats
Since 1898

—the ampersand enclosed in a flashing neon derby. The flashing neon clashed with the august gold leaf of the original sign, and in my opinion would have better suited a billiards parlor. As for that *& Son,* it referred not to my stepbrother, but to yours truly. My stepfather basked in the conviction that one day I'd be his partner and ultimately take over the business, a conviction I had no wish or intention to gratify.

❧

Bearing what looked like a medieval torture device or the brass and copper crown of an impecunious king, my stepfather returned. Mouthing a trumpet fanfare, he placed the spiny object on my lap.

"Gentlemen," he announced, though aside from my stepbrother I was the only person in earshot. "I give you…the Comformator!"

The object consisted of a dish-sized, oval-shaped brass ring, its circumference lined with a series of numbered brass thumbscrews. A set of copper buttresses connected the bass ring to a wheel divided into triangular slices, each numbered slice bristling with pins, like a carnival wheel of fortune.

"What do you think?" my stepfather asked, relighting his Calabash pipe. On the table next to his rocking chair at home he kept a rack of seven pipes, one for each day of the week:

Monday: Maple
Tuesday: Meerschaum
Wednesday: Cherry
Thursday: Brier
Friday: Olivewood
Saturday: Calabash
Sunday: Corncob

Walter J. Waple was a fuming human calendar.

I asked, "What is it?"

"Take a wild guess!"

"Something for measuring hats?"

"You're barking up the right tree, there, as it were," my stepfather said, grinning. "Sure, it sizes hats. Nothing new there. There've been many devices created to fulfill that humble purpose. *Conformators,* they're called, with an *n.* Ah, but, sport, the *Comformator* —with an *m*—is a whole 'nother kettle o' fish. You could even say the *m* stands for *more,* since it does much, much more. Here, allow me to demonstrate…"

So saying my stepfather picked the contraption up and lowered it onto my head. Despite its soothing compliant name, the thing snagged my skull like a crown of thorns.

"Now, if you'll permit me, I need to adjust the thumbscrews…"

While making said adjustments my stepfather explained to me how his invention, on which he'd labored in secret for the better part of a year, could not only arrive at the perfect size for a customer's hat, but—using data gleaned from observation—could also arrive at the perfect style, color, band and brim width. It could even calculate the ideal angle of rake with which a hat should be worn, whether or not to dimple the crown, and in which direction, if any, to snap the brim.

"Impressive, huh? Or as you kids like to say these days, *neat-oh*!"

I was impressed, all right. Of all my stepfather's schemes, this was by far the most ambitious—and the most ludicrous, since by then it was obvious that nothing would save his or any other hat store from the fickle winds of fashion. Already my stepfather had gone to great lengths to attract more customers. He'd ordered the neon sign, replaced incandescent bulbs with fluorescents (to better replicate office environments), installed maroon wall-to-wall carpeting and glass-and-mirror display cases. If all that wasn't enough, he'd instigated a series of radio ads with slogans he wrote himself: *Hats Make the Man! If You Want to Get Ahead, Get a Hat! Beautify America: Wear a Hat!* Still sales at Waple Hats kept falling.

For the decline in sales of men's hats, my stepfather blamed neither scientific studies nor wars nor airplanes nor automobiles. He blamed our thirty-fifth president, John Fitzgerald Kennedy, or "Hatless Jack," as he was known contemptuously to those in the hatter's trade. The mere mention of Kennedy's name was enough to make my stepfather's normally stiff upper lip tremble while making the usually tepid blood in his veins boil. As tolerant as Walter J. Waple was of most human beings, he was intolerant of President Kennedy, and had been ever since the snowy morning of January 20th, 1961, the day he took the oath of office—the first president ever to do so without, as my stepfather put it, "so much as a beanie on his hairy Irish Catholic head!"

Yet even for that indecent performance he had been willing to forgive Kennedy, who was, after all, in his view, a young man, subject to a young man's lapses in judgment and taste. And, to be fair, on that blustery bitter-cold day Vice President Eisenhower had likewise gone hatless, as had Robert Frost, our frail Poet Laureate, his hoary hair flapping like a ghost kite in the breeze, his octogenarian eyes so dazzled by winter glare he couldn't make out the words to his own inaugural poem: a calamity that—as my stepfather pointed out—might have been averted had Frost worn *his* hat.

Hence my future stepfather had given Kennedy a chance to redeem himself. He wrote him a letter, one that he typed himself on the Remington "Noiseless" in his office that, contrary to its name, sounded like a machine gun. He made two carbons, one of which hangs on the wall of my study.

"Dear Mr. President," his letter begins,

I was very sorry to read that you had a cold and hope you recover quickly and completely. The same paper that reported the story also carried a picture of you wearing a hat and coat, with the caption below explaining that you donned them because of your cold.

As the owner of the oldest hat retail store in Hattertown, Connecticut, I was naturally pleased to come upon this photograph of you wearing a hat. However, I must express to you my very strong conviction that there are reasons for wearing a hat other than as protection against the elements.

Not only does wearing a hat flatter your appearance, it endows you with an added air of maturity, authority, and dignity in keeping with your office. If that's not reason enough, 25,000 men and women work in the hatting industry. They, too, benefit from your wearing a hat.

And now may I take this liberty, dear Mr. President, to offer my services as haberdasher and come to Washington to personally prepare a hat wardrobe for you? It would be a great privilege. And you may rest assured that, assuming you accept, under no circumstances will I take advantage of this undertaking for purposes of publicity.

Yours Respectfully,
Walter J. Waple
Owner & Sole Proprietor
Waple Hats, Incorporated

To this missive my stepfather never received a reply. Again, in President Kennedy's defense, he may have had other things on his mind. The same week my stepfather posted his letter, a United States Air Force reconnaissance plane photographed a string of medium-range ballistic missile bases under construction near San Cristóbal, Cuba.

But rather than assuage my stepfather's resentment the Cuban Missile Crisis merely exacerbated it, since it had been Khrushchev—that pumpkin-faced, shoe-banging despot, the same Khrushchev who gave the homburg a bad name—who'd pulled a fast one on our hatless, hapless commander-in-chief. Proving, if proof were necessary, that not only was Kennedy uncouth, he was dangerous.

Despite this, and notwithstanding the persistent decline in sales, my stepfather remained steadfast in his devotion to men's hats. A few weeks after writing his letter to the president, he presented Governor Dempsy with a proclamation, typed on the same Remington typewriter, for a national holiday:

PROCLAMATION

Ever since the first cave dweller wrapped a reed of grass around his brow to bind his flowing hair, Man has busied himself with the adornment of his pate. In the passing of time his garland has evolved through an animated variety of scalp locks, feathers, bonnets, turbans, shakos, helmets, kerchiefs, caps, and crowns to emerge as the modern day hat.

Today, from its perch on every head, the hat stands as a crowning monument to the happiest marriage of craftsmanship and practicality yet styled to hug the human skull.

More than most states Connecticut has reason to pay homage to the hat; for the know-how of her hatters has won us world renown. We must take pause to reflect on the hatter's art, how it has ennobled our pretensions while warming us against the frosts of fall and winter's icy fingers.

Therefore, and by the presumed authority of a joint resolution to be passed in the General Assembly, I ask that you hereby proclaim that Saturday, September 30 henceforth be known as

HAT DAY

Have a good hat. The secret of your looks/ Lies with the Beaver in the Brooks.

To Walter J. Waple, hats were more than a protective covering for men's heads. They were symbols of progress and pride. A civilization without hats was as much a contradiction in terms to him as a mind with no brain.

As for men who went hatless, they were brutes, beasts, barbarians. Even the poorest fellow, if he had any self-respect, wouldn't set foot in public without a hat. It could be a hat of inexpensive wool felt, or a tweed or canvas cap, and battered to boot. Still he'd wear it with as much pride as a king wears his crown.

As for "Hatless Jack" and the revolting fashion he'd instigated, like all seasonal viruses it would run its course. In time the white corpuscles of good taste would prevail, and men would return to their fedoras, their trilbies, their pork pies, their derbies, their homburgs… The dark days of hatlessness would pass.

"Yes, sir," my stepfather said, brandishing his invention. "This baby's gonna launch hatting into the space age. We've already gotten nibbles for mass production deals from some big manufacturing firms. Ever hear of American Totalizer? Third biggest maker of vending machines in the country. We play our cards right, sport, there won't be a single hat store left in America without one of these babies."

I thought: *There won't be a single hat store left in the country.*

"Not a word of any of this to your mother, okay, sport? For the time being it's strictly on the QT, if you will—between you, me, and the Comformator!"

"Uhn haah dah," said Gordy, having by then traded my yo-yo for his fingertips.

My stepfather had reason for keeping his invention a secret from my mother. She would have been appalled. For two years she had been trying to get him to close the store, to engage in some more lucrative business. Having learned that Dick Stefansky—the same Dick Stefansky who fished me out of Lake Candlewood—had been promoted to vice president of the Wire Clothes Hanger Division of Consolidated Screw & Wire in nearby Waterbury, and was seeking a director of marketing, she urged my stepfather to apply.

This my stepfather refused to do. "I'm a hat merchant," he argued. "What in a ham sandwich do I know about wire coat hangers?"

"You're a salesman, Walter," my mother reasoned. "A good salesman can sell anything. You've said so yourself many times."

"I never said any such thing."

"You have, Walter. *Many* times."

It was past nine o'clock. My mother and stepfather were in the parlor watching *Perry Mason.* Raymond Burr was getting out of a black Ford. From my vantage point crouched behind the beaded curtain I listened.

"'A good salesman can sell anything.' Those were your exact words, Walter," my mother was saying.

"Be that as it may, I've no interest in selling wire coat hangers."

"People need coat hangers," my mother said, lighting a Chesterfield King. Less than a month earlier her doctor had gotten her to quit. Now she was at it again.

"If you're suggesting that men don't need hats, I beg to differ."

"President Kennedy doesn't need a hat."

"President Kennedy, if you'll pardon me, is an ignoramus."

"He may be an ignoramus, but he's still the president."

"He may be the president, but he's still an ignoramus."

"At least he doesn't wear brown suits."

"What has that got to do with the price of eggs, if you will?"

"Dick Nixon wears brown suits."

"Who cares what color suits Nixon wears?"

"Hitler wore brown suits," my mother said.

"Were we or were we not talking about coat hangers?"

"You voted for him."

"I voted for *Hitler*?"

"You voted for Nixon, dear."

It was a Wednesday. My stepfather re-lit his cherry pipe.

"At least let them interview you," my mother pleaded. "What have you got to lose?"

"I have no intention of selling coat hangers, much less wire ones. And that, as they say, is that."

Only it wasn't. A week later they were at it again. This time the argument took place in the kitchen. My stepfather ate his usual breakfast of Melba toast and Lipton tea. Sunshine dazzled the yellow curtains. The *Hattertown Gazette* lay spread open on the table under my stepfather's eyes where, having circled a want ad for a salesman in the men's accessories department at Sears & Roebuck in red ink, my mother had shoved it.

"Not interested," my stepfather said, shoving it back.

"Why? You'd still be selling hats!"

"A hat is not an accessory! A *scarf* is an accessory. A glove is an accessory. A hat is a *garment*!"

So saying my stepfather stood abruptly, donned his tan fedora, straightened himself in his suit, and—in a cloud of righteous indignation—left for work.

"Damn you, Walter Waple!" my mother shouted after the door slammed behind him. "You'll send us to hell with your damn hats!"

Then she burst into tears.

❧

"Now, then, sport," my stepfather said as I sat with his invention on my head. "If you've no objection, I'd like to make unto thee thy graven image, as it were, for the patent application. The face that launched a thousand Comformators!"

He went to get his Polaroid camera. I gazed through the plate-glass windows I had polished countless times at cars splashing through puddles on Felt Street. Winking taillights stained the puddles red. The red lights were absorbed by raindrops that slid sled-like down the window, putting them in competition with the flashing neon sign. Standing by his wooden kiosk, a policeman in a yellow slicker directed traffic. My stepfather returned.

"Now, sport, if you'd just hold the device by its sides like you would a hat in a breeze. That's it. Easy, now; don't tug." With cool, manicured, soap-scented fingers, he adjusted my posture. "Perfect!"

He aimed the Polaroid.

"Let's have a nice big grin, there, sport. On a count of three. One, two—"

"Uhn haah dah."

"Cheese!"

The flashbulb exploded, blinding me at first before setting off a fusillade of dazzling colors. As I blinked them away my stepfather counted: *One Mississippi, two Mississippi...* As the colored blobs dissolved, through glass and raindrops I watched refugees from the weather huddled over coffee mugs and ice cream sundaes at the soda fountain of the drugstore across the street. My stepfather took more Polaroids. Between blinding flashes I flipped through the latest issue of *Life*. The main story, about the seven Project Mercury astronauts, featured a grainy photo of them goofing around in their gravity-free space capsule, catching floating peanuts in their mouths, squirting orange ribbons of Tang at each other. Across vast expanses of space my stepfather's voice reached me:

Always remember to sight the protrusions first before you take the conform. That's very important...

The customer on the closest stool at the drugstore wore a windbreaker the same color as the Man in Blue's coveralls, reminding me of my guilt, since I'd screamed at and insulted him when all he'd done was save my life. Worse, I'd hidden his walking stick and the plaid robe with his glasses in it. Already the poor guy was lame and mute. Now, thanks to me, he was blind, too.

Forget to sight the protrusions first, you may as well throw the whole works out the window, if you will...

I flipped abstractedly through the magazine, thinking how for years I'd dreamed of outer space, peering through my mail-order telescope, wanting as much to be discovered by something out there as to discover it, to partake of something of the infinite. My dead father's words came back to me:

Follow your fears... Follow your fears...

What were my fears? What was I most afraid of?

As I watched the pouring rain it came to me: Water. *Drowning*, that was my biggest fear. If I was ever to partake of something of the infinite, to conquer outer space, first I'd have to conquer my fear of inner space, meaning of water. Meaning I'd have to learn to swim. Meaning someone would have to teach me.

That someone, I realized, was the Man in Blue.

Through fathoms of water my stepfather's voice bubbled:

Customer satisfaction, sport. That's the key to increasing sales. Fashion's got nothing to do with it…"

Tomorrow, I told myself as wet pedestrians flew past the store windows. Tomorrow I'll return to Fern Cottage. I'll find the Man in Blue. I'll ask him to teach me how to swim.

A man holding a newspaper triangulated over his head darted between parked cars.

Sport?

That's what I'll do…

Leo?

The Comformator tucked into the crook of his arm, my stepfather towered over me.

"You're free to move about now, sport," he said, adding with one of his hokey winks: "Your death sentence, as it were, has been commuted."

The next day I returned to Fern Cottage, but not before helping Zag at the dog pound as I did every Sunday morning. Volunteering there was the highlight of my week. To be responsible for all those dogs, even for just a few hours, gave me a sense of purpose and responsibility absent mostly from the rest of my life.

It was a bright sunny day. The rain the day before had washed every trace of cloud away, leaving the sky so bright it hurt my eyes. The dog pound, a cinderblock building with a fenced-in incinerator behind it, was by the town reservoir, close to the dam. When Gordy and I arrived Sergeant Pomeroy's canine control van wasn't parked in the gravel lot, meaning he was "stalking wild turkey," as Zag put it—i.e., parked along a deserted stretch of road somewhere nursing the pint bottle of bourbon he kept in the van's glove compartment.

Sergeant Pomeroy was a big man. His round ruddy face reminded me of a boiled Easter ham (minus the pineapple slices and cloves). His only son died in Korea, in the Battle of Pork Chop Hill. Since then he'd moved through existence in a perpetual state of torpor. You might reasonably conclude that someone in that condition would make a less-than-ideal dogcatcher. You'd be wrong. Pomeroy's sluggishness was the key to his success. The wildest, fiercest, most aggressively defiant dogs walked calmly straight into his arms, lured there by nothing more than a dog biscuit and the sergeant's imperturbably placid manner.

A tangy smell of dog shit scented the morning air. I leaned my bicycle against the incinerator's chain-link fence. The back door to the pound opened to a clamorous tunnel of caged dogs. Gordy and I walked through it to Pomeroy's office, where Zag sat behind the sergeant's metal desk, his sneakers propped up on it, sipping coffee from the sergeant's State Farm Insurance mug, puffing a cigar from the cedar humidor box the sergeant kept next to his CB radio, which spluttered.

Behind the sergeant's desk a wall-sized map of Hattertown bristled with various colored pushpins, with white pushpins standing for "animals" (Pomeroy never called them "dogs") that had been reported for excessive barking, yellow pushpins for those guilty of lesser offenses (shitting on neighbors lawns, digging up flower beds), blue pushpins for those that had bitten once, red for those guilty of two or more assaults, and black pushpins indicating animals suspected of carrying rabies.

Through a cloud of blue smoke Zag handed me a cigar from the humidor. He knew cigars made me sick. He also knew I'd take it if only to avoid having him call me a pussy.

"I can't stay long," I explained as he lit the cigar using Sergeant Pomeroy's grenade-shaped cigarette lighter.

"Why not?"

"My stepfather needs me at his store."

"What for? It's Sunday!"

"He's doing inventory," I lied, shrugging.

Zag's left eye was swollen and purple. Once a month on average Zag's father bruised his son with one of the crutches he hobbled around the ground floor of their home with. The black eyes had become a regular feature of his looks, which was too bad. Not only was Zag the shortest, strongest, and most athletic of the Back Shop Boys, he was the best looking—a young Humphrey Bogart, with Bogey's black hair and his habit of drawing his lip across his upper teeth when vexed.

I pointed to the shiner. Zag stared at me. He didn't want to talk about it.

We sat there for a while, filling the office with cigar smoke, deciphering the CB radio's staticky splutters, until at last Zag said, "Right, let's get to it."

With cigars fuming and me holding back an urge to vomit, we

transferred the dogs to their outdoor cages. Each cage had an indoor and outdoor compartment, with the compartments separated by a guillotine-style door controlled by a rope and pulley system. With the dogs in their outdoor cages, we hosed the inner cages down, and vice-versa. We let Gordon man the hose. My stepbrother loved watching the water pry up bits of dog shit and other crud and send them scuttling into the slop hole drain. In exchange for manning the hose, Gordon had to clean out the slop drain trap, which, when opened, exuded a week's worth of repugnantly fermented dog food and shit.

While Gordy hosed the cages Zag and I opened a dozen cans of Ken-L Ration. By then the dogs had stopped barking—all but one of them, Zag's dog. Zippo's barks reverberated off the tiled walls of the Isolation Room, where dogs were euthanized. Every Thursday afternoon Dr. Dillard, the town veterinarian, arrived with his black bag of lethal implements. Afterward he would stuff the dead dogs into burlap bags and haul them out to the incinerator, which turned them into dog ash and smoke. Zippo had been scheduled for euthanization the Thursday when, having taken a liking to him, Zag pleaded with the sergeant to grant him clemency and let Zag keep him. Pomeroy consented with the stipulation that should the dog return for any reason no further reprieves would be granted.

"What's Zippo doing in there?" I asked over Zippo's barks.

"I can't leave him home. The barking drives my old man crazy."

Zippo was the barkiest dog I'd ever known. He barked at everything: flowers, birds, bees, trees, insects, gravel, and grass. He barked at mailboxes, phone poles, lawn sprinklers, fire hydrants. He barked at butterflies, fluttering maple pods, dandelion puffballs. He barked at cars, trucks, shoes, bicycles, sneakers, raindrops, and snowflakes. If I whistled or hummed or played with my yo-yo, Zippo barked. He barked at the sun, the moon, the stars, the planets and galaxies. He barked at women, children, at workers (in or out of uniform), cats, and other dogs. He barked at Christians, Jews, Muslims, Buddhists,

Presbyterians, Pentecostals, Taoists, Zoroastrians, Seventh Day Adventists, atheists, and agnostics. He barked at odors, intuitions, and even at implications. Zippo's was the least discriminating bark in the world, dispensed as generously as God's supposedly infinite grace.

"He sure does bark a lot," I noted.

"He's expressing himself," Zag said testily. "He's got a lot to say."

"I've got a lot to say, too, but I don't bark my head off all day long."

"You're not a dog."

"True," I said.

"You have no idea what goes through a dog's mind. Did you know the average dog recognizes about a million times as many smells as you or I ever will? Think about it. Imagine going through your life noticing so many smells. Every corner you turn, everywhere you point your nose, another smell! And another! And *another*! It would be like walking down a street lined with...I dunno...candy stores, or stores filled with Matchbox toys or yo-yos or whatever it is that you're crazy about, and all of it free and yours for the taking—or the sniffing, rather. Now, you can't own a smell the way you can own a Matchbox toy, it's true. You can't take it home with you and put it on your shelf and collect it, can you? Of course not: it's a *smell*! You get to smell it, and that's that! Which is the point. Which is why dogs bark so much. It's not what they're seeing. That's only half the story. Hell, it's not even half the story, it's maybe one-tenth of the story. Smells—they're the other nine-tenth. The more intelligent, the more sensitive, the more sophisticated the dog, the more smells it's gonna recognize, therefore the more it's gonna bark, because it wants you and the whole rest of the world to know what a great smell it just smelled. Which is what Zippo's doing right now. He's letting us know he smells something interesting. He doesn't bark too much! He *smells* too much. The world smells too much!"

As it always did when his passions were excited, Zag's top

lip drew back Bogey-like against his teeth. He clenched and unclenched his fists. Zag was a man of obdurately bold convictions. Even when the facts were against him, or when he had no idea what he was talking about, Zag's convictions gave him the edge in any argument.

Anyway, once Zag made up his mind about a thing, he was about as likely to change it as Saturn is likely to shed its rings.

With the dogs fed and their cages hosed, we put a few on leashes. Holding two leashes each, we walked the dogs across the dam to the pump house. Driven by a vortex of baying snouts and swirling limbs, we ran across the top of the dam. Some days the door to the pump house would be open, and Mr. Silz, the pump house superintendent, would be there, with his red bandanna tied around his sunburned neck. He'd show us his latest pin-up girl and play darts with us.

That morning the pump house door was closed. We turned and headed back across the dam. We were halfway across when Zag said: "I need to find him a new home."

"Who?"

Zag gave me a look. "Zippo, who else? Everything was fine till the old man's gout started acting up. When Dad's gout flares up, it gives off a smell that Zippo finds exquisite, so he barks. It's called a vicious cycle. Even outside with the windows all shut Zippo still smells Dad's gout. It's a hopeless situation." Zag looked up at me. "I don't suppose you'd like to own a dog?"

I shook my head. "Nope."

We kept walking.

"Whatever happens I'm damned if I'll let Dillard get anywhere near Zippo with that needle of his. I'll put him down myself, first, if it comes to that."

We walked in silence a while longer.

Zag changed the subject.

"So—have you found out anything more about the man?"

"Who?"

"The Man in Blue. What other man would I be talking about?"

"Oh. No. Not much."

"Where does he live? Did you find that out, at least?"

"Not exactly. I got close, but then I lost him."

"How could you lose him? He's *blue,* for crissakes!"

Just then, a big smile broke over Gordon's face. Maybe it was the word "blue," or maybe it was something else. With Gordon you could never tell.

❧

With the dogs back in their cages, we drank ice-cold bottles of Yoo-hoo from the office refrigerator. I told Zag I had to go.

"You're not doing inventory at your stepdad's store," Zag said. "What's really up?"

"I need a favor," I said.

"Don't tell me you're still hung up on that Dalton girl?"

"Will you watch Gordy for me?"

"What? No way!"

"Unh haah dah."

"Just for an hour. That's all. It's important!"

"I'll bet." He smiled. "Snooty Highlander. Thinks her farts smell like roses and cinnamon buns. Just because her family used to own half the town."

"Will you do me a favor, or won't you?"

"All right, but only for an hour, not a minute more. After that, I swear I'll lock him in one of these cages."

I gave Gordon my yo-yo and rode to Lost Lake.

I couldn't find the man's robe and stick. He must have found them himself. I still owed him an apology. And I was still determined to get him to teach me how to swim.

I had arrived within a dozen feet of the cottage when I saw something on the stoop, a shortbread tin. There was a note attached to it with a ribbon. Even if she hadn't signed it, I would have recognized Belinda Dalton's handwriting.

I BAKED THESE YESTERDAY. PLEASE ENJOY!
BELINDA DALTON

Belinda Dalton knew the Man in Blue! At first this fact struck me dumb, but then it made sense, since the cottage's previous occupant had been Belinda's uncle, Brewster Dalton, the man who, in a fit of insanity (according to one theory) burned Hearthstone Manor—the Dalton mansion—to the ground.

As for what drove Brewster Dalton insane, most people assumed that it had something to do with the decision to shutter the Dalton Hat Works after 155 years of continuous operation, a decision that sealed not only the fates of the factory's hundred employees, but of tobacconists, cooks, shoe and watch repairmen, grocers, newspaper, and other vendors who provided them goods and services.

More upsetting still to Brewster was that the decision was made by his older brother Baxter, whom he detested, and who, subject to the will that Baxter himself prepared and that their father arguably signed in a state of *non compis mentis* (his mental capacities vastly diminished by the advanced stages of mercury poisoning), assumed the presidency of Dalton Hat Works, while Brewster inherited his brother's former role as operations manager.

While Brewster favored keeping the factory running for the workers' sakes despite increasingly narrow profit margins, Baxter believed that business is business, that their first obligation was not to the workers but to their shareholders. Proceeds from the liquidation of assets could be invested in more lucrative ventures.

Not only did Baxter shut the Dalton Hat Works down, he put Hearthstone Manor up for sale, having by then relocated his family to a less grand residence in Danville, on a thirty-acre plot adjacent to the state fairgrounds. As for Brewster, a provision in his father's will had left him a parcel of the estate, a dozen acres that included the former caretaker's cottage, into which he moved and where he lived out the remainder of his days in near-total seclusion.

Meanwhile, with no buyers in sight, Hearthstone Manor was boarded up and fenced in, and so it remained until the night of August 7, 1954, when the mansion burned down. In the ashes investigators discovered charred bits of human bone. That Brewster was never seen again led to the obvious conclusion that the bones were his, that in a fit of insanity he'd set fire to the mansion, killing himself (accidentally? on purpose?) in the process.

According to another theory, it was Baxter who set the blaze, wishing to rid himself not only of a mansion that he couldn't sell, but of an embarrassingly insane younger brother whose murder he concealed by means of the fire.

As I picked up the shortbread tin a sense of indignation welled up in me. I had come to think of the Man in Blue as my own personal mystery to solve, a secret passed on to me by the universe per Virgil Zeno's prophecy. Now I had to share that secret—with Belinda Dalton, of all people! It was like landing on the moon only to find someone else's flag planted there.

Absentmindedly I pried open the lid of the shortbread tin. A heady aroma of chocolate flared up into my nostrils. I peeled away a sheet of wax paper, unveiling a dozen fresh-baked brownies. Without thinking I took a bite out of one. Before I knew it, while gazing up at the blue sky through a web of tree branches, I'd eaten half a dozen of them. With my head resting against the cottage's green front door, to the drone of a small airplane flying by somewhere, I dozed off. And I dreamed.

I dreamed that I was being chased by dogs, hundreds of them, all snarling and yapping, trying to get at the shortbread tin under my arm. As I ran a stream of brownies fell out of the tin. In the dream I climbed a church steeple, all the while clutching the shortbread tin, climbing up and up and up. The steeple turned into a hat factory chimney. I kept climbing, my belly scraping against bricks. I climbed through the troposphere, the stratosphere, the ionosphere, into outer space. I kept climbing until I grew weightless, the Milky Way swirling around me, the stars caressing my cheeks…

Something jabbed my shoulder. The Man in Blue stood there looking down, the sun shining through the trees over his shoulders. I stood up. As I did the shortbread tin and its surviving brownies scattered across the cottage's front steps.

"Someone left these for you," I said, gathering them, holding them out to him like an offering to a temperamental god.

He stood there. He carried his rucksack and a bag of groceries.

I asked, "Do you remember me?"

The man stared.

"I'm the kid who fell in the lake. You saved me."

He kept staring.

"I came here to thank you…for saving my life."

"…"

"And to apologize…for saying…you know…what I said."

"…"

"That wasn't very nice of me."

"…"

"I was also wondering…if you'd be willing…if you'd consider…teaching me…to swim."

"…"

I nodded. "Thanks anyway."

I turned and started back to the gravel road.

The sun blazed through the trees. I'd reached the gravel road when I heard: "Who are you?" *(Hoo ahh hyew?)*

I turned. "Did you just say something?"

"*Who … are … you?*"

He had a foreign accent.

"You can *talk?*"

"I asked you a question." *(Hi esked hyew uh kvestchun.)*

"My name's Leo. Half, they call me."

"I didn't ask your name. I asked: Who—are—you?"

"You mean, like, where do I live, who my parents are, that sort of stuff?"

The man shook his head. "It is a simple question." *(Hids uh zimble kvestchun.)*

Had he asked me anything else, I'd have probably known the answer. Had he asked me, for instance, how big the moon would be if the sun were the size of a basketball, I'd have told him that it would be about the size of the period at the end of this sentence. Had he asked me how many muscles it takes for someone to smile (seventeen), or how many inches the *Queen Mary* moved per gallon of fuel (six), or what the highest point is in Pennsylvania (Mount Davis), or the lowest in Colorado (the Arikaree River), I could have told him any of those things. I could have told him that snakes can't blink, that tigers have striped skin, that peanuts were once used to make dynamite, that all polar bears are left-handed, that the spiral staircases in medieval castles run clockwise, that all New Hampshire license plates bearing the motto "Live Free or Die" are manufactured by prisoners, that bird droppings are the chief export of Nauru, a small island in the Pacific Ocean, that an ostrich's eyeball is bigger than its brain…

"I give up," I said. "Can you at least give me a clue?"

With a disgusted look, the man turned and walked into his cottage, slamming the green door behind him.

Part 4

Independence Day

That Fourth of July Zag shot his father.

Earlier that day, at two in the afternoon, Gordon and I straddled my bicycle to watch the Fourth of July parade's marching bands and floats make their way down Felt Street. In his DeSoto convertible, wearing his carpenter overalls, Virgil Zeno pulled the biggest float: a giant derby formed of crumpled black crepe paper affixed to an armature of chicken wire. Mothers jounced baby carriages, dads shouldered toddlers, old men in pointy VFW caps sat in folding lawn chairs on the sidewalks. As the gleaming fire trucks grumbled by, the old timers pumped their liver-spotted arms and shouted, "Got a siren on that baby?"

It wasn't long before Skunky and Victor joined us. Since that Sunday at the dog pound I hadn't seen Zag. No one had. That he wasn't at the parade didn't surprise anyone. Zag hated parades. "Colorful substitutes for war," he called them. Zag had a bunch of definitions like that for things that he disapproved of. Fly-fishing: *Cruelty to aquatic craniate animals dignified as masculine sport.* Algebra: *A branch of mathematics that uses a combination of numbers and letters to confuse people.* Public schools: *Minimum security educational penitentiaries.* Zagisms, we called them.

Over the tops of parade watchers' heads, on the other side of the street, my stepfather stood in front of his store, wearing a Panama hat with his blue and white seersucker suit. Across one of the two display windows he'd draped a large American flag. Seeing me, he smiled and waved. I smirked.

I scanned the sea of onlookers, hoping to see Belinda Dalton among them. Since my last visit to Fern Cottage, I'd been wanting to speak with her, to find out what she knew about its occupant. But she was nowhere in sight.

The cheerleading squadron marched by, led by the infamous Cecilia Kottlecamp. Cecilia was Hattertown's answer to Marilyn

Monroe, really more like a bad guess. She was said to have had some sort of sex with every member of the Hattertown Blockers, the high school football team. She wore a feathered majorette's cap and a pleated plaid skirt so short when she kicked up her legs we glimpsed her panties. The top she wore was as short in the opposite direction.

"Man," said Skunky, ogling Cecilia as she marched by. "They should have carved *those* on Mount Rushmore!"

With its dropped jaw, wide eyes, glossy lips, and bright teeth, my stepbrother's face was a compendium of delight. I put my arm around his waist and drew him closer to me.

When the parade ended, having agreed to meet at the carnival afterward, we pedaled home for supper.

The carnival occupied a grassy lot next to the feed store. It smelled of cotton candy, hay, peanuts, popcorn, and elephant shit. We pooled our funds for ticket rounds. Victor spent his predictably on candied apples and soda. Skunky favored nausea-inducing rides. I preferred games. The Moon Shot was my favorite. You had to shoot the planets—different-colored balloons hovering over jets of compressed air—and knock them out of orbit. The gun's barrel (I knew from previous experience) was curved. To hit the target you had to aim six degrees left of center. I won a wooden cup and ball. I gave Gordon my last few shots. Naturally he missed them all.

We were headed for the Ferris wheel when we noticed a man in a green corduroy suit standing on a small stage, holding a small bottle with a matching green label. At his feet a dozen similar bottles stood arrayed. The sign in front of the stage said:

Dr. DeGrasse's Amazing
Re-Vitalizing Tonic

We worked our way to the front of the line.

"Let me ask you all something," the man in the corduroy suit was saying. "Have any of you ever heard of a bovine with a bellyache?"

"A what?" someone in the crowd asked.

"A bovine, sir. A cow."

"Can't say I have," another onlooker answered.

"How would you know?" Skunky shouted.

"Say what?" said the man in the green corduroy suit.

"How can anybody tell if a cow's got a bellyache?"

Some in the crowd laughed.

"Fair question. Step forward, son, why don't you?"

Skunky stepped closer to the stage.

"What is your name, young fellow?"

"Wade. I go by Skunky."

"Skunky, huh? You ask a good question, a very good question, to which there happens to be an equally good answer. When you have a bellyache, how's your appetite? Good, or poor?"

"Poor," Skunky acknowledged.

"Now let me ask you this, Skunky, have you ever in your entire existence come across a bovine—a cow—with a poor appetite?"

Skunky owed that to date he hadn't.

"And what conclusion do you draw from this?"

"That cows don't have bellyaches?"

"Smart boy. That's right, folks! Cows don't have bellyaches. As a matter of fact, none of you has ever seen or ever will see a depressed, annoyed, angry, or otherwise less-than-contented cow. The reason? A consistent, invariable, wholesome diet of one-hundred percent pure grass. Yes, grass. Among the world's most abundant, nutritious foods.

"There's just one little problem, however," the man in the green corduroy suit continued after a pause. "Human beings cannot digest grass. It takes even a cow *four stomachs* to do so, whereas we humans have got only one little ol' stomach. Well, to that problem at long last a solution—pun intended, folks, ha-ha!—has been arrived at! Yes, ladies and—"

I yelled: "Cows haven't got four stomachs! They have one stomach divided into four compartments!"

"Yes, ladies and gentlemen," the man went on, ignoring me, "at long last the means for eating grass has become available to humans in the form of Dr. DeGrasse's Amazing Re-Vitalizing Elixir. Each of these bottles you see before you contain the distilled essence of seventeen—*seventeen!*—acres of fresh green grass. Imagine: all that good wholesome nutrition crammed into one little bottle, the very same goodness that has kept cows contented through decades!"

"Cows don't live decades!"

"Say what?"

"They live an average of fifteen years!"

"Who the hell are you? I mean, what's your name, son?"

"Half, they call me."

"Might that be because you have only half a brain?"

"No, sir," I said to the crowd's delight.

"Are you an agriculturalist, by any chance?"

"Am I *what*?"

"Have you worked on a farm?"

"No."

"What makes you an authority on cows?"

"I read it. In a book."

"Oh, book-smart, huh?" He leaned down and spoke to me sotto voce: "Get outta my hair, kid, or I swear I'll beat the living daylights out of you." Then, to his audience: "A teaspoon a day, folks. That's all it takes. Now then: who wants a bottle?"

As we walked off, Skunky shouted, "My friend may not know much about cows, but he knows a bunch of bull when he hears it!"

"Only a dollar per bottle, step right up…"

By the time we got on the Ferris wheel the sun was setting. Reflected by the river's black surface, the carnival lights resembled colored chalk marks on a blackboard. Victor and Skunky shared an enormous bag of popcorn. Halfway through the ride, to the consternation of those below, Skunky leaned over and shouted: "I think I'm going to be sick!"

We'd started on our fourth revolution when, among the people walking beneath us, I saw a pair of fiery pigtails bobbing. I shouted Belinda's name. The face with which she looked up at me was that of an astronomer confronting an aberrant asteroid.

"Wait!" I yelled down. "I want to talk to you!"

No sooner did I speak those words than a guy wearing a Minnesota Twins baseball cap stepped up to and put his arm around Belinda. Dwight Riddell, a transfer student from Minnesota, a place known to me then only for lakes and butter. Since his arrival the summer before, tall, handsome, athletic Dwight had been my chief rival for Belinda's affections—so I told myself, though this would have been news to Dwight.

By the time I got off the Ferris wheel Belinda and Dwight were gone. Darkness had fallen. It was time for the fireworks display.

❧

My feelings about fireworks were mixed. Yours would be, too, had you lost half your middle finger to a bottle rocket when you were six years old. Blame my father, bless his Rock & Rye-infused heart. On the humid evening of July 4th, 1956, he handed me a bottle rocket and watched, with unalloyed paternal pride, me scurry over to the torch he'd set up in our back yard. Per his instructions I aimed the bottle rocket away from the house, lit the fuse, took three steps back, and watched it *WHOOOSH* up into the evening sky, where it burst into a mélange of stars. Seeing it burst, I jumped up and down and clapped and watched the proud grin spread like peanut butter on warm toast across my father's stubbled face.

Such an auspicious debut demanded an encore. So I did it again.

And again.

The third bottle rocket exploded in my grip. I looked down at the blob of ground meat that had been my left hand.

Except for my middle finger's top two joints, which were pulverized by the explosion, the emergency room surgeon did a fine job of sewing me back together.

For the accident I held my father blameless. It seemed to me then as it does now that the bond between a father and son should consist of approximately one part each of affection and admiration to one part of terror—like fire, or a lightning storm. We're drawn to things we don't understand, that pose a danger to and can possibly even destroy us. I felt that way about my father: that I'd never understand him, that he'd always be a mystery to me; that, though he loved and would do just about anything for me, he could also hurt and possibly destroy me, as he almost did that time he threw me in the lake, out of love. Of all the threats posed to me by life none was graver than that posed by my father's love.

That years' fireworks display took place at the new football field. From behind the home team's end zone, Skunky, Victor, Gordon, and I watched the cloudless night burst into a heavenly garden in full bloom, a display supplemented by firecrackers from Skunky's private stash, until an off-duty cop hauled him away.

Watching the fireworks display, I imagined that I was witnessing the creation of the universe, seeing all matter born out of the Big Bang. A sense of my own total insignificance took hold of me then—a comforting sense, since it relieved me of the burden of having to be John Glenn, or anyone special. Not that I didn't *want* to be special; I just didn't want to *have to* be special, and thereby face the very real prospect of failure.

My need to partake of something of the infinite, what had it been born out of, if not the fear of not measuring up here on earth?

And where did that fear come from? When did it start?

When my father died. I blamed myself as much as mercury poisoning for his death.

I'd let my father down. And lost him.

To win him back, I'd have to touch the stars.

A shower of Roman candles brought the fireworks display to an end. As the last shell burst, on the far side of the field through the wavering haze I saw Belinda's face, glossy with sweat. Forgetting Gordon, I raced toward her yelling her name. I must have yelled it a dozen times before she turned.

"Oh," she said.

I scanned the surroundings, looking for Dwight, but didn't see him. Had she ditched him? It didn't matter. What mattered was that for the time being Belinda was mine to captivate with my vast intellect and rapier-sharp wit.

"What's up?" I asked.

"The sky," Belinda answered accurately.

"That was a pretty good fireworks display, wasn't it?"

"The stars are as beautiful and a lot less noisy."

A thought occurred to me. "Do you know why professional firework handlers wear clothes made from pure cotton?"

"No, Leo. Supposing you enlighten me?"

"Because the static electricity in synthetic clothes can accidentally set off fireworks."

Belinda nodded. "Fascinating. I'll keep that in mind next time I handle professional fireworks."

She turned and strutted off. I caught up with her. "Hey, you know that old caretaker's cottage? The one that used to belong to your uncle?"

"What about it?"

"Someone's living there."

"No kidding. My mom rented it out."

"Your *mom*?"

"Uncle Baxter gave it to Mom after Dad died. He figured Mom could rent it out to a hunter or somebody."

"She's the one who had it fixed up?"

Belinda stopped walking. "You know that's private property, Leo. You and your pals have no business being up there."

"I just happened to pass by, that's all."

"Well, next time you happen to pass by, read the No Trespassing signs and do what they say." She sped up her walk; so did I.

"What's his name?"

"Who?"

"The guy renting the place."

"Mr. Thomas."

"Where's he from?"

"How in the world should I know?"

"Have you talked to him?"

"He's not very talkative, unlike some people."

"What's he doing up there? Do you know?"

Belinda stopped and faced me. "I have no idea. Maybe he's a writer. He's writing a book. Or maybe he just likes being alone. He's Henry David Thoreau's long-lost grandson. What difference does it make?"

"Just curious, that's all."

"I really have to go, Leo. My mother's waiting for me in the parking lot."

She took off. To her back I yelled:

"Did you know that nutmeg is extremely poisonous? But only if injected intravenously!"

In the parking lot my stepfather held my stepbrother's hand. Gordy's face was damp and raw from crying.

"There you are, sport," my stepfather said. "We were starting to worry about you."

I hugged Gordy. As I did, his arms hung limply at his sides. A gob of snot clung to the tip of his nose. I wiped it off.

"Where's Mom?"

"I'm afraid your mother has had one of her attacks."

My mother suffered from migraines. She would be bedridden for days, sleeping and throwing up. Before she married my stepfather, she'd get them maybe once or twice a year. But afterward the attacks came more frequently. When they did the sounds of her retching would fill the entire house. Even with the TV turned all the way up in the parlor, or down in the basement playroom over the furnace's roar, the sound would reach me, a jagged roar like the sound Godzilla made in the movies. The Vomit Monster.

It started raining, a drizzle that blurred the headlights of cars as they maneuvered out of the parking lot.

"Can I give you boys a ride home?" my stepfather offered, pointing to his Shalimar blue 1959 Buick Electra. "We can put your bikes in the trunk. Heck of a trunk that Buick's got on her. You could fit the whole Tour de France in there, as it were!"

I turned to my stepbrother. "Gordon will go with you, won't you, Gordy?" I chucked his chin. While he giggled I turned to see the disappointed look on my stepfather's face.

A few minutes later I stood watching as, with its wipers thwacking and Gordon's bicycle in the trunk, my stepfather's car rumbled off, filling the rainy night with blue fumes.

I was in no hurry to get home. I pedaled slowly, looking up at the veil of clouds enshrouding the moon. Except for a few scattered fireworks and the howls of dogs set off by them, the town was as silent and somber as it had been festive earlier. The night clung to my face like a wet rag. The falling rain squeezed the shapes of streetlamps and headlights into lozenges. As I pedaled past them the hat factory smokestacks looked like giant straws sticking out of the ground. In the furtive recesses behind them, vague luminosities persisted.

I pulled into the town square. Though the rain was falling harder by then, I sat on a bench next to a statue of Barclay Moses Dalton. By the light of a streetlamp the hat mogul's bronze brow glistened. The shops along Felt Street looked eerily deserted, as if one of those bombs had gone off, the kind that vaporize people but leave buildings standing.

There are times when you forget that you exist. This was one of them. I sat there, on that wet bench, ignoring the rain that spread itself across puddles in the street like sheets over the victims of some epic disaster. Through the rain-swept darkness I gazed, wondering: what part of me belongs to infinity, and what part is mine alone?

Out of that rainy darkness two people, a man and a woman,

made their way toward me. The woman was holding an ice cream cone that each of them took turns licking while he held an umbrella with at least two broken ribs over them both. As they drew closer I made out the Minnesota Twin's baseball cap the woman wore and concluded that she was Belinda and the guy was Dwight Riddell.

I was wrong. The woman wasn't Belinda; she was Cecilia Kottlecamp. I should have been relieved. In fact it upset me even more. Not only had my beloved's heart been stolen by someone else, but that someone was a cad.

"Napoli!" Dwight exclaimed, approaching, smiling. "What are you doing sitting out here in the rain?"

"I'm sitting out here in the rain," I responded with my own wet smile.

By the streetlamp's pinkish glow I watched Cecilia Kottlecamp lick the ice cream cone, her tongue painted white by it.

"Ice cream in the rain. How romantic," I said.

"Isn't it?" said Cecilia, licking.

"Soft-serve?"

"Uh-huh."

"Carvel?"

"You bet."

"Say, did you know that Carvel ice cream was invented by mistake?"

"It *was*?"

"While out delivering ice cream one day, Tom Carvel got a flat tire and was forced to pull into a parking lot next to a pottery store. As the ice cream in his truck began to melt, he decided to sell it to people passing by in the street so it wouldn't be wasted. Turns out people loved the partly melted, soft ice cream. He sold out on his entire inventory! Eventually Carvel patented his own special process for making soft ice cream."

"Seriously, Napoli," said Dwight. "What are you doing here?"

I shrugged. "Nothing," I said, gazing upward. "Admiring the firmament of stars."

"What stars? It's *raining*!"

"Just because you can't see them doesn't mean they aren't there to admire."

"You're a queer duck, Napoli. You know that?"

"Did you know on a clear night in the Northern Hemisphere the naked eye can see 5,000 stars?"

"Queer duck—"

"Saturn is the lightest planet in the solar system."

"C'mon, Cecilia. Let's get out of here."

"A full NASA space suit costs ten thousand dollars!"

Holding hands, making quacking sounds, laughing, they walked off.

I sat there a little while longer, enjoying the sense of total abdication that went with the rain sliding down my cheeks. Then I hopped on my bike and pedaled home, racing my shadow past the girders of the green iron bridge.

When I got home everyone was asleep. In the kitchen I mixed myself a glass of Cocoa Marsh and milk that I meant to take up to my room but guzzled down before I reached the top of the stairs. In my room I lay on top of the covers in my underwear with the lamp burning. The *How and Why Wonder Book of Interplanetary Travel* sat on my nightstand, but I didn't feel like reading it or even looking at pictures.

Instead I stared up at the dogfight tableau, more intent on the wires that held them in place than on the airplanes, listening to the attic fan's steady thrum combined with the gurgles of water draining into gutters and downspouts, a symphony punctuated by crackles of leftover fireworks that, by then, sounded more forlorn than celebratory.

I'd been lying there that way for a while, intent on what those crisscrossing wires did to the moonlight, when something struck the window. At first I thought it was an acorn or a twig blown into it. When it happened twice more, I got up, opened the window, and stepped out onto the telescope platform.

The sky had cleared. A crescent moon hung full and bright. An owl hooted. From where I stood, I could see a section of the front porch.

An oblong shadow sat on the porch swing.

"Who's there?" I called down in a loud whisper.

The shadow blew a party noisemaker.

"Zag?"

"Happy Fourth of July!" he said.

"Shh! You'll wake everyone!"

In my pajamas I hurried down and switched on the porch light. A cloud of mosquitoes swarmed around it. *The average mosquito drinks five-millionth of a liter of blood per serving.* I switched the light off. Even in the dark I could see the dark blotches on Zag's white T-shirt, which fluoresced under the moonlight.

Fireflies flicked on and off. *Also known as lightning bugs, fireflies are neither flies nor bugs.* From her bedroom window Mom's retchings spiraled down like confetti from the deck of an ocean liner.

"I could use a drink," Zag said.

"I'll mix you a chocolate milk."

"I was hoping for something stronger."

"Cocoa Marsh or plain milk. Those are your choices."

"Gimme the hard stuff."

"One Cocoa Marsh coming up."

In the kitchen I grabbed the quart milk bottle from the refrigerator and returned to the porch with it, the jar of Cocoa Marsh, a tumbler, and a teaspoon. Zag grabbed the milk bottle from me and guzzled straight from it—breathless, greedy gulps. He'd drunk half the bottle when, coming up for air, he said:

"Guess who's in the hospital?"

"Your dad?"

Zag nodded. "Good guess!"

"What happened?" I asked, though I was pretty sure that I knew, gangrene being the obvious conclusion. For weeks the smell of gangrenous flesh had filled the Lengyl home. It emanated from the den where Mr. Lengyl slept on an army cot, his gout having made it too hard for him to climb the stairs to his bedroom. Already he'd had two of his toes amputated, one from each foot. I guessed this latest trip to the hospital had a similar purpose, with another toe or two to be sacrificed to the Gout God.

"Someone shot him," said Zag, lighting a cigarette from the pack he'd removed from his rolled-up sleeve.

"Someone shot your *father*? Who? *Why?*"

Zag offered me a cigarette that I refused. With me sitting there on the porch swing next to him he explained.

After I left him at the dog pound that Sunday, Zag had arrived at what he felt was an ingenious way to stop Zippo from keeping his father awake with his incessant barking. Like most good ideas, this one was as simple as it was obvious.

That same night, with his father snoring away in his army cot, Zag tiptoed into the downstairs bathroom. In the medicine cabinet, among his father's many prescriptions, he found the vial of Benadryl tablets and extracted a pink pill from it. By moonlight, on the kitchen counter, using an ashtray as a mortar and the handle of a screwdriver as a pestle, he ground the pill into a fine powder, sprinkled the powder into a bowl of milk, gave the bowl to Zippo, and watched, with a mixture of pride and guilt, Zippo lap up every drop.

That night for the first night in weeks Mr. Lengyl and Zippo both slept soundly. So did Zag, knowing that as long as he had a healthy supply of Benadryl on hand he and his dog were golden.

"And we would've been too," said Zag, "if it weren't for Thomas Jefferson."

"Thomas Jefferson? What's he got to do with it?"

"He wrote the Declaration of Independence."

"Oh," I said.

The morning of the Fourth of July Zag took Zippo up to Lost Lake. He sat by the dam, throwing a stick in the water for Zippo to retrieve. Once the fireworks started, Zag knew Zippo wouldn't stop barking. They stayed at the lake till long after sundown, when it started to rain. By the time they got home Zag's father was sound asleep. In the kitchen Zag ground up two Benadryl tablets and gave them to Zippo in his bowl of milk. Before going to bed he gobbled down a peanut butter sandwich.

He'd barely drifted off when Zippo's barks woke him. Soon they were met by his father's curses. Like ripples from a stone tossed into a lake, the barks and curses radiated into the night.

In his striped pajamas, slowly, as though in a trance, with his father's curses growing louder, Zag went down the stairs. As he did a strange blue wavering light met him on the staircase, as if an aurora borealis had entered the house: the same blue light Belinda Dalton described to me on the playground the week after both of our fathers died.

"I felt like a deep-sea diver," Zag explained, "the kind with the big brass helmets, descending into the ocean's darkest, deepest, most mysterious depths."

At the bottom of the stairs Zag turned into his father's study. There, in a pine cabinet next to the rabbit gun his father gave him for his tenth birthday, stood the Harrington & Richardson Topper Model 48 Single-Shot. To the odors of gun oil and stock cream, Zag's father had shown him how to clean and oil the shotgun, his heavily veined, muscular hands caressing the chamois cloth up and down the barrel's gleaming blue shaft. How possessed of authority and wisdom his father had seemed to him back then. Like the sun, he'd existed, or seemed to, at the center of all things.

In the drawer of his father's desk, Zag found a red and yellow box of shells. With the shotgun loaded, he carried it into the kitchen. Zag opened the refrigerator, took the milk bottle from it, poured milk into a saucer, and carried the saucer and the shotgun onto the patio, where moonlight fragmented things into geometrics of blue light.

Delighted to see his master at such an odd hour, Zippo slapped his tail against the patio floor. Zag put the bowl of milk down. As he did the shadows of tree branches rippled across his pajama sleeves. Watching Zippo lap milk from the saucer, Zag smiled.

"Dumb mutt," he said, shaking his head.

He'd aimed the shotgun and was about to pull the trigger when, hearing something, Zag turned. His father stood there, a pajama-clad Christ crucified on the cross of his crutches, his swollen gangrenous foot looking like a beached harbor seal.

"Put the gun down, moron."

Though Zag's aim was purposefully wide, twenty-six pellets of lead shot found their way into his father's gangrenous, putrefying flesh.

"They'd have had to amputate the damn foot anyway, sooner or later," Zag said between gulps of milk. Zag's body shook with laughter as he went on guzzling. His laughter blew bubbles in the milk. Soon both of us were laughing out there on the moonlit porch. Zag laughed so hard he lost his grip on the bottle, which fell and broke, spraying milk all over.

With Zag gone, on my knees on the porch with mosquitoes eating me alive and my mother retching in her room high above me, I gathered up the milky shards.

Part 5

Inner Space

The next day I rode with Gordon up to Fern Cottage. This time I didn't hesitate to knock on the door. The man wore his plaid robe.

"You again!" *(Hyew eggen!)*

"Teach me to swim."

"Teach yourself." *(Deech yuzelf.)*

He tried to close the door. I stuck my foot in it. Under his round glasses, the man's eyes hardened, but then they softened again. He pointed to my stepbrother.

"Who is this?"

"My stepbrother," I answered. "He's retarded."

"He can't be much more stupid than you."

The man indicated that I should wait. When the door re-opened, he had his walking stick with him. He walked past me and Gordon down the slatestone path to the gravel road, then turned left and kept walking, headed for Fool's Hole. Taking Gordon by the hand, I followed him. *Follow your fears.*

Soon we stood on the swimming rock, facing the water. Behind us Gordon sat on a patch of lichen playing with his fingers.

"Uhn haah dah."

"What's your brother doing?"

"It's this thing he does with his fingers, an optical illusion. And he's my stepbrother, not my brother."

Through the branches of a nearby tree the wind made a whistling sound. A gust sent a gray parabola shivering across the lake's surface. With his beard the man nodded down at Fool's Hole and said:

"Take your clothes off."

"What?"

"Or keep them on. It's all the same to me."

"You don't expect me to jump, do you?"

"Do you want to swim, or don't you?"

"Swim, yes; die, no!"

The man dropped the plaid robe. Compared to his sunburned arms his chest was pale, the hairs on it mostly gray. I noticed that scar again. It ran all the way up from his calf to his groin. What scared me more just then I'm not sure, the thought of jumping off that rock or just standing there next to this naked stranger.

"I will count to three." *(I vill kown do tree.)*

"Why do we have to jump? Why can't we just walk in?"

"Vun...doo..."

"At least let me put on my bathing suit!"

With my heart racing, I sat on the rock and unlaced my sneakers, all the time thinking, *Why am I doing this? I must be nuts!*—at the same time feeling it was inevitable, that I had no choice, that it was all part of the cosmic plan whereby at long last I would partake of something of the infinite. *Follow your fears...*

With my clothes in a pile and my swim trunks on, I walked over and stood next to the man at the rock's edge. All this time Gordon sat there, behind us, engrossed in his fingertips, oblivious of his stepbrother's impending watery death.

"Vun...doo—"

I shook my head. "I can't do this," I said.

"Why not?"

"Because—I'm scared!"

"What is your name?"

"I thought you didn't care about names."

"I don't. Tell me anyway."

"Half, they call me."

"Hoff? Silly name. Tell me, Hoff: how scared are you?"

"Very."

"Whose fear is it? Yours, or someone else's?"

"Mine, I guess."

"If a thing is yours, you can do what you like with it, right?"

"I suppose."

"Supposing your fear were an empty bottle that you're holding in your hand. You could throw it away, couldn't you?"

"I guess, though I'd be littering."

"Never mind that! Could you throw it away?"

"I guess."

"Stop guessing and answer!"

"Yes!"

"Good. Do it! Throw it away."

"The bottle?"

"Imbecile! Your fear. Here, now—into this lake!"

He took my hand.

"Vun, doo—"

"Please god no!"

"Tree!"

We jumped. We hurtled down; a wall of lake rushed up. In a collision of bodies three states of matter met: mine (gas, liquid, solid), the man's (ditto), the lake (liquid).

Then I was inside the green wall, in and under it, flailing in a bedlam of bubbles. Under its green skin the lake was brighter and darker and deeper in all directions. I couldn't tell up from sideways or down: they were all the same, churned together into a greenish froth. I thrashed my way toward the palest green, my legs and arms flailing, eyes burning, lungs yearning for air. Just when I was about to breathe in water, I burst through the lake's skin. Sunlight poured into my eyes. My lungs cringed; my ears popped. I gasped and went down again. Then up, then down, then up again, like my Duncan Midnight Special yo-yo. Each time I came up, like a dog trying to claw its way up a tree, I thrashed at the surface.

I was thrashing that way when the man swam up and held me from behind.

"You're fighting the water! Don't! Let it hold you!"

The next time I came up, I took an extra deep breath and tried not to flail quite as much. I did it again the next time, and again after that. After five or six times I wasn't thrashing as much anymore. I wasn't treading water either, exactly, but I wasn't drowning.

The man swam up to me again.

"All right?"

"Yeah," I spluttered. "Yeah, I'm all right!"

"See?"

"How did you know I wouldn't drown?"

"I didn't."

I looked up then to see Gordon looking down from the top of the swimming rock.

"It's okay, Gordy!" I shouted up at him. "It's okay; I'm okay!"

I was better than okay: I was ecstatic. I'd taken my father's advice.

I'd followed my fear.

I'd thrown it into Lost Lake.

That summer the Man in Blue taught me how to swim. More than that, he taught me to love water. He turned my fear of it into a love that endures to this day.

We started out in the shallows. Lesson #1: treading water. Since the human body consists mostly of water and has almost the same density, people are predisposed to float.

"The problem," the man, whose name was Jack Thomas (so he told me) explained, "is that though we float, most of us don't float well enough not to drown." *(Ve dunt vlote vell enuff nuh doo trown.)*

Once I'd mastered the art of treading water, we advanced to basic swimming strokes: backstroke, sidestroke *(Bick an abble, bood id in de basked, bick anudder abble…)*. From there we progressed to flutter kick and crawl. *(Spear de woddah wid yu hands. Leddem glide ahead uff hyew. Open yu hibs. Glide, Hoff, glide!)* "The first rule of swimming: trust the water," Jack said. "Since you and the lake are both made of water, it's the same as trusting yourself."

Gordon would sit and watch from the shore as I practiced my drills in the shallows. Meanwhile, having left me with my latest instructions, Jack would swim the full length of the lake, zipping across the water with perfectly timed strokes. I wondered when and how he had learned to swim and dive so well. When I asked him, to my surprise he answered.

"When I was around your age," he said (we were sitting on the edge of the dam, with Gordon between us), "I contracted diphtheria. Do you know what that is?"

"A serious infection caused by the *Corynebacterium diphtheriae* strain of bacteria."

"Very good. I couldn't go to school or play with other children. By then I was living with my aunt and uncle. My aunt gave me alcohol baths. When not confined to my room I took long walks. While walking one day, through the tall hedge surrounding the municipal pool, I watched a group of boys diving off the high board. Once their feet left the platform, they hung there momentarily, or seemed to, frozen like statues, before plunging with hardly a splash. It was the most beautiful thing I'd ever seen. Then and there I decided, once I'd recovered from my illness, I'd learn to dive like that. And I did."

I asked, "Who taught you?"

"The municipal pool lifeguard. His name was Günter. 'Straight, stiff, and smooth' were Günter's three words of instruction. 'With a perfect dive,' he said, 'there should be hardly a splash. The better the dive, the smaller the splash.'"

Otherwise Jack never talked about himself; in fact, he made it clear that with respect to questions his past was off-limits. The few times I asked him anything to do with it—where he was from, that sort of thing—he slammed the door on the subject, saying, "What do you care?" or "That's none of your concern."

Though otherwise unwilling to talk about his past, other subjects Jack was happy to discuss. Among those subjects: lakes. Jack loved lakes. He seemed to know all about them, how most lakes were formed after the last ice age, when rifts, valleys, and basins filled with water from the melting glaciers that had formed them, while others were formed by rivers silting up and damming, and still others—the so-called ancient lakes, as old as two and a half million years—were formed by tectonic plates shifting, carving enormous potholes into the earth that torrential rains filled with water. From Jack I learned that there are tectonic lakes, volcanic lakes, fluvial lakes, meteoric (or "crater") lakes, aeolian (produced by wind action), and anthropogenic (man-made) lakes. While some lakes are classified based on their origins, others take their names from their composition and surroundings. Hence: salt lakes, peat lakes, lava lakes, acid and alkaline lakes. There are lazy lakes, industrious lakes, even over-ambitious lakes: lakes overwhelmed by the nutrients in them, by phosphorus, nitrogen, carbon dioxide, and other things that make algae thrive, killing off not just fish, but all forms of life dependent on them. Jack explained to me how, as they age, lakes pass through different stages: oligotrophic, mesotrophic, eutrophic, hypereutrophic...how, before they die, they go senile, turning into marshes and bogs.

"Like people," I observed.

"Yes," said Jack. "Like people."

"Uhn haah daah," said Gordon.

"Why do you know so much about lakes?" I asked Jack one day as we were sitting on the rock after a swim.

"For the same reason you know so much about the planets and stars. Because they interest you."

Jack went on to say that he had long been fascinated by water. "It may have started the day I watched those boys diving at the municipal pool." He explained how, returning to the pool often after that visit, he became more and more entranced not just by the divers, but by what their plunging bodies did to the water, by the sizes and shapes of their splashes, and the patterns of waves that radiated out from them to create more waves and splashes at the edges and corners of the pool.

"Of all the things that make up the world," Jack said, "water is by far the most mysterious. Tasteless, odorless, colorless, nearly transparent, it's the most equivocal and adaptable of substances, having no identity of its own. Its form is determined strictly by circumstance. As Hesse wrote, it 'flows to fill whatever form it finds.'"

It struck me then that water and the universe had a lot in common. No matter how much we knew about them, they remained unfathomable. And since we're made mostly of water, it stands to reason that human beings are just as unfathomable.

Jack summed it up neatly: "The deepest water you'll ever drown in is yourself." *(Ze deebest woddah hyewl evah trown in iss yohzelv.)*

❧

Usually we swam in the mornings. I'd leave the house after breakfast and on most days be home in time for lunch. The other Back Shop Boys rarely went to the lake before mid-afternoon, so the odds of running into them there were small. For all kinds of reasons I didn't want them to know about my friendship with Jack.

Sometimes after swimming we would sit on the dam. From its top, Jack, Gordon, and I took turns skipping stones across the water. Jack's stones skipped dozens of times *(plif, plif, plif, plif, plif, plif, plif—spludge)*, mine just two or three *(plif, plif, plif, spludge)*. Gordon's were gulped down instantly on impact *(. . . spludge!)*.

We were skipping stones one morning when Jack told me about The Water Master.

"The *who*?" I said.

"The Water Master. He's a creature of Nordic myth, with burning eyes, green hair, and a matching green beard that turns white in the moonlight. He comes from a watery planet from which all the water evaporated as the result of an explosion, so he had to escape."

"Uhn haah dah," Gordon said.

"How did he get here?"

"Through the migration of cosmic dust."

With a primordial squawk, a heron took off from a nearby rock, its pterodactyl wings flapping slowly as it skimmed the lake's surface.

"The Water Master lives in an underwater palace made of crystal garlanded with ornaments of gold and silver," Jack continued. "He feeds on the corpses of drowning victims. At sunset when the water is like a mirror, that's when he claims his victims. He shoots out his claw, pulls them in, and drowns them."

I had my own underwater monster to share with Jack: not a mythical monster, or a purely mythical one, but Benedict Dalton, uncle to Brewster and Baxter, brother to Bradshaw, great grandson of Barclay Moses Dalton (the trapper who discovered felt after plugging a hole in his shoe). According to the legend, Benedict spent many summers at his brother's estate, where he enjoyed plying the lake's waters with a steam launch he built for that purpose. With its gay striped awning, the launch made gentle circles around the island with the stone lighthouse. Benedict named his launch the *Haberdasher* and took great pride in her—until his wife, Cassandra, started using the launch for her raucous, drunken parties.

This was during the Roaring Twenties, era of gangsters, speakeasies, bathtub gin, and flappers doing the Charleston. With the exception of Benedict Dalton, the country was in a celebratory mood. A man of great reserve, Dalton found his wife's "bacchanals" intolerable. So fed up grew he with them that, early one morning, with a cape flung over his pajamas and his wife sleeping off her latest hangover, he made his way to the gardening shed. Pickaxe in hand, from there he walked down to the boathouse. Having lashed a rowboat to the *Haberdasher's* stern, he fired up her engine and piloted her to the middle of the lake, where he scuttled her.

"But something went wrong," I explained. "He must've caught his leg in a rope or banged his head or something, 'cause when the *Haberdasher* went down, Benedict Dalton went down with her.

"They say he's still down there," I added, "or his skeleton is, at the bottom of the lake, clinging to the remains of his launch."

"Could it be," said Jack as we both gazed out across the lake, "that your Benedict Dalton and my Water Master are one and the same?"

One morning, near the end of my swimming session, it started raining. Jack invited us into his cottage. It was the first time he'd done so. By the time we arrived there the rain was falling in sheets. From a hook next to the door, he took down a lantern with a long sooty snout. He lit it and put it on a table.

"No electricity?" I said.

Jack shook his head.

"Is there running water?"

He nodded toward a sink with a curved pump-handle.

"Bathroom?"

Jack pointed out the window at the outhouse—the one with the wooden box next to it filled with ammonia.

"All the amenities," he said. *(All zamenitees)*

By the lamp's glow I got my first glimpse of Fern Cottage from inside since the day the Back Shop Boys ransacked it. In place of the moldy carpet of travel brochures, a wooden floor gleamed, its wide planks painted a deep grayish blue, the color of a storm at sea. There was a counter with a sink, an old-fashioned icebox, a cast-iron stove. At the room's center was a square wooden table. A chess set took up most of the table, its hand-carved wooden pieces arranged in their initial formation. Tucked into the room's far corner was a bed with a quilted coverlet above which a shelf holding a dozen or so books had been screwed into the wall. Everything neat, tidy. Mixed in with the books, serving as bookends, were some of the railroad insulators Jack collected. These were the only adornments to the place. Otherwise no paintings or photographs, no sentimental objects of any kind, nothing to suggest a past life or even much of a present one.

I touched one of the glass insulators.

"Please don't," Jack said.

He got a fire going in the stove, then filled a kettle with water, pumping the handle over the sink. The gushing water reminded me of a comet's tail. As Gordon and I watched with blankets wrapped around us, Jack carried the kettle to the stove and added a log to it. By then the rain was coming down hard. It sounded like gravel being dumped onto the roof.

We were sitting at the table with the chessboard.

"Do you play chess?" asked Jack.

I shook my head. (My father and I played checkers.)

"A pity."

I asked Jack who he played with. He pointed to himself.

"How do you do that?"

He demonstrated, moving a piece, then turning the board and moving another.

"Who wins?" I asked.

Jack poked himself in the chest.

"Who loses?"

He repeated the gesture.

The kettle whistled. Jack poured us tea.

"Uhn haah dah," said Gordon.

"Don't you get lonely out here?"

On a windowsill there was a clump of green moss. Jack took it and held it in front of me. "Do you know what this is?" he asked.

"It's a piece of moss."

"One of ten-thousand species. And twice as many varieties. More than enough to keep me company."

On the counter next to the sink there was a bowl of apples. Jack offered us each an apple and took one for himself. From a pocket of the coveralls that were draped over a chair, he took what I didn't realize at first was a knife until he flicked out its long, narrow blade. He peeled an apple with it, rotating it with the ball of his thumb against the blade. The skin came off in a leathery spiral. Jack handed the peeled apple to Gordon. He was going to peel one for me when I said: "I'll do it."

Jack handed me the apple and held the knife out to me.

"I've got my own, thanks."

I got my Swiss Army Knife out of my knapsack.

"Pretty knife." *(Priddy nive.)*

"My father gave it to me."

"He must think well of you."

"He's dead."

"Oh. I'm sorry."

"My mom remarried. That's where he comes from." I pointed to Gordon. "His father is my stepfather."

We ate our apples and sipped our teas and listened to the hissing stove and the sound of rainwater dripping from the cottage's eaves. After a while Jack said: "That explains a lot."

"What does?"

"To lose your father at so young an age isn't easy. I was quite young when I lost my parents."

"What happened?"

"They were both killed in a railway accident."

I wanted to know more but knew better than to ask.

We went on sipping tea, listening to the stove and the rain, just like that, just sitting there. I don't think I've ever been as quiet with anyone before or since. It felt strange but good, comfortable. I felt more comfortable there than in what was supposedly my own home. I think Gordon felt comfortable too, though it was hard to say. Once Gordon lost himself in a yo-yo or his fingertips he could have been anywhere.

"Unh haah dah," Gordon said.

We stayed there like that until the rain stopped completely and our clothes were warm and dry.

Though I came to trust and feel comfortable with him, still, I knew nothing about Jack. Who was he? Where did he come from? Where was his family? Why did he collect that stuff in his rucksack? How did he get that limp? Once or twice I dared to ask him about this or that to do with his past. Each time he either shrugged and said nothing or put me off in other ways.

"The past is garbage," he said to me one day. We were in his cottage playing chess. He'd taught me how to play. I had just nabbed one of his pawns with my knight.

"Why is it garbage?"

"Because—it's useless." He took my bishop with his queen.

"Don't you want to remember things? The places you've been, things you've done?"

Jack shook his head. "Memories are like tea balls. Some people use them over and over again. Me, I throw mine away."

He snatched one of my rooks. I nabbed another of his pawns.

I changed the subject:

"I'm going to be the first man on the moon," I said.

"Congratulations."

"President Kennedy says we'll land there before the end of the decade. I'll be twenty years old. Old enough."

"May I share an observation?"

"Go ahead."

"You talk too much."

"Unh haah dah," said Gordon.

"If only everyone spoke as little as your brother."

"My stepbrother. Since I let you share an observation, may I ask a personal question?"

"As long as I may not answer." He got my queen with his bishop.

"Do you believe in God?"

Jack made a puffing sound.

"Is that a yes or a no?"

"Some people embrace the God of things unknown and unknowable. I embrace things unknown and unknowable. My way is simpler. Whether one names the mystery or not, it's still a mystery. Anyway, why insist on answers when the questions are so beautiful?"

Jack moved his rook.

"Checkmate. You really must pay more attention to your game, Hoff."

❧

One day between rounds of chess Jack went out to use what he called his "privy." I was sitting there contemplating my next move when my eyes drifted toward the canvas rucksack leaning against the wall next to Jack's stove, its opening secured with a leather drawstring. With Gordy occupied with my yo-yo, having looked out the window to make sure the privy door was closed, I rose from the table, went to the rucksack, crouched, loosened the drawstring, looked inside, and saw five more glass insulators just like the ones on Jack's bookshelf. I extracted one and gazed into it like a crystal ball, as if by staring hard enough I could force it to reveal its secrets to me.

After peeking again through the window to make sure the privy door was still closed, I flung open every drawer in the cottage, searching for anything that might tell me who Jack Thomas was and where he came from. Candlesticks, matchbooks, assorted tools, a flashlight, sweaters, socks, underwear, and other clothes. In one drawer under a ropy sweater, I found a padded envelope, the kind you mail books in. I was about to open it when I hesitated. The privy door squeaked when opened so I'd have known if Jack was headed back. Still, to be sure, I looked out the window again.

There were two things in the envelope. The first was a small black-and-white photo with crinkly edges of a man, a woman, and a boy standing in front of a body of water, a pond or a lake in which, to the right of the photo, was a small sailboat. The woman was tall, as tall as the man, almost. She wore a large rolled-brimmed floppy hat that cast a shadow over most of her face except her hawk-like nose, which protruded into the sunlight. The boy looked about ten or eleven years old. The man could have been Jack, possibly, but a younger Jack, without the beard.

The second item inside the padded envelope was a book. Slim, with a badly worn leather cover. The pages were foxed and brittle. It had to be very old.

I opened it to the title page:

A
Short introduction for
to learne to Swimme.
Gathered out of Master Digbies Booke
of the Art of Swimming.
(...)
And translated into English for the better
instruction of those who understand
the Latine tongue.
By Christofer Middleton
★

AT LONDON
printed by James Roberts for Edward
White, and are to be sold at the little North
doore of Paules Church, at the signe
of the Gun. 1595.

I'd slid the book back into the padded envelope and was putting it back under the sweater when something slapped the back of my head. I hadn't heard the privy door squeak.

"Ouch!" I said.

"You've been snooping!" Jack said.

"I wasn't! I was just—!"

He slapped me again. Like its predecessor it was a loose, half-checked slap that hurt just enough to make its point.

"I asked you not to snoop!"

"I'm sorry! I—"

He slammed the drawer shut. He grabbed my arm, forced me to my feet, and pulled me back to the table, where he sat me down—hard—on the chair. Tears blurred my vision. Gordon stopped playing with his yo-yo and looked at me.

"If you persist in snooping, you and your stepbrother will no longer be welcomed here. Understood?"

I nodded. More tears tugged at my eyes.

"Stop crying."

I couldn't speak. My voice was trapped deep down in my throat. My face was all screwed up. It hurt. But what hurt the most wasn't my face or Jack's slaps but my having betrayed his confidence. I felt deeply ashamed.

"You cry too easily," Jack said.

He tousled Gordon's hair, then he sat back down in front of the chessboard.

"Whose move is it?"

❧

Sometimes after swimming, if the lake was high, we'd climb under the sluiceway, under the Saran Wrap-like sheet of tumbling water, and stand there looking out through it, watching it turn the landscape into a blurry watercolor, the water thundering so loudly we couldn't hear ourselves talk over it. We were doing so one day when from the left-hand side two brightly colored blobs entered the watercolor, a fat blue blob and a skinny red blob. I recognized the blobs as Victor and Skunky.

They stopped and stood there on the path not far from where we had left our clothes. Even with the waterfall turning them into blurry blobs, I could tell they were looking our way, seeing us there, or seeing three flesh-colored blobs, since we must have looked as blurry to them as they did to us.

Though I couldn't hear them over the thundering water, I could see my stepbrother's teeth chattering. Mine did, too, not from the cold, but out of fear. I was terrified that Victor and Skunky would recognize us and know that I'd been hanging around with Jack, with the Man in Blue. To make matters even worse, it so happened that on that of all mornings I'd arrived at Jack's place to find that I hadn't packed my swimming trunks into my knapsack, so I had done without. Not wanting to feel left out, Gordon, too, shed all of his clothes. Why not? Who'd see us? Well, we had our answer now.

We stood there, the three of us, frozen, waiting for the blobs to move on.

At last our interlopers stepped out of the watercolor. Had they seen our clothes piled on the dam, with Gordon's conspicuous red Boy's Club cap on top of the pile?

The next time I saw them Victor and Skunky didn't say a word about seeing us. Still, I didn't care for the way they kept looking at me, the knowing gleam in Victor's eye, the sly curve of Skunky's lips. I made up my mind then and there to find some way to keep them away from Lost Lake.

On my next visit to Fern Cottage, with a one-inch trim brush and a can of red enamel that I found, I painted a sign on a slab of plywood and nailed it up to the tree at Fool's Hole:

DANGER!!!
FLESH-EATING BACTERIA!!!
SWIM AT YOUR OWN RISK!!!
State of Connecticut
Dept. of Public Health

Were flesh-eating bacteria a thing? Did Connecticut really *have* a Department of Public Health? Anyway, for the rest of that summer, Jack, Gordon, and I had Lost Lake all to ourselves.

By August I was able to swim in deep water. It was time for my first long solo swim.

"The lake is all yours," Jack said. *(Sze lek hiss all yohrs.)*

"Is there anywhere I shouldn't go?"

"Yes," Jack said. "The bottom." *(Sze boddum.)*

With Jack and Gordon watching from the top of the rock, I set out for the island with the miniature lighthouse. By then Jack and I had swum there and back at least a dozen times together. There was no reason for me to be afraid. If I got tired for some reason I could always stop and tread water.

All the same with each stroke the lake grew deeper and darker, or seemed to. I imagined Benedict Dalton's skeleton somewhere down there, his grinning weedy skull looking up at me. I thought of the Water Master, too, with his slimy beard and treacherous claw lying in wait. *The deepest water you'll ever drown in is yourself,* I said over and over to myself in time with my strokes, each stroke pushing more of the lake behind me. The harder I stroked, the farther away the island with the miniature stone lighthouse appeared, as if I were swimming backward, or the island was swimming away from me.

Follow your fears. Follow your fears...

Then, suddenly, I was there, scrambling up the rocks at the base of the lighthouse, weak and wobbly, but alive. With the last of my strength, I climbed the rusty ladder and stood at the top of the lighthouse, waving back to Jack and Gordy.

Though I'd swum less than a quarter mile, I felt that I'd gone much further. I was the first man on the moon, Colonel Leo Half Napoli IV, waving at all the poor suckers stuck back on dreary, dismal, gravity-bound Planet Earth.

Part 6

The Thing in the Woods

For shooting his gouty father, the juvenile judge remanded Zag to the State Reform School for Boys in Cheshire, a forty-five-minute car journey, where he would remain until a week before Christmas. The second weekend after school started I visited him there.

My stepfather drove Gordon and me there. It was a warm breezy cloudy day. Gordon rode in front with my stepfather, who wore his seersucker suit. Unlike my father, who used to drive his Studebaker slouched in the driver's seat, with one loose hand on the wheel, the other guiding his cigarette from mouth to open window and back, my stepfather gripped the Buick's wheel rigidly, hands at ten and two o'clock, knuckles white, shoulders hunched, as if not merely steering his precious Buick, but grimly holding its parts together.

Along the way he tried to engage me and Gordon in a game of Bridge—not the card game favored by hoary retirement home residents, but one wherein the first person to spot a bridge on the highway yells, *Bridge!*, thereby scoring a point. A dozen bridges into the game, however, both my stepfather and Gordy had proven no match for me, and I lost all interest in playing. Instead I spread myself across the Buick's roomy back seat. As we glided down a newly constructed Interstate-84, while watching clouds ("*formed in clear air and ragged in appearance, cumulus fractus are a precursor to cumulus humilis and larger cumulus types*") lumbering past the rear window, my mind likewise wandered. I thought about Belinda, with whom I'd hardly spoken since the Fourth of July, exchanging cursory smiles and nods in the hallways between classes at the new high school. And I thought about Jack, of course, trying to imagine the past about which he was so secretive. What was he hiding? Who was he hiding from? What had he done—or what had been done to him?

Only as we were passing through Waterbury, with its shabby wire and screw factories, when an enormous cross thrust itself into the view through the Buick's rear window, did my interest in the passing scenery revive. The cross was the centerpiece of a biblical theme park named "Holy Land, USA," constructed on the Southern slope of Waterbury's highest hill by a lawyer and self-styled evangelist with the unlikely name of John Baptist Greco. Ever since my parents took me there on my seventh birthday, I'd been fascinated by the place. I recalled how, as Mom looked on anxiously, like a pair of low-budget monsters Dad and I trounced through miniature scale models of Bethlehem and Jerusalem, complete with Wailing Wall, Harem al-Sharif, and Church of the Holy Sepulcher. Hand-in-hand we negotiated the park's convoluted trails, through its hokey assemblages of holy junk. Down a muddy passageway we descended into the so-called "Catacombs," a fiberglass and concrete tunnel decked out with glass-encased newspaper clippings of various miracles. The tunnel led to a claustrophobic chamber awash in green light that was supposedly the tomb of some dead pope. As we left, saying, "Need to drain the ol' lizard," Dad hurried on ahead of us. Moments later with a Rock & Rye-infused "*Boo!*" he leapt out from behind a miniature Noah's ark, scaring the crap out of me and nearly giving my mother a heart attack. For three days she refused to speak to either of us.

Now, as my stepfather's Buick rolled past that enormous metal cross, I recalled with enchantment that afternoon so irrevocably claimed by the past. Was it Proust who said, "The only true paradise is a paradise lost"? If so that Madelaine-dunking Parisian knew what he was talking about. The fabricated holy hill my parents and I traipsed through that sunny afternoon had been a Paradise for me, a nirvana wherein fathers loomed invincible over their progeny. Childhood: the true Holy Land…

The ticking of the Buick's turning signal dislodged me from my daydreams. We swung off the interstate onto Route 70, then headed southeast past rows of red tobacco barns toward Cheshire. Twenty minutes later, the Buick crunched up a long stone drive lined with giant beech trees, past a pond teeming with swallows. As we drove past, the swallows rose in a crescent-shaped mass and flew off toward the sun, which painted their wing tips silver.

We passed a tiered fountain and then through a set of ornate iron gates to the front of the administration building, with its crenellated turrets and pointy arched windows of leaded glass. *Some boy's reformatory,* I said to myself. *It's a damn castle!* I pictured Zag wearing a full suit of armor, complete with a plumed visor and heraldic shield, like a knight of the Round Table.

On the administration building's sandstone turret two flags flew, an American flag and the state flag, with its grape vines and acorns over a dark blue backdrop: *Qui transtulit sustinet.* We pulled into a vaulted portico where, as if we were visiting royalty, a guard in a white-belted uniform greeted us.

"Welcome to Cheshire!"

Leaving my stepfather and his newspaper behind in the parked Buick, Gordon and I entered the main building, where the receptionist made us wait on a bench. Refracted through the windows of leaded glass, dusty rays of sunshine spread spectral colors across the marble floor. From the reception area bright corridors fanned out in different directions. Though the temperature outside couldn't have been much over seventy, inside it felt more like a hundred. A tall fan stood in the corner. I went and stood in front of it, plucking my shirt from where it stuck to my chest.

I was still plucking it when Zag arrived, escorted by a woman whose white hair contrasted sharply with her young face. Zag wore a blue chambray shirt two sizes too large, the excess fabric bunched behind him. By the looks of it someone had given him a haircut with kindergarten scissors. Seeing me, his face lit up with a big smile.

"How's it hanging?" he asked, shaking my hand firmly, like

the president of a Fortune 500 company. As if she was his secretary, Zag introduced me to the white-haired woman.

"Miss Ingols, meet my best friend, Leo Napoli. Miss Ingols is the best thing about this place—not that that's saying much!" he added, winking at her.

"That will do, Mr. Lengyl," Miss Ingols said.

She escorted us to a meeting room. On the way Zag put his arm around my shoulders and asked me about my family, how my mother and stepfather were doing.

"Has that hat store of his gone out of business yet?"

"Not yet," I said. "He's got this new thing he invented that's supposed to help out with sales. The Comformator. For measuring hats, though it does other things too."

"I'll say this much for your stepfather, he doesn't give up easily."

"What about your old man? How's he doing?"

"He's still learning how to walk on one foot. It's been hard for him. He can't keep his balance. The weird thing is, he still feels the missing foot. He even gets cramps in his missing toes, bad ones. He says it's the worst pain he's ever experienced. Can you believe that? A 'phantom limb,' is what the docs call it. Who knows what evil lurks in the hearts of man?" Zag recited. "The Phantom Limb knows!"

We laughed.

"The even weirder thing is that ever since I shot him Dad and I get along better than ever. It makes me think I should have shot him a long time ago. Better late than never, I guess."

The room Miss Ingols took us to had a round folding table and four plastic chairs. After reminding us that visiting time was a half-hour, she left, leaving the door halfway open. When he sat down I saw the rolled-up sleeves of Zag's chambray shirt straining against his upper arms.

"Been working out?" I asked him.

Zag smirked. "Exercise and read. That's all there is to do around here."

"Oh, that reminds me..." From inside the crotch of my pants

where I had hidden them, I pulled out three rolled-up comic books. *Twilight Zone Number 4, Doctor Solar, Man of the Atom,* and *Tales of Suspense #46* ("featuring The Crimson Dynamo, more powerful than the Iron Man!"). I handed them to Zag.

"Thanks," he said tucking them into his own crotch. He took a cigarette from his pocket, stuck it in his mouth, and lit it with a contraband match that he ignited along the inseam of his jeans. A NO SMOKING sign loomed on the wall. I pointed to it.

"Who's smoking?" Zag asked, blowing smoke.

"You are," I said.

Zag shook his head. "Impossible," he said. "Smoking isn't allowed here." With his thumb he pointed over his shoulder at the sign. "That would be breaking the rules, and we can't be breaking the rules, now, can we? After all, without rules you can't have a society, and without societies you can't have civilization. Right?"

He sounded a lot like my stepfather. "Right," I said.

"The thing about rules is—there has to be accountability, but there also has to be flexibility. It's like a dance where one partner leads and the other follows, only it's not that simple—dancing, that is. A good dancer knows that you don't just drag your partner across the floor or let them drag you. You feel each other out; you try and anticipate the other person's moves. If you're leading, you anticipate what the person you're dancing with is anticipating. Here, now, for instance, in this room, the sign says, 'No Smoking.' But who is the sign for? And who's to say the sign knows what it's talking about? If I were smoking," said Zag, smoking, "which of course I'm not, then the sign would be wrong, wouldn't it? It would no longer properly represent conditions within this room. On the contrary, under the circumstances to properly represent given conditions within this room the sign would have to say, 'Yes Smoking.' But you can't tell a sign what to say, correct? Correct. Nor, it stands to reason by logical if inverted extension, can a sign tell you what to say or do. Right?"

"Right," I said, not wanting to press the matter further, knowing my doing so would only invite another round of Zag's reasoning, which had as many twists to its logic as a bowl of spaghetti. I changed the subject.

"How have they been treating you here?"

"Not too bad," Zag said. "The people who work here, they're mostly pretty cool, the guards and the counselors. We all get along. Except for Mr. O'Dell, the farm crew supervisor. The Nazi, we all call him. He's about yea tall." Zag held his palm up to his chin. "To make up for being short, he wears cowboy boots. I swear, he wears them to bed in case there's an emergency. Smokes cigars and shows off his one-armed push-ups. Makes us salute and call him Captain. Captain Asshole." Zag smiled. "Everyone else is okay. There's a few loudmouths and crybabies and troublemakers, but otherwise everyone gets along, including the ghosts."

"Ghosts?"

"Uhn haah dah."

Zag leaned in close and lowered his voice conspiratorially. "I'm not supposed to talk about it," he said, "but this place is haunted. The dorms especially, especially down in the so-called 'Pit,' the basement where they used to keep the *real* troublemakers. It's sealed off and empty now except for a bunch of old mattresses and a few tortured spirits that wander upstairs now and then." Zag snuffed out what was left of his cigarette on the sole of his shoe. Then he went to the door, opened it, stuck his head out into the corridor, and yelled: "Miss Ingols!"

The pretty white-haired woman arrived. She sniffed the air.

"Who's been smoking in here?"

Zag faced me.

"There's no smoking allowed in here, young man," Miss Ingols scolded me. "Don't you see the sign? You're too young to smoke anyway, both of you," she added with a look combining disgust, pity, and a trace of sympathy, indicating to me that she herself smoked and would have lit up then and there had she been permitted to.

"He's very sorry, Miss Ingols. Aren't you sorry, Half?"

"Yes." I nodded. "I'm very sorry."

"And he promises not to do it again. Right, Half?"

"I promise," I said.

"Say, Miss Ingols, would it be okay if we step out for some fresh air?"

"For a few minutes. And as long as you don't smoke."

"Don't worry, Miss Ingols. I'll keep an eye on him. God knows we've got enough troublemakers around here."

Outside in the yard a dozen delinquents played basketball, their sneakers slapping asphalt. Across the clouded sky stretching behind the reformatory's purely cosmetic battlements a helicopter whirred. Zag lit another cigarette.

"What's this I hear about you and the Man in Blue?"

No sooner did he say it than my mouth went as dusty dry as a vacuum cleaner bag. Meanwhile my conscience took off into outer space, leaving behind a blank-faced husk.

"The guys say they saw you swimming with him."

There was a plastic comb in my pocket. I ran the ball of my thumb over its teeth—so hard I felt the tines breaking off one by one.

"Is it true? Did you?"

"What do you think?"

"I'm asking you."

I laughed. "Of course not! Hell," I said, "Victor's a liar! And even with his glasses Skunky's as blind as a bat!"

Zag said nothing. He watched the kids play basketball.

"Besides," I felt compelled to add, "you know I can't swim!"

The basketball rolled our way. Zag tossed it back to one of the kids. A silence filled with sounds of basketball passed before he spoke.

"The thing about lying," Zag said, "is you can always tell when someone's doing it. Their inflections give them away. I ask you again: is it true?"

"You wanted me to spy on him," I explained meekly.

"I said spy, not skinny-dip. What the hell, Half!"

"It's not what you're thinking."

"What am I thinking?"

"I forgot my bathing suit!"

"What were you doing hanging out with him in the first place? And when did you learn to swim?"

"He taught me."

"Who?"

"Jack."

"Jack? That's his name?"

I nodded. "Jack Thomas."

"What else have you found out about him?"

"A few things."

"Like?"

"Where he lives. By the lake. In the old caretaker's cottage."

"What else?"

"I found out what he's been collecting in his bag."

"You told me already. Glass insulators. What else?"

"I know he's not from around here."

"No shit."

"He has a foreign accent."

"What sort of accent?"

"German, I think."

"German?" Zag nodded. "Then he's either from West or from East Germany."

"Does it matter?"

"East Germany is Communist. He could be a Commie spy!"

"Unh haah dah."

"I don't think so," I said.

"Think again. Right now there are more spies in this country than ever before in its history. Spies and provocateurs sent by the Commies to undermine our way of life. They're everywhere. They'd like nothing better than to see this country and the entire system of free enterprise collapse. It's called the Cold War, in case you haven't heard of it."

"I've heard of it," I said.

"Ten-to-one your skinny-dipping German friend is spying on our industrial secrets or putting fluoride and other agents into our drinking water and doing whatever else he can to undermine capitalist democracy. Meanwhile he goes around collecting junk and acting like a nutcase so no one will suspect him."

Zag had worked himself up into a froth of wrathful patriotic fervor. He clenched and unclenched his fists; he drew his upper lip back over his teeth so hard it turned white.

"So," I said, "what are we supposed to do about it?"

"I'm thinking." Zag rubbed his jaw. "Calling the cops won't do any good. We don't have enough to go on yet. We need to catch him in the act."

"*What* act?"

"I don't know. Something. We'll know it when it happens."

"Supposing nothing happens? What if he doesn't do anything?"

Zag shook his head. "Trust me, your German pal is up to something. Whatever it is, you can bet it's no good. Meanwhile you better watch your step. If he finds out you've been spying on *him*..." Zag slid a finger across his throat. "Then again now that you've started you can't just stop hanging around with him. He'll know something's up then. You'd better just keep doing what you've been doing. Don't give him any reason to suspect anything."

A gong sounded. The basketball game ended. The players walked off the court. From the doorway Miss Ingols called out to us:

"Visiting time is over!"

Except for that awkward encounter after the sluiceway incident, for the rest of that summer I didn't see Victor and Skunky. Only when school started again that September, while waiting for the bus at the Spitting Pole, did we see each other again.

The Spitting Pole was our name for the street signpost at the corner of South Carrot and Knox streets, where they caught the school bus. Long ago we'd reversed the two signs, an act of vandalism that, to our dismay, wreaked only minimal havoc, South Carrot being a dead-end street rarely sought out by motorists. After I moved into my stepfather's house and officially became a Highlander, that corner was no longer my school bus stop. Still, out of loyalty to the Back Shop Boys, with Gordon on the seat behind me, I'd pedal my Royce Union there every morning and keep them company while they waited for the bus.

On frozen winter mornings, to distract ourselves from the cold, we'd take turns spitting on the sign's green-painted shaft, then stand watching our boogers creep down to the sidewalk, taking nickel bets on whose booger would arrive first. Over time our combined DNA offerings formed a crust thick enough to render fresh coats of green paint unnecessary.

While hocking and spitting and awaiting the bus we'd listen to Victor's latest lies. Victor's lies were as big as Victor. And Victor was big, very big. Playing touch football, he'd tackle you and you'd be under him, screaming through squashed lungs, *Get the hell off of me, you fat tub!* His flesh would jiggle its way deep into your suffocating lungs. Being tackled by Victor Szentgyorgyi was like being tackled by an enormous bowl of sweaty Jell-O.

Most of Victor's lies had to do with his dad, a World War II veteran who according to Victor had

a) skippered a submarine during World War II
b) skippered a PT boat during World War II

c) killed a Nazi soldier in a foxhole with his dagger and brought home his coalscuttle helmet
d) helped build the bridge on the River Kwai

The helmet, which sat on Victor's dresser in his bedroom, had a provocative dent in it. Seeing it I'd picture Mr. Szentgyorgyi leaping into a Nazi foxhole like Audie Murphy in *To Hell and Back*.

Of his acts of bravery we were instructed by Victor never to speak to his father. "It might set off a flashback," Victor told us. He then went on to describe the time his father, in the grip of a nightmare, lurched out of bed and tore down all the bedroom curtains.

"Dad dreamed he was on bivouac and the krauts set fire to his tent," Victor told us.

I didn't know what a bivouac was, none of us did, not that it mattered, since we all knew Victor was lying. We didn't mind. We enjoyed Victor's lies. They were so much more engaging than our truths. He lied for all of us, Victor did. He made heroes of all our dads. Along with Victor's father, our dads climbed the Matterhorn. They swam the Hellespont, descended the Mariana Trench in a bathysphere, outran the bulls at Pamplona, piloted Chuck Yeager's X-1 as it broke the sound barrier.

Victor's lies embraced our deepest hopes and darkest fears. Bitten by a mosquito in the jungle, Mr. Szentgyorgyi contracted malaria. The hundred-and-ten-degree fever raged for twenty days and nights. A priest was summoned to Mr. Szentgyorgyi's bedside.

"In his delirium, Dad saw the Virgin Mary," Victor recounted. "She stood at the foot of Dad's hospital bed wearing a plaid skirt like the girls at St. Mary's. After the priest finished dispensing last rites, she gave Dad a blowjob."

The disasters and diseases we most dreaded, fat Victor endured for us. Like most boys of our generation, we Back Shop Boys had fallen under the sway of television's Don Herbert, also known as *Mr. Wizard*, whose Saturday morning science show enchanted us with its vast array of edifying stinks and bangs. Following Mr. Wizard's example, in the name of scientific research Victor and Skunky performed an experiment in the course of which they set Victor's asshole on fire.

"We wanted to see if farts are ignitable," Skunky explained.

For the experiment Victor ate an entire sixteen-ounce can of baked beans. "Cold," Skunky specified. Taking an empty Coca-Cola bottle and a box of wooden matches with them, they repaired to Victor's bedroom, where, on all fours with Skunky manning the bottle, Victor farted. Moments later he and Skunky watched intently as Skunky brought a lit match to the bottle opening. Sure enough, a modest puff of blue flame materialized.

"A blue angel, that's the technical term for it," Skunky disclosed.

Unwilling to leave it at that, they repeated the experiment, this time with a larger specimen that they ignited at the source. The result: Victor as *Hindenburg,* exploding. *The lives, the humanity.* According to Victor, he was subsequently treated—not for second, or even third, but for *fourth* degree burns the likes of which the doctors and nurses at the New Haven Hospital Burn Unit had never seen before.

"They had to peel all the burned skin off my butt," he elaborated. "A nurse with the biggest bazoomas I'd ever seen did it using a pair of forceps. It took her six hours. She looked exactly like Sophia Loren in *El Cid.* Before becoming a nurse she'd been an opera singer. While peeling off my skin she sang Violetta's aria from *La Traviata.* Then she gave me a blowjob."

Through Victor, we underwent the cure for rabies, a series of hypodermics administered with a twelve-inch needle through the chest wall straight into the heart's ventricle. So long was the needle, it tickled the back of Victor's throat. The doctor who administered the shots looked like the wizard in *The Wizard of Oz.* After injecting him the doctor offered Victor a blowjob, but Victor declined.

❧

During our second meeting at the Spitting Pole that September, Victor shared his discovery of a box of rubbers found by him in a desk drawer in his father's home office while he had been searching for a pack of playing cards. The box held hundreds of male prophylactics.

"My dad must've bought 'em wholesale," Victor surmised.

From his jacket pocket he produced a sample. For the life of me it looked like a white balloon. As I marveled at its exalted purpose Skunky snatched the thing from Victor's grip and inflated it, which cracked us all up, but not as hard as when Victor pointed out that the rubber had been used.

As for the cards he'd been looking for, Victor found them. From his coat pocket he withdrew them. The back of each card held a different pornographic image, the degree of obscenity commensurate with the card's value, with the ace of spades the most obscene of all. From then on, starting with the lowly two of hearts, morning after morning Victor would flash us a card.

"Fifty-two cards," he'd remind us, pocketing the deck as the school bus grumbled into view.

Thus for the next two weeks he held us spellbound, so eager to reach the ace of spades we nearly died in the waiting. We had arrived at the Jack of Clubs when, one morning, Victor broke the news that the cards had been stolen back from him.

"Dad must've missed them," he concluded.

As the school year progressed I spent fewer and fewer mornings at the Spitting Pole. Without Zag there to lead us, the Back Shop Boys lost much of their charm. By October I'd abandoned the Spitting Pole altogether.

Meanwhile I spent as much time with Jack as I could. We swam, played chess. The more time we spent together, the more questions I had about him. Among many other things I wondered what he did with the glass insulators he collected.

I wouldn't have to wonder much longer.

One Sunday I arrived at Fern Cottage earlier than usual.

Gordon wasn't with me. He'd gone with his father to visit his mother's grave as they did every year on the anniversary of her death. Though officially the cause of Margaret Waple's death was "accidental poisoning," it was widely believed that she committed suicide. Why else would someone swallow a whole bottle of Lysol disinfectant?

The former Mrs. Waple was buried on the far side of the Hudson River, in Tuxedo Junction, New York, where she'd been raised. Every second Sunday of October my stepfather drove there with Gordon to place fresh day lilies on her grave. On the way back, they'd ride the creaky wooden funicular that rattled and groaned its way to the top of Mount Beacon. Though it had a canopy, the funicular was otherwise open to the elements. Seeing the gloomy sky that morning, it struck me that they'd chosen a perfect day for a graveside vigil but a lousy one for the funicular.

A ragged corkscrew of smoke rose from the cottage's chimney. I'd walked up the stairs to the green front door and was about to knock when from somewhere behind the cottage I heard what sounded like bottles being tossed into a pit and went to investigate.

Through a sea of ferns I stepped around the side of the cottage to see Jack pushing a wheelbarrow into the woods. I almost called his name, but something stopped me. Instead, I followed him.

Jack and the wheelbarrow—with his walking stick laid across it—went up a trail, or what became a trail as Jack cleared brush and other obstacles away. The trail rose crookedly up a steep incline past the remains of a stone wall to where it ended, or seemed to end, at a rusty chain-link fence. From a dozen yards away, I watched as he peeled back a part of the fence, creating an opening through which he passed. Before pushing on he closed the fence behind him. The objects in the wheelbarrow made clinking sounds.

I waited until he was far enough away then did as he had done, rolling the fence back and sealing it behind me before going on. Keeping my distance, I followed him up the trail. He'd pushed the wheelbarrow another two dozen yards before he stopped to wipe his forehead on a sleeve. Then he pushed on another hundred yards, up the trail along which to either side dark pits had been dug into the earth, some shallow and dry and covered with leaves, others deep and filled with dark, angry water. Next to one pit was a rusty old winch, next to another a spool of equally rusted cable.

I passed a mound of rocky rubble with what looked like bits of ground glass glittering in it, and more rusty things: a crushed bucket, a metal grate, rusted pipes jutting out of the ground like colossal straws, the wheels of an ancient mining gondola...

The path climbed up to a pine copse where, momentarily, I lost sight of Jack. He must have gone over the other side. On all fours I crawled across a bed of moss and pine needles. A low branch snagged a shoulder of my jacket. The brown needles gave off an acrid smell. Where the pine needles ended, so did the ground.

I found myself looking down into a hollow dug into the earth big enough to hold the foundations of two houses: the pit of an abandoned mica mine. The woods of Connecticut are full of mica. The mineral's crystals form clear, heat-resistant sheets, ideally suited for making fireproof windows for lanterns and furnaces, insulating tubes, and other things no one uses anymore. This mine had to be at least a hundred years old.

But this was no ordinary abandoned mica mine. Encrusting its jagged walls, embedded in their chiseled nooks and ragged crannies, were glass insulators like the ones Jack had been collecting, hundreds of them in assorted watery blue shades. And other shiny things, too: light bulbs, bottles, sparkplugs, and other gleaming objects made of porcelain, metal, and glass. Even under the cloudy sky's stingy gray light, they glittered like diamonds.

At its deep end the drift was flooded with water. From out of its dark submerged depths, like earth's earliest life forms emerging from the primordial soup, figures of junk, with hat-block heads, rusty nail hairdos, sparkplug eyes, radio tube and doorknob ears, and other parts formed from hat factory and other refuse, emerged. Two-by-two, the figures marched in procession out of the flooded drift and through a scree of jumbled rock toward a mass of tree branches, twigs, and more rocks arranged in the shape of a boat. No, not a boat: an *ark*. The mythical ark on which Noah rescued two of each species from God's watery judgment.

In the nearby woods more junk creatures foraged: a peacock (its body made from a corroded dynamo, its tail an arrangement of tube brushes); a rhinoceros (its armored head a ventilator cowl, its horn a galvanized metal funnel); an alligator or crocodile (its bumpy back a discarded conveyor chain). It was as though a space-aged Noah had crash-landed his ark deep into the woods of the former Dalton Estate. It reminded me of something. Then it came to me: *Holy Land*—that other folly perpetrated by a lunatic lawyer. Compared to this, Holy Land had been a sober business venture!

My belly resting on that bed of pine needles, gazing down at this bizarre installation, I wondered: had Jack Thomas done this? Could any one person possibly have done it, alone in the woods with no help? If so, why? Why would anyone create such a thing, especially where no one could ever see or appreciate it? What purpose could it possibly serve?

I was wondering all these things when something struck the hollow space between my shoulder blades.

"Spion!"

A second blow.

"Verräter!"

With each cry a fresh blow. The pain was white hot and luminescent. A lightning-bolt of molten lead shot up my spine to the base of my skull. I rolled onto my back to see Jack Thomas bending over me, framed by pine branches, his walking stick drawn back, his mouth contorted with rage.

"Schwachsinniger! Widerling!"

More blows. I covered my head.

"Stop! You're hurting me!"

The pain ricocheted in my brain. Stars danced in my eyes. The air burst out of my lungs. I drew myself into a tight ball.

"Please—!"

He tossed aside his stick. Then, dropping to the ground on his knees, he grabbed me by the neck and hoisted me up to my feet.

"Walk!" he said.

Gripping my T-shirt behind my neck, he led me back down the trail. Tears blurred my vision. My breath caught in my throat.

I spoke through sobs. "Where are you—?"

"Shut up."

He marched me back down to the cottage. Inside, he sat me down at the table where the chessboard was set up. With me seated, from the pocket of his coveralls he pulled his knife, opened it, and stood there gripping it, as if he wasn't sure what to do with it. At last he brought the knife down hard on the table, stabbing it. With the knife still vibrating there, he looked down at me, his face dark with fury.

"What else have you learned?" he snarled.

"What *else?*"

"Your heard me! What else?"

"Nothing."

"Liar!"

"I swear, I haven't learned anything! I don't even know what you're talking about!"

Jack stared at me. No sooner had he asked the question than I myself wondered: what else *was* there to learn? What else had Jack Thomas done that he was keeping from me and the rest of the world? Who was Jack Thomas, really? Of one thing only I was sure: he was a man with more than one secret.

We stayed there like that for a while, with Jack glaring murderously down at me and me sitting there looking apprehensively up at him. I was reminded of the time a screech owl got itself trapped in Mr. Waple's house. Morning, winter, a few weeks after my mother and I moved in. My mother and Mr.

Waple were both working. Gordon and I were watching TV in the den when I heard a rustling sound coming from the fireplace. I guessed a squirrel had gotten caught in the flu. It wasn't a squirrel. Having flown into a dozen rooms and twice as many walls, at last the owl came to rest atop the dining hutch. And there it remained, never once taking its big yellow eyes off me, fixing me with the same terrified look I directed now at Jack as he stood there, wondering what to do with me.

Finally, with a weariness I'd never seen in him before, Jack sat at the table across from me. The knife was still stuck there, its black handle jutting into the air. Jack yanked it from the table, folded it, and put it back in his pocket. As he did I said:

"That thing I saw . . . in the woods . . . did you—?"

Jack shook his head. "It was here already when I arrived."

"But then . . . who . . . ?"

"I don't know. Presumably the person who lived here before me."

"Brewster Dalton?" Did I speak the name, or just form it on my lips? "But how is that possible? He couldn't have done it. Not by himself. Besides, he was crazy!"

"Perhaps that is what made it possible."

Jack went on to explain that he'd been living in the cottage for several weeks when, one morning while exploring the woods, he came upon a path and followed it.

"The path ended at the fence that you saw," he said. "Naturally this made me curious. The next day I returned with a pair of wire shears, cut through the fence, and continued up the path. And I saw what you've now seen, but in far worse condition."

"What *is* it?"

Jack snorted. "I've no idea, Hoff. Not the foggiest."

He started laughing then. He threw his head back and laughed at the rough-hewn timbers running across the cottage's ceiling. As he laughed I thought of Brewster Dalton and the rumors that had him burning Hearthstone Castle down and himself with it. Had he really built that crazy thing in the woods? It seemed incredible. On the other hand, it made sense, but only because Brewster Dalton had been insane. Which didn't explain why Jack Thomas had taken up his cause. Unless Jack Thomas was crazy too.

Jack was still laughing when he noticed me rubbing a bleeding welt on my arm.

"Did I do that?"

"It's my fault," I said. "I shouldn't have spied on you."

He stood up and crossed to the sink. From a drawer near it he took out a small brown bottle. "I'm sorry," he said, returning with it and some cotton. "Will you forgive me?"

The iodine stung.

It started raining. Rain slid down the windows. With my wound dressed, Jack filled the kettle and put it on the stove. He added a log to the fire. As he did I said: "Why would anyone build something like that? In the middle of the woods? Where no one can ever see it?"

"As I said: I have no idea."

"I don't mean Brewster Dalton. He was crazy. I'm not talking about him! I mean you. Why are *you* doing it?"

"There once was a man," Jack said as he fiddled with the wood fire, "and this man had inherited a watch from his grandfather—a lovely gold and silver pocket watch. The watch wasn't working, so the man brought it to the local watchmaker. As the watchmaker took the watch apart, the man noticed something on the balance wheel. At first it looked like a scratch. In fact it was a tiny engraving of a rose. So small was this engraving, it couldn't possibly be read without a jeweler's loupe. In any event it would have been invisible, hidden there inside the movement. Said the man to the watchmaker, 'Why engrave something where no one will ever see it?' 'God sees it,' said the watchmaker." The kettle whistled.

"I thought you said you don't believe in God?"

"I believe in the watchmaker. And the watch."

Jack poured us tea. We sat there for a while, at the table, dunking our tea bags, saying nothing, listening to the rain. After a few minutes to break the stalemate I got up, went to the stove, opened the door, and blew uselessly on the fire.

"I still say it makes no sense," I said, blowing.

"Life makes no sense," Jack said. "Yet here we are. This business of going to the moon with which you're so taken: does that make any sense? Yet you believe in it with all your heart. Why? Because it's so unlikely. Because like all miracles it's impossible; it makes no sense! And you want to believe in miracles; everyone wants to believe in miracles. You look for them on the moon. I say why look so far when impossible things exist so much closer to home?"

I sat back down. Jack squeezed his tea bag. With the used tea bag in it, he held his hand open for mine. Smiling, I gave it to him.

"Why are you smiling?"

"You know that saying, 'If a tree falls in the forest and no one is there to hear it…'?"

"Where I am from, we have the same saying. *Wenn ein Baum in den Wald fällt und niemand ihn hört…*"

"If a crazy person builds something crazy in the woods," I said, "and no one's there to see it…?"

"God sees it," Jack said.

He laughed then and so did I.

The cottage resounded with our shared laughter.

Part 7

A Gantry

I lived in two worlds: the world of school, of the Back Shop Boys and the Spitting Pole, of my stepfather's hat store and my mother's cream sherry and drunken rants…and the world of Fern Cottage, of Jack Thomas and the Thing in the Woods, of swimming and chess and sipping tea to the crackles and pops of his wood stove.

My two worlds even had their own separate weather. Everywhere else in Hattertown it could be pouring rain, at Fern Cottage the sky would be blue and the sun would shine. Or the sun would be shining everywhere else, while up at the Dalton Estate an exclusive black cloud emptied itself onto the roof of Fern Cottage.

Like oil and water the two worlds repelled each other. It never occurred to me that they would soon combine with disastrous results.

Though high school took place in a larger, more modern building with different classrooms and different teachers, it didn't take long for me to realize it was no great improvement over Junior High. Not that my new teachers had nothing to recommend them. Our science teacher, Mr. Blum, had a novel method of demonstrating Newton's Laws of Motion: he hurled chalk erasers at disruptive or dozing students. Miss Delvecchio (art) wore a paint-splotched smock, brought fresh-cut flowers to class every day, and let us call her by her first name, Madge. Mr. Oates (algebra) stood in front of his equation-slathered blackboard, his stubby legs spread apart and short arms bowed, like a gunslinger squaring off with his opponent[s]. They weren't bad teachers, really. Some were pretty good, as a matter of fact. Still, I couldn't see any of them ever helping me partake of anything of the infinite.

That fall squirt guns were the rage. Armed with plastic Soakermans, Splashshooters, Green Avengers, Squirt-O-Matics, and Water Finks, we prowled the school corridors, a Wild West wherein the bullets were made of water. At a quarter to fifty cents a pop, the squirt guns would last less than a week before their plastic triggers snapped or their rubber gaskets failed. Still, we considered them to be worth every penny.

Our enthusiasm for squirt guns wasn't shared by Miss Stanhope, known to us as "Ol' Purple Puss," so named for the large purple birthmark on her lower left jaw (a flagrant case of body shaming commensurate with the times). Middle-aged, heavyset, with features several sizes too small for her ample face, she carried a wooden yardstick with her at all times, and not for measuring things. Her "Board of Education," she called it.

As for that purple birthmark, depending on Miss Stanhope's mood, it changed color and shape, looking one moment like a rooster's comb, the next like the head of a rhinoceros. On certain days it looked more like one of the United States, Florida or Texas, though Michigan too made an occasional appearance, as did the Great Lakes. While she droned on about the Founding Fathers and the division of powers (social studies was her subject), Miss Stanhope's birthmark held me in thrall, convinced as I was that at any moment the thing would explode, splattering me and the rest of our class with a mixture of puss and grape jelly, a prospect more terrifying to me than that of the nuclear attack for which we had been instructed to duck and cover.

That fear, along with my still raging crush on Belinda Dalton, was all that kept me awake during class. That Ol' Purple Puss' class was the only one Belinda and I now shared did little to diminish my ardor for her; on the contrary: it inflated it to a sense of longing that, knowing it would never be fulfilled, amounted to despair. Something had changed in me over the summer. Now when I thought of Belinda it was no longer a matter of being enchanted by her paisley dresses or her fiery pigtails. My thoughts were haunted by the parts of her I couldn't and most likely would never see, by her belly and her breasts and—yes—by the orifice that, thanks to Victor's pornographic playing cards, I now knew beyond any doubt and against the tortured logic of my sentimental heart existed in Belinda Dalton as it did in all females of the species homo sapiens. *Belinda Dalton's Cunt:* such a bold, novel, radical concept—one that, when it first occurred to me, I had trouble framing. Yet there it was, lurking irrevocably under those paisley dresses. Now, given the chance, rather than rushing up to her and—in a conspiratorial whisper and all innocence—invoking some item of trivia pertaining to Saturn's rings or the reproductive habits of pygmy shrews, while I froze with yearning my mind would rush in for me, lurching and tumbling, descending like Hell's elevator to my knees on the ground before her, to worship at the altar of Belinda's no longer purely hypothetical sex.

A month into the semester Miss Stanhope went on a rampage, confiscating squirt guns from all who carried them, stashing them in the drawer of her metal teacher's desk. I knew she stashed them there since that's where I watched her stash my Flash Gordon Rocket Ray (ruby red, cigar-shaped, featuring a brass-knuckle handgrip). As she slid the drawer open I caught a colorful glimpse of the tutti-frutti arsenal, enough squirt guns to equip a small army.

The next day, while Miss Stanhope pulled hall monitoring duty, Victor, Skunky, and I sneaked into her classroom. With Victor keeping lookout, using my Swiss Army knife I pried open the drawer. Fast as we could Skunky and I jammed squirt guns into our pockets, up our sleeves, and down into our crotches (where they leaked embarrassingly). That same afternoon out in the high school parking lot, as they awaited their rides home, to cheers we re-distributed the rescued squirt guns back to their rightful owners.

It was a short-lived victory. The very next day all the squirt-guns we'd rescued and as many more were recaptured. This time instead of locking them in her desk drawer, with the entire student body gathered ceremoniously as if at a hanging, Miss Stanhope fed the squirt guns to the school incinerator.

Such a despicable act cried out for vengeance. Two days later, using pushpins from the bulletin board, we booby-trapped Miss Stanhope's chair. With breaths held we watched her cross to her desk and sit down and…nothing happened. She proceeded to take role as usual, checking off our names in her roster. When she rose from the chair the pushpins rose with her, holding her dress up like the curtain over a stage. Only as she made her way back to her desk did the pushpins start falling, *snap, snap, snap,* onto the linoleum-tiled floor. On the third *snap* she turned to see the trail of pushpins she'd left behind, at which point we all lost it. As the room burst out laughing Miss Stanhope's entire face turned as deep purple as her birthmark.

Eventually, by way of Hattertown High's first underground newspaper, Miss Stanhope's fury delivered me straight into my heartthrob's arms. That wouldn't happen until toward the end of November. Meanwhile, on weekends and after school, Gordon and I helped Jack work on the Thing in the Woods.

In the junk figures we replaced socket eyes, gear sprocket ears, vacuum tube and spark plug noses. To work on the partly submerged figures there I had to wade into the drift up to my hips. It took a month to refurbish most of the sculptures. Replacing the broken insulators along the drift walls took another month. Time, moisture, and insects had reduced much of the ark to spongy toadstool-covered sticks crawling with vermin. We spent a whole weekend replacing rotting branches. Birch being scarce, we substituted poplar and sassafras.

At the shallow end of the drift, a shaft of stone two feet wide at its base and twelve feet tall, cut square and pointed on top, lay half submerged in the ink-black water. Where not covered in lichen, the obelisk was badly scarred and chipped, but still intact. Not far from it was the rocky pedestal where it had once stood or was meant to stand. The obelisk, Jack pointed out, was made of blue stone. It was the only blue stone around. Everything else was granite. Someone had to have moved it there.

"Impossible," I said. "The thing must weigh a ton!"

"Two tons would be my guess. Nonetheless, it didn't walk here by itself."

"Uhn haah dah," Gordon said.

"We must raise it," said Jack.

"How?"

"There's a way, I'm certain."

"It's called a crane!"

Jack shook his head. "No. No machines."

"Without a crane or something there's no way we can lift it!"

"How old are you?"

"I'll be fourteen in March."

"Does the name 'Archimedes' mean anything to you?"

"The astronomer."

"'Give me a place to stand,' Archimedes said, 'and I can move the world!'"

"Great, let's get Archimedes to move the thing!"

"We'll need a tower, something to give us leverage." (*Sometink to gif us lefrej.*)

"A gantry," I said. *The framework that supports a rocket before launching.*

"Yes, a gantry. I don't suppose you know how to build one?"

I didn't, but I knew someone who probably did.

"I see you've made contact," said Virgil.

Gordon and I sat on the edge of the flying saucer. Virgil handed us each steaming hot mugs of Ovaltine. Though I'd promised Jack I wouldn't breathe a word about the Thing in the Woods to anyone, with Virgil I made an exception.

"Extraterrestrials have a long history of leaving evidence behind during their sojourns to Earth," Virgil explained. "Crop circles, Stonehenge, the Easter Island statues, the Stones of Carnac... engineering marvels, all. By those standards I'd say your man is thinking pretty small."

"Are you telling me Jack Thomas is an alien from outer space?"

"Based on what you've told me there can be little doubt."

"What about the obelisk?"

"What about it?"

"Do you think we can we raise it?"

"Sure, if the right principles are applied. Pull up a stool."

Virgil wheeled himself to a workbench and opened a notebook.

"Let's take another obelisk as a point of departure," he said, sketching. "The obelisk at St. Peter's in the Vatican. Around 1580, a guy named Domenico Fontana moved it from the Roman circus just south of the basilica to where it stands now, in St. Peter's Square. It took Fontana four months—that's with a thousand men, dozens of horses, and fifty winches. St. Peter's obelisk is twenty-five meters high. It weighs a million pounds, or about five hundred tons. Yours weighs—how much did you say?"

"Two tons."

"Uhn haah dah."

Virgil sketched away, muttering, making calculations in the margins of his sketch. Finished, he snapped the pencil eraser against what looked like a teepee with a hangman's noose dangling from it.

"Twenty-five feet, that's how tall a gantry you'll be needing. I recommend a four-legged rather than a three-legged job. Use hemlock. Grows locally, strong and flexible, gives a lot before it breaks. Choose trees that are dead and leafless but not fallen. Twelve inches at the base. That ought to give you your desired height."

Virgil tore out the notebook page and handed it to me.

As we were leaving his back room I pointed to Virgil's saucer in-progress and asked, "When do you plan to launch this thing, anyway?"

"When the time comes, son. When the time comes." Virgil

put his arm around me. "Why? In a hurry to get rid of me?"

Per Virgil Zeno's instructions we built a gantry. Using a rope harness with all three of us pulling, we dragged the downed hemlock trunks to the mine pit. That took a day. Up at the mine we laid the cut trunks out in an 'A' configuration, with the wide ends forming the bottom of the 'A,' and two trimmed-off tops serving as crossbeams. At the top of the 'A' we cut a forty-degree miter joint, then drilled two holes a few inches down from it for the half-inch bolts that would secure the peak. With both A-sections moved into position, we tied a rope around one of the bracing timbers and slung it around a suitably large nearby tree branch. Then we yanked the frame into a vertical position, leaned it against the drift wall, dug holes to secure the legs, and piled heavy stones around them to keep them from shifting. With one of the two A-frames standing, we raised the second into position.

With the gantry finished we looped a three-foot long, quarter-inch, 1,800-pound breaking-strength rope (courtesy of Hattertown Hardware) twice around the gantry cap, then secured its ends with a sheet bend. Using another section of the same rope we'd raise the obelisk, or try. All we needed was a block and tackle.

I knew just where to find one.

We walked along the railroad tracks, the same ones where Jack collected the insulators. Like most railroads it went through the worst-looking parts of town, past sandlots, dumps, and the sewage treatment plant: a landscape of drab grays and browns that even the sunniest days couldn't brighten. A rusted siding veered off into what remained of the Dalton Hat Works. The factory's brick chimney still stood, the name

D
A
L
T

O
N

running down its weather-beaten brick shaft. The factory's outer walls bristled with barbed and razor wire and NO TRESS-PASSING signs. Still, from the siding it wasn't hard to get in.

We entered a cavernous space of blown-out windows and piles of used tires, hundreds of them. There, dangling from a beam up in the loft, just where I remembered seeing it, hung the block and tackle. As Jack and Gordy watched from below I climbed out on the beam and cut it down with my Swiss Army Knife.

Leaving the block and tackle behind, we explored the rest of the abandoned factory, making our way from dusty room to room, each room a ghostly museum of rusted machinery. Seeing those old rusty machines, I recalled the first time my father brought me with him to the hat factory where he worked. I was six years old. I remember it being extremely hot and wet, with all kinds of chuffing, flapping, pounding machinery, and steam oozing and hissing and floating in clouds everywhere, so much steam I felt like a ship lost in a foggy sea. The steam rose to the rafters, where it condensed and fell like rain—a deadly rain, back in the days when mercuric nitrate was still used as a fur processing agent. Most of the back shop workers wore leather aprons; some wore masks over their mouths. As I stood with my father a man dumped a cart of half-finished hats onto a wooden slab.

"Are they done?" a worker asked.

"Stick a fork in 'em and find out!" my father said, getting a laugh from his fellow Back Shop workers. How proud I'd been of him then!

As we made our way from one room to the next I pointed to the various rusted machines, explaining to Jack as I did the process for making hats, how the pelts of rabbits and beavers were cut, sorted, and cleaned, how by a process called "carroting" they were cured with mercury salts until 1948, and other chemicals afterwards, how the cured pelts were fed into a machine that cut the fur away from the skin, how the loose fur was then fed through a "picker" for sorting, how after they were bagged and baled the bales went into another area of the Back Shop called the Rough Body Plant, where the different types of fur were weighed and blended for different styles of hats, how the blended fur passed subsequently through a machine called a "feeder," which broke it down and made it softer, how from the feeder the softened fur was fed into the "blower" where any leftover rough fibers were picked out by hand, how on a conveyor the resulting mixture was pressed into long sheets that were subsequently blown into bell-shaped domes. Those domes were then stretched over a "spinner" that spun them, tightening the fibers like the spinners that wrap cotton candy around cardboard cones at carnivals.

"That's just the first step," I explained. From there the domes went through a sequence of hot water, steam, and rolling pressure treatments to further tighten up their fibers. Next, they went through a "hardener" that shrank them to half their original size.

Once dyed the cone-shaped felt was ready for blocking. The "blocker" consisted of two large concave aluminum pans, an upper and a lower one, mounted horizontally and controlled by foot pedals and hand wheels. Heated by open flames, the pans were dangerously hot.

"It took three men to operate each blocker," I explained. The first man, called the "tipper," stretched the moistened felt over the lower pan. The second man, the "brimmer," formed the band-line and the brim, while the third man, the "blocker"(Dad's job) pressed down extra hard on the foot pedal, forcing the lower pan up into the upper one. Using the hand-wheel, the pans were tightened further.

The blocking process resulted in a crudely shaped hat known as a "capeline." After it was varnished, dried, and sandpapered, a two-ply band of rayon or silk was stitched around the capeline's crown where it joined the brim. From there, the capeline went into the Front Shop to be blocked again, this time on a wooden block that gave the crown its ultimate shape. From there it passed through the "pouncer," following which more excess fur was removed with super-fine sandpaper. To soften the felt even more and give it a richer tone, a colored powder was rubbed into it. By an application of dry heat and pressure the brim got its final shape, with resultant excesses cut away by a "trimmer." For some hats—a Homburg or a derby—the brim was rolled and "flanged" (bound with a strip of silk). After that the hat passed under a steaming hot sandbag known as an "elephant's leg" where it was set into its final style.

"Such an elaborate process," said Jack.

"We're still not done."

"You mean there's more?"

"One more step."

The last dusty room was the Finishing Shop. There, I explained, a leather sweatband with a tiny, ornamental silk bowtie was stitched into the crown. From there the finished inspected hat was packed in tissue paper and boxed for shipment to the retail store.

"And that is how hats are made," I said, our tour having come to its end.

"All that for a hat!" said Jack. *(All sed chust voh uh het!)*

"I beg your pardon, sir," I said indignantly, imitating my stepfather. "Upon my word, without hats there'd be no civilization! Why we would all be apes!"

From under a pile of debris I yanked out a capeline and plopped it on Gordon's head, raising a cloud of dust that had us all choking. Two more capelines found their ways onto my head and Jack's. Wearing our capelines, coughing and laughing, we returned to the room full of old tires. I had just hefted the block and tackle over my shoulder when through one of many paneless windows I saw a police car pull into the weedy lot.

"Cop car," I said. "We'd better scram!"

Soon we were back walking along the train tracks. We came upon the carcass of a dead dog lying beside them. Flattened and desiccated, it had obviously met its end under a train. Jack poked it with his stick.

"Everything is contingent," he said, poking it.

"Contingent? What does that mean?"

"Dependent on other things."

"What is everything dependent on?"

"On everything," said Jack.

By then I assumed we were in the clear. As we cut over to the road, though, the police car crept up and started shadowing us.

"Damn," I said.

Jack said nothing but he looked nervous. We kept walking. I had always been afraid of cops, since I was little, when they came to the house one day and arrested my father, what for I forget or was never told. We were eating lunch when they took him away in handcuffs.

The police car shadowed us for a while longer before it rolled up next to us. There was just one cop inside. He rolled down the window.

"Were you fellas just in the old Dalton factory?"

"Nossir," I answered. My legs were shaking. The block and tackle was draped over my shoulder. The cop nodded toward it.

"Where'd you get that block and tackle?"

"We found it," I said. "By the railroad tracks."

"Who's your friend?" The cop pointed to Jack who stared straight ahead and kept walking. "Hey—mister!"

"He doesn't talk," I said.

The officer pointed to my stepbrother. "What about him?"

"He doesn't talk, either."

"Must be an epidemic. What's your name?"

I told him.

"What about your friend here?"

"His name's Jack."

"Are you in trouble, boy?"

"No, sir."

"Are you sure?"

"Yes, sir."

"If I catch you near that factory again, I'll arrest you."

"Yes, sir."

The cop shadowed us a while longer before speeding away.

Every chance we got Gordon and I helped Jack with the Thing in the Woods. We'd work for a few hours in the morning, go for a swim, eat lunch, then work some more. Afternoons, when it got warm, Jack would unzip his coveralls down to his waist and let the sleeves dangle. Gordon and I would take off our shirts. We'd eat lunch by the dam or back in the cottage. Bread, apples, cheese, tea. Sometimes after lunch we'd play a round or two of chess.

Raising the obelisk proved to be much harder than we had hoped. We tried hoisting nautical style, with Jack hauling and Gordon and me "tailing on." Jack took hard pulls, gaining some leverage by pulling the rope out like a bow, easing up only after Gordon and I secured each gain. With the first few pulls, the obelisk rose an inch or two, but afterward every pull grew increasingly harder, until by the seventh or eighth pull the obelisk refused to budge. A few more pulls and the block and tackle would give. Like a torpedoed battleship the obelisk would slide back into the inky water.

With all three of us hauling and the load split between four ropes we still couldn't get the obelisk to rise more than a foot before the block and tackle broke. The fourth time it broke I said: "Face it, Jack—it's hopeless!"

"Nothing's hopeless," Jack said. "Even if it is, one must never say so!"

Through October we kept swimming. Jack had a technique for swimming in cold water. The trick was to not go in too fast or slow, to just step in without giving it much thought. "Tell yourself the water feels fine, and it will." Per Jack's instructions I'd slip in, feeling only a brief chill that the first dozen strokes would eradicate. A half-dozen more strokes and the water felt fine.

The days grew shorter. Across Fern Cottage's windows morning hoarfrost spread fern-like patterns. Meanwhile the real ferns skirting the cottage shriveled and turned brown. Along the edges of the lake crusts of ice formed. Mornings we'd arrive at the gantry to find its ropes glazed with rime. The cold air burned our ears and cheeks and made it hard to breathe. Our gloved fingers froze. Even for Jack the lake was too cold to swim in. We played chess and sipped tea, kept warm by the stove.

It was while playing chess with Jack one Saturday afternoon that I uncovered the secret to his mysterious past. He was filling the kettle at the sink. As he did, while setting up the board for our next game, I noticed that the bottoms of each of the hand-carved wooden chess pieces were lined with discs of colored paper: pink, orange, red, green. On the bottom of one rook a disc of purple-colored paper had started to peel off. On its underside something was printed: two lines, one thick, one thin, followed by the letters "PR," and under them the letters "CA." With Jack still busy at the sink, I picked up another chess piece, a knight, and peeled back the yellow paper disc under it, revealing the bottom part of an "I" or possibly the number 1, with the letters "CEN" printed below it.

During my next few visits to Jack's cottage I peeled away more of those colored discs, a dozen of them. I put them in my pocket and took them home. There, at my bedroom desk, using paper paste, like a paleontologist piecing together the bones of a prehistoric creature, I assembled the pieces. Soon I realized that the colored discs were from some sort of currency in denominations of five, ten, and twenty-five cents. Even more enticing were parts of words: "SONER," "INOIS," "CAMP." Most enticing of all, at the center of one disc, the letters "W," "A," and "R": WAR.

By three in the morning I had pieced together:

—SONER—WAR

CAMP—ADOTTE, —LINOIS

With a little help from my World Atlas:

PRISONER OF WAR
CAMP BERNADOTTE, ILLINOIS

Under those words was a black line, and under the black line "No." followed by a series of numbers and letters stamped in red:

81G-93p---

The next day at the town library I did some research. Like most people I had no idea that there had been Prisoner of War camps in the United States during World War II, let alone over 700 of them, let alone that those camps once held over 430,000 POWs, most of them Germans captured in North Africa. Though hastily constructed, the camps were well-organized and clean. Prisoners were well-fed and well-treated, entertained and educated. Works details were voluntary and remunerated. So agreeable were the camp's accommodations, critics referred to the camps collectively as "the Fritz Ritz." It's no wonder then that, according to an article I found in the May 1953 issue of *Collier's Magazine,* of those 430,000 prisoners, only 2,803 escaped. Most of them, the article went on to explain, were caught in a matter of days…

> …but a number who spoke English well attempted to assume new identities and melt into obscurity. Tracing them was a needle-in-a-haystack operation: a scant 6,000 FBI men combing almost 160,000,000 people. A Chicago police officer said: Any prisoner of war smart enough to go to work in a big city, or lose himself on some remote farm, ought to be able to remain at large forever. Yet today, only five escapees are still free. The FBI has weeded out and captured all the others.
>
> For the remaining five, it's probably only a matter of time before the G-men catch up with them (although it might be a

> different matter if their fingerprints and other identifying data were not on file). You may be able to speed up the process.
>
> Here are the photos of the German POWs still at large; if any of these men look familiar to you, notify the nearest FBI office at once.

The article included photographs of the five men with the dates of their escapes and descriptions under them. Though clean-shaven and younger than the man in the deckle-edged photo (the one with the hawk-nosed woman, the blond boy, and the sailboat), the man in the fourth photo *could* have been Jack. However the name underneath it wasn't "Jack Thomas." It was "Johann Verhoff." He was described as twenty-two years old, tall and fair, with a scar on his chin. The caption went on to say he'd escaped from the POW camp in Bernadotte, Illinois, in August of 1945.

Is there any point in my trying to parse the heady mixture of emotions that found me in that library at that moment? Shock, fear, disbelief, dismay: all went through me as I sat there in front of my pile of books, newspapers, and magazines. But more than anything I felt exhilarated, as if I had discovered some new planet, star, or galaxy in the universe.

I had never known a German or a soldier, let alone a German soldier, let alone an escaped German prisoner of war. The little that I knew about the Second World War, I had learned mostly from movies like *The Guns of Navarone* and television shows like *Combat.* German soldiers were "Krauts," "Fritzes," "Jerrys," "Heines," and "Huns." They wore piss-pot shaped helmets like the one Victor's father gave him, marched in goose-step formation, barked *jah vol* and *Sieg Heil* to stiff-armed salutes, and were buffoons and/or sadists. If in a game of war you got stuck playing a German, it meant certain inglorious death. Krauts were the enemy. They were despicable. They existed in my adolescent conscience for one purpose and one purpose only: to be deployed and despised.

I supplemented my minimal knowledge of World War II with volume nine of the *Golden Book History of World War II,* from which I learned about Hitler and the Nuremberg Laws, about concentration camps and six million Jews killed in gas chambers. Could Jack have had anything to do with all that? With difficulty I inserted him mentally into one of the book's many illustrations. No sooner did an image of Jack goose-stepping down the Champs-Élysées along with other German soldiers form itself in my mind's eye than a wave of nausea swept over and through me. No, I said to myself. It's *impossible!* That couldn't be Jack Thomas—not the Jack Thomas I knew! I had to remind myself that there was no such person, that the Jack Thomas I "knew" I hardly knew at all; he didn't exist.

Under the subject heading "Johann Verhoff," a further search of periodicals turned up the following microfilmed item in the September 1945 issue of the Illinois *News-Gazette:*

ESCAPED GERMAN POW SOUGHT

> Federal Bureau of Investigation agents Thursday were searching for a 22-year-old German prisoner of war who escaped on Wednesday night from the prison camp at Bernadotte, Illinois. The former lance corporal in Field Marshal Erwin Rommel's Afrika Corps, Johann S. Verhoff, was captured in Tunisia in 1943.
>
> Verhoff is described as five feet eleven inches tall, weight between 160 and 175 pounds, light brown hair, narrow face, and a small mustache. He was last seen wearing dark trousers and shoes, a plaid shirt, and a green cap. It is believed that he may have jumped a freight train and is making his way west.

What to do? I wondered. Do I tell Zag and betray Jack? Or keep Jack's secret to myself and betray not only Zag, but my country? Worse: I'd be an accessory to a crime, aiding and abetting a Nazi fugitive. Then again (I told myself), World War Two had been a long time ago. Eighteen years! Wasn't there a statute of limitations for being an escaped German POW? For all I knew the "authorities" weren't even looking for Jack anymore. Could they possibly still be looking for him, after so many years? If they had really wanted to find him, they'd have done so long ago.

A trip to the local post office was all that it took to dissuade me of that notion. On the bulletin board there, buried under more recent notices, was a poster distributed by the FBI, the word WANTED spread across its top in letters as black as the storm clouds in the sky that day. Under a set of thumbprints were three black-and-white photos of the same person taken from different angles. The central photo was the same one I had seen in *Collier's*. To its left I read:

> Johann Verhoff, German Prisoner of War, escaped on or about August 5, 1945, from a Prisoner of War Camp located near Bernadotte, Illinois. Any person having information which may assist in locating Johann Verhoff is requested to immediately notify the Director of the Federal Bureau of Investigation, U.S. Department of Justice, Washington, D.C., or the Special Agent in Charge of the Division of the Federal Bureau of Investigation listed in the back hereof which is nearest your city.

Spread across the bottom of the poster:

Identification Order No. 2103
Issued by: J. Edgar Hoover, Director

When no one was looking I pulled the poster down, crumpled it up, and tossed it in the wastebasket.

I lead a double life: on one hand, a more-or-less typical high school student, on the other: the secret friend of an escaped fugitive German POW.

Meanwhile in Hattertown High the seeds of insurrection were being sown. Though in other parts of the nation the student protest movement that would define mid-'60s America wouldn't start in earnest for a few more years, somehow Hattertown got ahead of the game.

It all started the night of October 31, 1963, Halloween, when Dwight Riddell bashed his skull open on a tombstone at Backwards Hill.

Backwards Hill was the site of an abandoned Episcopal church off a one-lane road that rolled through the hilly outskirts of town. According to local lore, if you parked at the bottom of Backwards Hill facing the church (headlights on, transmission in neutral, foot off the brake), your car would roll slowly uphill all the way to the church's front steps. When it did, if immediately afterward you jumped out of the car, ran to the front door of the church, knocked three times, and pressed your ear to the door, you'd hear werewolf howls coming from inside, supposedly.

Though at thirteen I was too young to drive and knew no one who had personally undergone this experience, the rumors were so rife we never questioned them; anyway, until one of us had a learner's permit, we couldn't disprove them. Meanwhile we settled for riding our bikes to Backwards Hill and challenging the devil to a footrace.

The race worked this way: you had to run up the hill, knock three times on the church door, climb over the graveyard fence, run to the farthest tombstone, touch it, then run and climb back over the fence again. If, after climbing back over the fence, you felt the wind blowing past you, you knew you'd won, the wind being the devil catching up with you. But if the wind blew past you *while* you were still running, you'd lost the race.

While those who won their races with the devil could look forward to years of good fortune, losers could anticipate nothing but misery.

Of what might befall you if you lost your race with the devil Ernie Applebaum was our supreme example. Back in '61, at a Halloween party three nights after Ernie lost his race, he and two friends of his were putting their fire-breathing skills on display. They took turns squirting butane from a cigarette lighter into their mouths, then, with the still-flaming lighter in front of them, exhaled sharply, producing twin fireballs. They had done so successfully twice on the rear porch of the house and were doing it a third time when Ernie coughed, sucking the flame into his lungs. At first, he didn't seem at all fazed. He'd gone inside to party more when suddenly he fell writhing to the floor. By the time the ambulance arrived Ernie Applebaum was dead.

It made the front page of the *Hattertown Gazette.*

The consequences of Dwight Riddell's losing his race with the devil were far less severe. While running back from touching the farthest tombstone Dwight tripped and fell head-first into another grave marker, one with a carved angel on it, bashing his skull on it.

To stitch his fractured skull together the emergency room doctors had to shave off all of Dwight's hair. Dwight was extremely vain about his hair. It was dark brown and thick and he wore it in a Ricky Nelson flip. For Dwight having a shaved head was worse than having a split skull. To hide his bald scalp he wore his Minnesota Twins baseball cap. He wore it everywhere, including in school, violating the school dress code forbidding the wearing of headgear indoors: a paradoxical rule, considering Hattertown's past as "The Town that Crowned America." When Dwight refused to remove his cap he was suspended.

It was Dwight's suspension that resulted in the creation of Hattertown High's first ever underground newspaper. Called

The Hatted Tattler (among considered titles: *Hat City Free Press, Mad Hatter Rag, The Hattertown Harbinger, The Mercury Muckraker*), the newspaper was Belinda's idea. In its typewritten pages we students aired our grievances about "the Riddell Affair," as well as our views on other matters of urgency. Belinda, the self-appointed editor-in-chief, wrote the feature story, "A Crown for Dwight Riddell."

On Friday November 22nd, at seven-thirty in the morning, Issue #1 of *The Hatted Tattler* rolled damp and warm off the spirit duplicator in the English Department office, to which Miss Delvecchio had graciously provided the key. Belinda turned the chrome-plated crank; I collated and stapled. We made seventy-five copies. In solidarity and protest everyone wore hats to school that day. I wore one of my stepfather's fedoras; Belinda wore a scarlet Bonnie Parker-style beret. As I stapled the last of the newspapers, she said:

"I really appreciate your helping me with this, Leo."

"It's my pleasure," said I.

Belinda did something then that I was completely unprepared for. She bent forward and she kissed me—a chaste kiss at first, on the cheek, but one that nevertheless sent waves of bliss coursing through my body. She drew back and studied me then, like a doctor examining a patient. Having arrived at her diagnosis, Belinda administered the treatment—another kiss, but not a chaste one. As though it were a spade and my tongue was a weed she was trying to dig out by its roots, Belinda jammed her tongue into my mouth. I had the start of a head cold; my nose was all stuffed up. With my mouth full of Belinda's tongue, I couldn't breathe. I felt like Lloyd Bridges in one of *Sea Hunt's* many underwater battles in which the hero's scuba hose gets sliced by a bad guy's knife. When she finally stopped kissing me I came up for air so fast I got the bends.

"Come on," she said as I sat there trying to catch my breath. "We have an underground newspaper to distribute!"

❧

The Hatted Tattler was still warm and reeking of mineral spirits when, armed with her Board of Education, Ol' Purple Puss barreled toward us down the school hallway, to where we'd been distributing it ahead of the first period bell. Having confiscated all of our remaining issues, she marched us to Principal Laurelton's office.

Because it was secreted behind panels of frosted glass, we referred to Principal Laurelton's office as the "Cloud Chamber." While waiting to be called inside I raised the blinds on the only window in the vestibule, exposing a view of the Caxton-Dumont factory chimney, the tallest in town, already belching thick smoke at that hour. Five years earlier Tove Jennings, who worked the blocking machine with my father, stood atop that chimney. Distraught at having been laid off a week earlier, despite pleas from his wife, his priest, a brother-in-law, the chief of police, and the town selectman, he hurled himself to the ground. You could still see stains on the pavement where he landed. The Jennings used to come over to our house for barbeques. I played with their kids. As I watched the smoke belch from the chimney a shiver ran up my spine.

"Would you mind please sitting down, Leo? You're making me nervous."

Before I could sit down we were summoned inside.

Short, bald, with a paunch and a wispy mustache, to me Principal Laurelton looked a lot like Wimpy, the guy from the Popeye cartoons who's always cadging hamburgers. You never would have guessed that he survived the sinking by kamikaze attack of the minesweeper he had captained during WWII, or that he personally rescued several of his crew, suffering terrible burns in the process, an act of bravery for which he was awarded the Distinguished Service Cross. A black-and-white photo of the *USS Perry* hung on the wall behind his desk. Pats on the back were Principal Laurelton's trademark, as was his standard greeting: "Glad ta see ya!"—a sentiment that under present circumstances wasn't reciprocal.

Brandishing her "Board of Ed," Miss Stanhope stood between Principal Laurelton, who sat at his desk, and the United States flag, with its eagle-topped gold stand.

"Have a seat, please," Principal Laurelton said.

The Cloud Chamber reeked of cloves. To help him quit smoking, Principal Laurelton chewed clove-flavored chewing gum. Five ruddy packs were lined up on his desk between a staple gun and the principal's Executive Decision Maker roulette wheel. Principal Laurelton eased himself back into his chair.

"Now then." He folded his hands over his stomach. "It's my understanding that you've been distributing contraband material in the school hallways. What have you to say?"

"Guilty as charged," I said.

"Not guilty!" said Belinda.

"Your defense?"

"You call it contraband," Belinda argued. "I call it free speech."

"It's radical filth!" said Miss Stanhope, brandished a copy of *The Hatted Tattler* with pinched fingers, like a dead rat by its tail.

"We're expressing our opinions."

"Maybe so," said Principal Laurelton, leaning forward over his desk. "But that doesn't give you the right to distribute unauthorized material in the school hallways."

"Or the right to use school equipment without permission," Ol' Purple Puss added. She turned to Laurelton. "They broke into the English Department office after hours and used the spirit duplicator. I'm sure of it."

"We didn't break in," said Belinda.

"Who let you in, then?"

Belinda and I both said nothing.

"School rules forbid displaying or distributing materials without prior approval," Principal Laurelton informed us.

"We weren't aware of that," I said.

"We are so aware of it," Belinda corrected. "And it's a rotten rule. It amounts to censorship!"

"Censorship!" Miss Stanhope said.

"That's right—censorship!" Belinda faced Principal Laurelton. "I don't suppose either of you bothered to read our newspaper before confiscating it?"

"You didn't give us much of a chance," said Laurelton.

"We're under no obligation to read your propaganda," said Miss Stanhope.

"Hold on a second, Margaret," said Principal Laurelton.

"You mustn't let them get away with this, Herbert. If you do, I promise you it won't be long before this school is entirely overrun by radicals."

Until Ol' Purple Puss uttered it that morning, except as applied to algebra equations the word "radicals" had been unfamiliar to me, which may help explain why it reached my ears as "radishes," and I wondered what Belinda and I had to do with a pungent red root vegetable.

Smiling, Principal Laurelton leaned back in his chair. I had the feeling at that moment that he was getting a kick out of the proceedings.

"What say we examine the evidence?"

So saying, the principal put on his bifocals, picked *The Hatted Tattler* up from his desk, and had started reading it aloud when Belinda snatched it from him.

She summed up its contents: "A Consumer Reports-style survey of popular water pistol models, two editorials—one by yours truly protesting Dwight Riddell's suspension, the other by Leo endorsing the so-called off-string method of performing yo-yo tricks."

"Versus looping or sleeping," I interjected.

"Lastly, a review of the hot lunch program, in which the pizza is described— accurately—as 'tomato sauce and cheese covered shirt cardboard.' Highly inflammatory!" She tossed the paper back onto the principal's desk.

"Still," said Laurelton, "you don't deny having broken the rules."

"We don't deny it," said Belinda, "any more than you can deny denying us our First Amendment right to free speech! Or doesn't it apply to Hattertown High students?"

"What impudence!" Ol' Purple Puss snarled. By then the dimensions of her port wine stain had expanded in all directions; the stain had also darkened by at least three shades. "You mustn't let them get away with this, Herbert. I'm telling you! It will only incite them to bigger and bolder acts of insurrection."

"Insurrection!" said Belinda.

Extracting a stick of clove gum from one of the packs on his desk, Principal Laurelton slowly unwrapped and folded it into his mouth. As he did one eyebrow of his shot up to where his hairline used to be. A smile crept under his wispy mustache, the same smile I'd seen there the day Coach Reardon sent me and a caricature that I'd done of him to the principal's office back in sixth grade. Though Principal Laurelton agreed that the drawing was disrespectful, he also conceded with a barely suppressed smirk that I had gotten Coach Reardon "dead to rights."

That same day after lunch Belinda and I and the rest of the student body were summoned to the GP (General Purpose) Room, the auditorium where school plays and other events were staged. We Back Shop Boys sat together in the front row. From behind a wooden lectern at the center of the stage, on behalf of the whole school administration, Principal Laurelton apologized for having "inadvertently violated [our] First Amendment right to free speech." As he gave his speech, we nibbled symbolic radishes from our hot lunch salads.

Principal Laurelton ended his address with two announcements. First: Dwight Riddell's suspension had been overturned; second: until further notice, the rule forbidding hats in school had been lifted.

The assembly over, in celebration we carried Dwight Riddell on our shoulders out onto the school lawn. While still holding him up, we threw our hats into the air. They hovered briefly like flying saucers silhouetted against the cloudy bright November sky. While they hovered, I fell in love with Belinda all over again. But this time it was a different kind of love, not the stomach-churning, cross-eyed, mouth-drying, sickeningly helpless love of adolescence. I loved her as a friend, a comrade, for having a dead father like me and for being the sister I'd never have. I loved her for all the times we would never have together, for the lives we would never live with (or, for that matter, without) each other. But mostly I loved her for the mortal creature she was, for every finite breath of air that of all the air on earth was hers alone to breathe.

Two hats were still hovering when Wesley Conklin, a tenth grader known chiefly for his accordion playing skills, burst out of the school and ran toward us, waving his fists, shouting:

"They shot him! They shot President Kennedy!"

Part 8

The Cloud Chamber

Dismissed early from school that day, I arrived home to find my mother in her bathrobe and slippers on all fours on the kitchen floor, an empty sherry bottle overturned not far from her.

"Well, now, look who's here," she said as Gordon and I stood there, looking down at her. "My interplanetary enigma of a son. You are my son, aren't you? Juss wanna be a hunnerd percent sure. It's been so darn long, I forgot what your face looks like."

My mother's laugh was a cynical cackle. There was bright orangish-red lipstick smeared across her upper teeth. I heard a newscaster's voice murmuring from the Zenith in the parlor. As discretely as possible I asked my mother what she was doing down there on the floor.

"I'm sitting here. What the heck does it look like I'm doing?" (For the record she wasn't sitting; she was on all fours, but never mind.)

"*Why* are you sitting there?" I asked.

"That's good question, a very good question. Help me up on my feet, and I'll do my very best to answer your question. How's that?" She hiccupped.

I helped my mother to her feet. As her face came up level with mine I smelled the sherry and peanuts on her breath. Though I'd seen her drunk many times before, I'd never seen her quite like this. At first I assumed it was the assassination, that she'd been watching the news. My mother liked Kennedy, she always had—for his looks, if for no other reason. I assumed that the news had devastated her. I was about to ask her if she'd heard when she said: "Dance with me!"

"What? *No!*"

She pulled me into a jitterbug.

"Mom—!"

"Quit talking and dance!"

To the music of Walter Cronkite's voice coming from the parlor, amid a leaf storm of cancelled checks, we danced in the kitchen, my mother and I, or rather my mother danced while I stood there, seeing her whirl herself around me like a ribbon around a Maypole.

"You aren't dancing!"

"Please, Mom! You know I can't dance!"

"Nonsense! Your mother and father were both superb dancers. You wouldn't be here otherwise. I didn't marry that father of yours for his money or his brains, that's for sure. Look at *me,* Leo, not down at your feet! Your feet aren't your dance partner; *I* am!"

By then Gordon had joined us, gripping my mother's free hand, whirling himself around with her, his other hand flapping, his tongue sticking out, uttering indecipherable sounds of joy.

"Your brother's got the right idea, see?"

"Stepbrother," I said.

"Remember how you and I used to dance at the Grand Union?"

Would that I had forgotten! The Grand Union was the local supermarket, and my mother and I had indeed danced there when I was three-and-a-half—barely old enough to walk, let alone do a jitterbug or the Lindy Hop. A grainy memory finds us in the frozen food aisle, encircled by rubbernecking housewives, their grocery carts piled with Wonder bread, toilet paper, and Campbell's soups, watching us go at it like Fred and Ginger amid frozen peas and ice cream. It's a wonder the Grand Union didn't sign us up, we were such a big hit. Years later people who had seen our act would remark, "Why your mother must have loved you *to death*!" or something to that effect, though I had to wonder if forcing me to dance with her that way had been more my mother's means of sublimating her thwarted dance career than showing me affection. Was it motherly love or a unique form of child abuse?

Now there we were at it again in the kitchen, with Mom

whirling herself as I stood there shuffling lamely back and forth in my P.F. Flyers. By then out-of-breath Gordon had retreated to the breakfast nook, leaving my mother and me alone to cut a rug—or rather the linoleum—across which a sea of torn-up checks floated.

"What's with all the torn checks?" I asked.

"Oh, *those* checks? They're cancelled checks that your step-father wrote."

"Why are they all torn up?"

"Because I tore them up, that's why."

"What are they doing all over the floor?"

"That's where they landed after I tore them up."

"Oh," I said.

Without breaking her dance, my mother explained:

She had been balancing my stepfather's checkbook as she did every last Friday of each month, when something caught her notice: a check in the amount of one hundred and fifty dollars made out to one Harvey Gilmore, Esq. Memo: "Mortgage." It was one of many checks like it that she'd noticed.

"At first I just assumed Harvey Gilmore was the loan officer at your stepfather's bank, that he'd been paying down the principle."

This time, however, on a hunch my mother had a closer look at all of those checks. That's when she saw that they had all been deposited—not by the bank in Hattertown that held the mortgage on our home, but at a bank in Hartford.

"'Hmm,' I said to myself. 'Now that's peculiar. Why were the mortgage payments going to *Hartford*?' So I phoned the Union Trust and asked to speak to the accounts manager. 'Does your bank have a Hartford branch?' I ask. 'Not as far as I know,' the accounts manager tells me. Not only is there no Hartford branch, there's no Harvey Gilmore: none that works for the Union Trust, anyway. So then I asked the accounts manager—Mr. Slocum, that's his name—I ask him when was the last time he got a mortgage payment from your stepfather? So he goes and looks it up. 'Well, let's see now,' Mr. Slocum says. 'Yes, here we go. The last payment was in August.' 'That's four *months* ago!' I say. 'That's im*possible*.' So Mr. Slocum double-checks for me. And it's true. It's been four months since your stepfather made the last payment on the mortgage. So now I'm *really* curious. I go look through your stepfather's desk, and what do you suppose I find in there? A stack of letters from the bank. *Thirty days due. Sixty days due. Notice to accelerate. Notice of default*... All this time your stepfather's been writing checks for a hundred and fifty dollars to this Harvey Gilmore, Esquire, whoever he is, *not* paying the mortgage. So then I call your stepfather at his store and ask him straight out, 'Who is Harvey Gilmore?' And guess what he tells me?"

I shrugged, having no idea.

"Well, first he *lies* to me, tries to cover it up. When *that* doesn't work your genius of a stepfather admits to me that he's got himself involved in some scheme, some dopey business scheme, that this Harvey Gilmore is his patent attorney slash business investment partner and their 'business venture' comes down to a machine he's invented for measuring hats. Can you *imagine?* Have you ever heard of anything dumber? I mean seriously, *what's* to invent? Put the darn hat on your head and see if it fits!"

All this time my mother orbited me like Sputnik.

"I don't suppose you happen to know anything about this?"

"Who, me? Why should I know anything?"

"Well, I don't mind telling you, your stepdad and I, we had it out then and there on the telephone. Not that your stepfather listened; not that he's ever listened to me—or to anyone else, for that matter, when it comes to that darn store of his. I swear, Leo, your stepdad is the single most stubborn person I've ever known in my entire life. That's including your father, which is saying a lot!"

With that my mother switched from a jitterbug to something like a Carmen Miranda routine, minus the head-borne fruit basket. Poor Mom, I thought, watching her samba across the kitchen. She'd struck out. Strike one: her aborted dance career. Strike two: marrying my rye-whisky-soaked hat factory worker dad. Strike three: marrying my fuddy-duddy bankrupt stepfather. When she married him, had my mother known—did she have any inkling—that Walter J. Waple was in dire financial straits? Had she known, would she have married him?

But she hadn't known. She'd known only that Walter J. Waple was a widower who lived in a grand stone house on Crown Heights Boulevard, with a sweeping wraparound porch, stained glass windows, a turret, and a circular driveway edged with tulips—or were they calla lilies? He had a mentally retarded child, the dear poor man; maybe that's what had driven his first wife to poison herself, though it hardly seemed like a good reason. My mother knew he owned and operated a retail hat store, so he must have been well off. At least he didn't work in the Back Shop of a hat factory. He smelled not of fusty damp wool and sour chemicals, but of sweet pipe tobacco and dignified cologne. His fingernails were polished and trimmed square with no trace of factory grime under them. He didn't curse or drink to excess, was courteous and good mannered and never failed to present himself to her with a dozen long-stem roses. Maybe he wasn't all that wealthy; maybe he merely earned a comfortable living. Still he'd buy her fancy gowns and in his gleaming Shalimar blue 1959 Buick Electra take her to dine (not to *eat,* mind you, but to *dine*) at genteel establishments with names like The Cobbs Mill Inn, The Spinning Wheel, The Wild Turkey, The Old Oak...or to that Swedish place, the one by Lake Candlewood, the one with the model of a Viking ship in the vestibule. The smörgåsbord. They'd order cocktails: him a Gin Gimlet (with a droll little onion), her a Brandy Alexander (not that she cared for brandy, but she liked the sound of it, *Brandy Alexander,* beverage of world-conquering Macedonian military commanders)... At the endlessly long table resplendent with silver-tureened meatballs wading in golden-brown gravy, glazed, clove-studded hams, gasping one-eyed fish and pantied racks of lamb, Mr. and Mrs. Walter J. Waple would fill their plates to brimming and life would be good.

Only it wasn't good. Mr. and Mrs. Walter Waple could afford

no smörgåsbords. They couldn't afford fancy restaurants of any kind. Walter Waple was in debt up to his ears, with the bank now holding two mortgages on his Crown Heights house.

"What will you do?" I asked.

"About what?" my mother said, dancing.

"The mortgage. It has to be paid, right?"

"I don't feel like thinking about it. I feel like dancing. C'mon, Leo! Quit standing there like one of those striped poles they have in Venice!"

With my mother's discovery of my stepfather's financial deceptions, what had been a stuffy atmosphere at home turned dismal. I'd come home from school to find them, my mother and my stepfather, in the parlor, the TV broadcasting what seemed like an endless funeral cortege, my stepfather puffing one of his pipes, her eating her peanuts and sipping her sherry, both of them not talking to each other, their mutual silence dividing them no less than the beaded curtain divided the parlor from the hall.

Is it any wonder I preferred being with Jack at Fern Cottage?

By then the woods of the Dalton Estate were white with snow. While Gordon played with my yo-yo and gawped at his fingers, Jack and I played chess, sipped tea, and listened to logs snapping in his stove. I had told no one about Jack—or about Johann Verhoff. Including Jack. I'd already experienced his response to my uncovering one of his secrets. How would he react to my having uncovered this much bigger and far more potentially damning secret? The memory of Zag dragging a finger across his throat by the boy's reformatory basketball court flashed into my mind.

By then I'd made up my mind that Jack was guilty of nothing more than having been caught fighting on the wrong side of a war, then having had the temerity to not only escape his captors, but to evade them for eighteen years. That the FBI was still after him struck me as extremely unfair if not inhumane. Whatever crimes Jack had committed, it seemed to me that by then he had more than paid for them. I couldn't imagine what he'd been through.

As long as he remained hidden away in Fern Cottage I thought Jack was safe, or did until the morning Principal Laurelton's voice over the school intercom summoned me once again to the Cloud Chamber. This time I waited more than a half hour before the door to Principal Laurelton's office opened and he came out to greet me. On the lapel of his suit he wore an American flag pin.

"Good ta see ya, Leo," he said.

With a hand on my shoulder, Principal Laurelton guided me into the Cloud Chamber, where, to my surprise, my mother and stepfather sat waiting. Mom wore her beige winter coat and navy pillbox hat. My stepfather sat in the chair next to hers, clutching his grey homburg in his lap by its rolled brim, as if a sudden wind gust might somehow penetrate the Cloud Chamber and snatch it away from him. Also present in the room were Miss Stanhope, aka Ol' Purple Puss, standing next to the principal's desk, clutching her Board of Ed as always, eyeing me with a mixture of curiosity, pride, and disdain, as though she were a lepidopterist and I a rare specimen she had mounted on a pin. On the opposite side of the principle's desk stood a uniformed Hattertown police officer who looked disarmingly familiar.

"Hello, there, sport," my stepfather said with none of his customary chipperness, his eyes skidding off mine like a pair of wet marbles.

"Have a seat, Leo, why don't you," Principal Laurelton said, indicating the empty chair facing his desk while taking his own seat.

"Now then..." He cleared his throat, the fingers of both of his hands splayed on his moss-green blotter. "I don't suppose you know why I've asked you here this morning?"

"If it's about those kids breaking into McMullin's Five and Dime last night," I blurted, "I had nothing to do with it! I was home. Right, Mom?"

I turned to my mother who gave me a pitying look. Her face had the chalky pale complexion that came with her migraine attacks.

Principal Laurelton gestured toward the cop, who stood there with his hands crossed over his groin.

"Do you recognize Officer Prentice?" Laurelton asked.

I did but pretended I didn't.

"According to Officer Prentice, you and he made each other's acquaintances a few weeks ago walking on Hood Lane near the train tracks. Remember?"

I looked up at the police officer who smirked at me.

"You were walking together, you, your stepbrother, and this other person, a man," said Laurelton. "A Mr. Thomas."

"Leo, who *is* this person?" my mother interjected.

"Mrs. Waple, please. Let's let Leo explain things, if he can."

They all looked at me. I kept my mouth shut.

"Officer Prentice here also tells me that he's seen you and your stepbrother walking toward where this Mr. Thomas lives, up by the old Dalton Estate. Apparently you and this Mr. Thomas person have spent a good deal of time up there together lately. Is that right?"

I shook my head.

"Tell the truth, kid," said the cop. "I passed you walking up there. More than once."

"You may have seen us walking," I protested. "That doesn't mean we were going to visit anyone!"

"Where were you going?" asked Miss Stanhope.

"To Lost Lake."

They all looked at each other.

"He means the lake on the Dalton Estate," said Officer Prentice. "It's the only lake up there. Private property."

"What business do you have there?" Laurelton asked.

"No business," I said. "We like going there, that's all."

"You mean to say you've never visited this man's home?"

"Nope."

"The word is no, sport, not nope," said my stepfather.

"And tell the truth," said my mother.

"Yes, sport, tell the truth," my stepfather reiterated.

"I'm telling the truth!"

"You haven't done anything wrong, Leo," said Principal Laurelton. "We just need to know some things, that's all."

"No one's accusing you of anything, sport," said my stepfather.

"For God's sake, Leo," my mother said. "Who the heck *is* this person? This man? I *demand* to know!"

My eyes wandered to the wall behind the principal's desk, to the framed photo of the minesweeper he'd captained, the *USS Perry*. At that moment I felt as if *I* had been kamikaze attacked and was burning and sinking.

"Do you deny spending time with this person?" asked Ol' Purple Puss, her birthmark having by then transformed into an octopus waving its tentacles. "Answer me!"

"A crocodile can't stick out its tongue."

"What?"

"What did you say, sport?"

"Clouds fly higher during the day than at night."

"He's protecting him! That's what they do!"

"Leo, please—"

"The opposite of a vacuum is a plenum."

"Sport?"

"Dirty snow melts faster than clean."

"For god's sake, Leo!"

"The dot over the letter *i* is called a *tittle*."

"We're concerned about you, sport, your mom and I. We both feel that you've been keeping us in the dark, as it were."

"You never said a word to me about this... this person! All this time I thought you and Gordon were playing with friends. You *lied* to me, Leo! Your own mother. You've been lying to everyone!"

"What have you and this Jack Thomas man been up to? You can tell us that much at least, can't you?"

"The longest one-syllable word in English is *screeched*."

My mother thwacked the back of my head. Everyone was staring at me: my mother, Officer Prentice, Principal Laurelton, Ol' Purple Puss... everyone except my stepfather, who looked down at his homburg. On his mossy desk blotter, Principal Laurelton's hands formed the prow of a ship, the *USS Perry*, with his U-Boat stapler poised to fire a torpedo into it. A lonesome stick of clove chewing gum sat in the principal's Decision

Maker roulette wheel. It took all my strength to resist grabbing it, unwrapping it, and shoving it into my desert-dry mouth. Ol' Purple Puss spoke:

"Since you refuse to tell us who Jack Thomas is, I'll tell you. He lives at the old Dalton Estate, in the former caretaker's cottage that he's been leasing from Betty Dalton. Where he's from no one seems to know, but he's a foreigner. Beyond that, no one knows anything about him. He has no relations, not in the area, anyway, or friends to speak of, present company excepted." Ol' Purple Puss eyed me with unmitigated contempt. "That's all anyone knows. Unless you care to enlighten us any further, Mr. Napoli?"

"Well?" Principal Laurelton said. "Is there anything else you care to add, Leo?"

"Ketchup was originally sold as a medicine."

"Has this man—has he *touched* you or Gordon?" my mother asked in a trembling voice. "Has he ever—"

"*What?* No!"

"Are you sure?"

"Jack hasn't done anything!"

"So now he's 'Jack'?" said Ol' Purple Puss.

"I don't want you going anywhere near this person anymore! Is that understood, Leo?" my mother said.

"Proportionally, Earth's atmosphere is no thicker than the skin of an apple."

"I strictly forbid it!"

"In ancient times, vinegar was the strongest acid. At any given moment, there are approximately 1,800 thunderstorms in progress."

"All right, Leo." Principal Laurelton stood. "That will do. You may return to class."

I left the Cloud Chamber, thinking, *The earth gets heavier each day by tons as meteoric dust settles on it.*

I made up my mind to stop visiting Jack. I did so for his sake. I'd drawn enough attention to him. If I kept on visiting him, I'd only draw more.

Still I couldn't just stop seeing him without saying anything. I considered leaving a note on the door to Fern Cottage. Then I thought, No, Half, you need to tell him yourself, in person.

So I paid him one last visit.

I waited until the following Thursday after school. Gordon had gone with my mother to the dentist. The week before we both had gone to the dentist for our annual cleaning and checkup. I had no cavities; Gordon, with his passion for Jujyfruits, had three.

To lower the risk of being seen, I cut through yards and avoided main roads. On the way I thought about what I'd say to Jack. The simplest option would have been to just tell the truth, that I had been forbidden from seeing him, but with that went the suggestion that he was some kind of pervert, a thought that I couldn't bear myself, much less tell Jack about. I needed a less distasteful motive. As I turned down the gravel road to Fern Cottage it came to me: my stepdad was shifting inventory at his store and needed me there. It was only a half-lie. Lately I had been spending more time at the store, helping put up the Christmas display as I'd done every year for the past two years. This years' display was a fedora-clad Santa presiding over six elves in belted green tunics, candy-striped leggings, and trilby hats, each at work at his elf bench, hammering, sawing, or chiseling away at…what else: a hat!

I was a few dozen yards from the cottage, still fine-tuning my excuse, when I saw Jack standing in front of the green door, smiling.

"I wondered if you were coming," he said.

He asked about Gordon. I explained about the dentist.

"You're just in time for tea."

We went inside. Jack made us tea. As he did, as I was about to explain that I wouldn't be seeing him for a while, he said:

"There's something I want to show you."

He went to the dresser, took something from its drawer, and brought it to me. It was the book about swimming, the battered old leather one I'd found that day in the same drawer of the same dresser, the one that also held the photograph of Jack standing with a tall, hawk-nosed woman and a blond boy, and the letter.

"It is the oldest known book on the subject of swimming," Jack explained. "There are only three known copies in existence. This is one of the three."

I turned the brittle pages carefully. The book was illustrated with woodcuts, each showing a different swimming technique, with a description written on the opposite page:

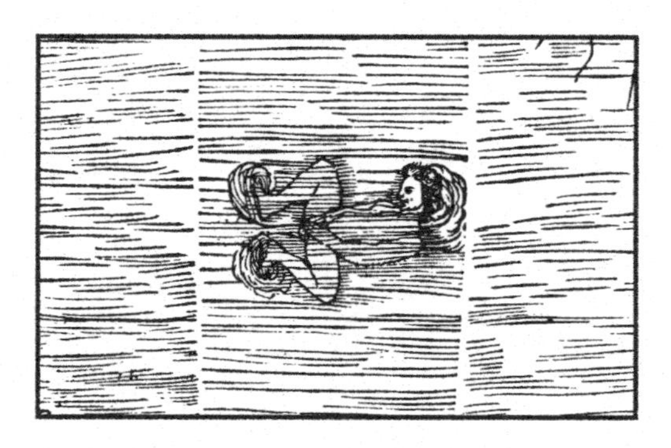

To Swim on the Back

And when he is thus laid upon his back, he must lie very straight, not bending or bowing with his body any way, save only his legs which must easily pull out and in, and when he was on his belly, to put him forwards in the water.

To Swim with Hands and Feet Upward

To swim with hands and feet upward is nothing else but the swimming upon the back as we taught before, saving that he useth his hands as a boat doth her oars, casting them out on both sides and drawing them in again, which maketh his motion swifter.

To Swim Like a Dog

Into this kind of swimming many do at the first fall, before they perfectly learn the right stroke. And there is this different betwixt them, that whereas in the right kind he stretcheth out his hands and his feet, in this he rudely beateth the water with his hands and feet, first lifting his right hand out of the water and then his right foot, and forcibly striking them into the water again.

"Where did you get it?" I asked.

"That's a complicated story. It was more or less given to me by my wife."

"You're *married*?"

"I was. For a time."

I thought: the tall woman with the hawk nose.

"What happened?"

"That, too, is complicated. Do you like the book?"

I nodded. "It must be worth a lot."

"It's quite valuable."

Distractedly I flipped through the rest of the book. I still hadn't told Jack what I'd come there to tell him. After a time I managed to blurt out some version of my hat store excuse. Jack nodded and said, "I see," or something like that. He didn't seem at all surprised or concerned, as though he'd been expecting it. "Well," he said. "Given that we won't be seeing each other for a while, shall we play one last round of a chess—for the time being, that is?"

I was setting up the board when Jack picked up one of the chess pieces and shoved it, torn bottom exposed, under my nose.

"You did this, didn't you?" he said with a weird, twisted smile. *"Didn't* you?"

I licked my lips.

Jack nodded. "Clever boy." *(Klevah boy.)*

He flung the piece away, reached into his pocket, pulled out his knife, and snapped the blade open an inch from my nose. As he held it there I thought, So this is how I'll die, stabbed to death in a cottage deep in the woods of the former Dalton estate.

"Who have you told?"

"No one!"

"Whom do you intend to tell?"

"No one—I swear!"

He drew the knife away, retracted its blade, and put it down on the table.

"Why should I believe you?"

"Because—you're my friend?" It was a strange thing to say to someone who'd just pulled a knife on me. "Why would I want to tell anyone?"

"I am a fugitive from justice. You're a citizen. It's your responsibility to report me."

"Who says I'm responsible?"

I heard thunder. Rain pattered against the cottage's roof. Soon it drizzled down from the eaves, forming a curtain of rain. For a while we both sat there in silence. Then I said:

"All this time—you've been hiding?"

He nodded.

"That must be rough," I said.

"I don't recommend it."

"Supposing they do catch you? What's the worst they can do? Arrest you—for what? Being on the wrong side of a war that ended eighteen years ago?"

"You don't understand."

"I don't!"

"They'd send me home."

"What's wrong with that?"

"There's no such place. My homeland no longer exists. What was once my home is now a prison far worse than the one from which I escaped."

Jack stood up. He rubbed his face.

"I still don't get it," I said. "What did you have to escape for? The war was over!"

"It's a long story, Hoff."

"Tell me!"

"Why? What difference would it make? Even were I to tell you everything, Hoff, you still wouldn't understand. You still wouldn't know me, not really, no more than you can possibly know any human being, including yourself. We're each of us as mysterious and unreachable as the stars you look at through your telescope."

"I still want to know," I said.

He rubbed his face again. I'd never seen him looking so weary.

"All right," he said. "Under one condition."

"Name it."

"You sit there and listen until I've finished. Unless I ask you something, you're not to say a word or to move from that chair. Understood? When I've finished, you may do as you wish, but not till then."

"I was born and grew up what is now Czechoslovakia but then still belonged the Republic of German-Austria. We lived in a city of textile mills. 'The Town of a Hundred Chimneys,' they called it, there were so many textile mills there.

"The town's streets were lined with chestnut trees," Jack told me. "Day and night one heard the sounds of chestnut hulls falling. They covered the sidewalks and gave off a pungent, sweet, rancid smell. When I stuffed them into my cheeks they tasted bitter. Whenever she caught me about to do so, my mother would slap the hulls out of my hand.

"Like most children I was afraid of ghosts, a fear augmented by a lurid imagination. I was convinced that, if I got out of bed after midnight and peeled back the damask curtains of my bedroom window, I'd see a milk truck hovering there, level with the second story, its driver wearing his peaked cap, its headlights blazing into my terror-stricken eyes. The first time I reported this phenomenon to my parents, my papa made a great show of throwing on his robe, rushing downstairs, grabbing the fire-poker from its stand, and—crying, *'Weg mit allen Monstern!'*—hurling himself into the frozen night. He did so several times until finally he said, 'Enough, Johann! There is no Milk Truck Monster!'

"I told you my parents were killed in a railway accident. They'd been traveling from Dusseldorf to St. Petersburg for their wedding anniversary when their train derailed. I lived with my aunt and my uncle, a trainmaster who kept a dovecote in the yard. I mentioned as well my coming down with diphtheria and the long walks I took. Along those walks I'd collect 'wishing stones,' smooth pebbles with rings around them with which I adorned the windowsill in my room. For Christmas my uncle bought me a tumbler with which to polish them but I preferred the stones as they were, dull and rough like little potatoes freshly dug from the earth.

"And I told you about the municipal pool and those boys I saw diving there? And how afterward I signed up for swimming and diving lessons with Günter, the lifeguard? There's a little more to that story, however. Do you recall the first words you ever spoke to me, Hoff?"

"Am I supposed to answer?"

"When I ask you something, yes."

"You mean the day I asked you to teach me to swim?"

"Before then."

"The first time we spoke—when you asked me who I was?"

"Before that as well."

I thought about it. Then I remembered. I felt my cheeks flush.

"Yes," I said. "I remember."

"One of the boys I'd seen diving off the high board that day was named Gerhard. He and I became very close. By then I'd joined and been on the swim team for years. When not meeting for matches and tournaments the team met several times a week for practice drills. When we weren't swimming or diving together, Gerhard and I played games. We went for walks, studied together, did all the things friends do. After a time, though, it became clear to me that my feelings toward Gerhard went beyond friendship or brotherly affection or what you call 'puppy love.' What I felt for my friend was, I'm guessing, more or less what you feel for my landlady's daughter—what's her name?"

"Belinda."

"Belinda. Do you understand?"

I nodded, though I couldn't imagine Jack wanting to do with another boy the sorts of things I longed to do with Belinda. I didn't want to imagine it. Still, I kept my promise: I sat there; I listened.

"One day in the locker room after a swim meet the other boys having gone, finding myself alone there with him, for the first time I let my feelings for Gerhard be known. Oh, I'd shown them in other ways: holding hands while walking with him, that sort of thing. But such gestures could easily have been construed by him as meaning something less than what they meant for me. And so in the locker room that morning I spelled my feelings out." Jack smiled. "Suffice it to say his reaction was hardly what I'd hoped for. He drew back and looked at me. I'll never forget that look, Hoff: a look of complete horror, of total disgust—not unlike the look you gave me that time we first met, though of course our circumstances were entirely different. You didn't know me; you had no reason *not* to be frightened by me. But the way he looked at me, as if I'd turned into some sort of monster before his eyes, as if my skin had turned green and horns had sprouted from my skull and my hands had curled into claws. Then Gerhard did something much worse: he started laughing. It was nervous laughter at first, I thought, but it quickly turned malicious. Soon he was seething, saying he never wanted to see me again, that he'd punch my face if I so much as tried to come near him. 'Do I make myself clear?' he said. He was snarling; his lips were coated with spittle. I ran out of the locker room. When I next returned to the pool for practice, Günter the lifeguard took me aside. I was off the swim team. We'd been training for the Olympics. Gerhard had reported me. He'd told all the other boys on the team. It wasn't long before word got back to my aunt and uncle. My uncle couldn't look me in the eyes. My aunt called me a monster. Beyond that, neither of them would speak to me.

"Soon after that Germany was at war. Troops conducted maneuvers on the outskirts of town. Word of my 'condition' having spread to the authorities, I was declared unfit for military service. While other boys my age enlisted or were accepted into officers training school, I found myself alone in a town full of women, children, and old men, living with an aunt and uncle who refused to speak to me. At last my solitude grew unbearable, so much so that I volunteered for the one outfit that was sure to have me, the so-called bucket-and-spade brigade. I spent the next two months draining swamps and digging ditches for latrines when—possibly because word of my condition had somehow reached my unit commander—I was suddenly transferred to a tunnel-digging detail in the Harz Mountains. The tunnel crews there worked ten-hour shifts. The tunnel's anhydrite walls stank of sulfur. My clothes, my hair, my bedclothes...everything reeked of it. Conscripts worked alongside prisoners and were treated as badly. The tunnel foremen doubled as guards.

"Among the prisoners working with me was a young man named Romulus, a Romanian Jew, an engineer who also worked in the machine shop and who for reasons unknown to me was the principal subject of our foreman's abuse. One morning, the foreman having delivered a particularly nasty blow to Romulus' shoulder with the butt of his Mauser, I went to his aid, earning a blow for myself. From that day on Romulus and I were subjected to routine beatings by the foreman, until we finally decided to escape.

"One night, with the full moon hidden under clouds and the pockets of our workers' coveralls stuffed with rusks, to the air-raid siren's wail, my Romanian friend and I crept across the scree to the latrine, where, with a grappling hook Romulus had made in the machine shop, we lowered ourselves down a concrete wall that divided the latrine from the river that coursed by the camp. While crouched there contemplating the dark, rushing waters, I confessed to my friend that, although I was a champion swimmer, so far my experience had been confined to a brightly lit, supervised, municipal pool. The dark rushing river frightened me and I told him so. He said to me what I said to you that first time we jumped off the rock.

"'Whose fear is it?' he asked as we crouched there. 'Yours—or someone else's?'

"'Mine,' I answered.

"'If a thing is yours, you can do what you like with it, right? You can throw it into this river, can't you?'

"I nodded; we jumped.

"The current wasn't as strong as we'd expected, but the water was much, much colder. Milk-colored moonlight fanned across the surface. Where the rushing water met rocks, pale phosphorescent plumes spread. With Romulus' help I made it to the opposite shore where we collapsed into a bed of pine needles. We spent the rest of that night hiking, smelling acacias, avoiding columns of soldiers. It wasn't until dawn that we stopped to rest in a field of gorse. By then we had eaten the rusks the river had turned to mush. Hugging each other for warmth, we curled up in the gorse. Neither of us said a word. We were too tired to speak.

"Another day's hike brought us to a small village where a goatherd shared his lunch of turtle soup. The goatherd directed us to the headquarters of the local field commander. On the way there we contrived an excuse for being in worker's clothes without papers. While marching with our work unit we'd come upon a pair of officers whose Kubelwagen had gone into a ditch. Having promised to drive us back to our unit afterward the officers ordered us to dig them out. As we dug the officers shared a bottle of schnapps. By the time the Kubelwagen was freed they'd grown boisterous, telling lewd stories, laughing, singing drinking songs, slapping each other's backs. The proffered ride wasn't forthcoming. Instead the officers drove off with our papers. Unable to catch up to our unit by foot, we decided to volunteer for the nearest Panzer division.

"That's what we told the officer who we believed to be the field commander, but who turned out to be the kommandant's sublieutenant, as we learned when the door to the field office burst open and the real kommandant entered.

"'Who are these two?' he asked, removing his scarf.

"The subordinate briefed his commander, adding that he didn't believe our story.

"'Who cares?' said the commander. 'If they're foolish enough to volunteer, give them their damned orders and get them the hell out of here!'

"We were given fresh uniforms, provisions. A long train journey took us to an induction center above the Crimean Peninsula. There Romulus and I spent a sleepless night, knowing we were going to have our physicals in the morning. For his circumcised penis, my Jewish friend had contrived a clever excuse: in his youth he'd contracted the 'Spanish collar,' a disease wherein the foreskin gets trapped behind the glans. Left untreated, the condition is prone to infection, the common treatment back then being circumcision. If the medical examiner bought this excuse, Romulus would be conscripted as a soldier. If not, he'd be sent off to a concentration camp.

"Apparently the medical officer didn't buy my friends' excuse. After that morning I never saw Romulus again.

"I was assigned to a horse-drawn reserve leftover from the Great War. I groomed and fed the horses, shovelled manure, moved heavy artillery. That winter it got so cold the canon shafts froze. When I touched them with gloveless hands bloody patches of skin tore off my fingers. I caught pneumonia.

"It was while recovering in the infirmary that I learned that Rommel was seeking volunteers in North Africa. Not long after my recovery, I found myself aboard a ferryboat packed with soldiers, all very young or very old, bound from Athens to Crete. From Crete a plane took us to Libya, where we joined a Panzer division in its retreat to Tunisia. I was put in charge of a 105mm gun. The shells weighed over thirty pounds. With each tug of the lanyard the earth shivered and my ears were left ringing.

"When not firing ordinance I spent most of my time crouching in foxholes, ducking from American bombers and fighter planes on strafing runs, wiping sand off the epaulets of my desert uniform. When neither firing nor crouching we marched under a scorching sun along roads littered with charred hulks of tanks and armored vehicles. Sandstorms provided the only relief from the heat. When not baking under the desert sun we had to contend with swarms of mosquitoes and gnats.

"One advantage of belonging to an army under defeat: one rises quickly through the ranks. By that March I had been promoted to lance corporal and made adjutant to a captain. I polished his boots, prepared his teas, chauffeured his SdKfz 222. Herr Hauptmann had a taste for American novels. While polishing his boots one morning I noticed a bookmarked copy of *Huckleberry Finn* on his nightstand.

"April brought an eerie silence. No artillery fire, no bombers or strafing planes. I spent the better part of that month in the turret of my captain's SdKfz, reading his copy of *The Grapes of Wrath*. By then the war was lost; we all knew it. For Herr Hauptmann and me the end arrived after a long day spent driving over bombed-out roads. As darkness fell I could barely make out the craters. My captain ordered me to pull over. 'No point in us getting ourselves killed now,' he said. 'Let's get some sleep. We'll worry about the war in the morning.'

"We parked behind the hulk of a charred tank. With nightfall the temperature fell below freezing. 'Come morning,' Herr Hauptmann said as we huddled together under a thin blanket, 'you and I will be prisoners of the British Army. Goodnight.'

"It was still dark when we heard shouts and a searchlight beam awakened us. Speaking German, a British-accented voice through a loudspeaker ordered us out with our hands up.

"We were taken to a collection center in Tunis. Stripped of badges, documents. Fingerprinted, photographed. From there they packed us into a truck and took us to a camp near Casablanca, a patch of desert enclosed with barbed wire. They gave us shovels and ordered us to dig holes for our latrines. No blankets or covers. Two cans of food per day. On sunny days, the camp was hot but tolerable. But when it rained or when they turned the fire hose on us for drinking water the camp became a muddy hell. Everything became moldy. The books provided by the Red Cross turned to pulp. I was there for three months. Then, that September, they packed me into another truck and drove me to a port, where, along with hundreds of others, I was herded onto the ship that brought me here, or rather that brought me to a processing center north of New York City. From there I was put on a passenger train, a coach with roomy, upholstered seats. At regular intervals a porter passed up and down the aisles with coffee, tea, and sandwiches. At the far end of the car a uniformed MP stood guard with a pistol. To go to the bathroom I had to raise my hand like a schoolboy.

"I had no idea where the train was taking us. I knew only that the journey was very long. With my nose pressed to the window, I saw river-like highways streaming with traffic, and night cities burning—not from German incendiary bombs as had been rumored, but with electricity. Where not filigreed with highways the countryside was a checkerboard of fields, mainly of corn. Corn, corn, corn! I'd never seen so much corn! At last, after a journey of two and a half days, we arrived at our destination: Camp Henderson, Bernadotte, Illinois…

"The camp was orderly and clean, with tarpaper barracks arranged in neat rows. Everything new, smelling of sawdust and Lysol. We were welcomed by the camp adjutant, issued good shoes, a belt, four pair of trousers, an overcoat, a raincoat, winter gloves. We were fed three hot meals a day, with ice cream sandwiches and fruit salad for dessert. We played horseshoes, tennis, volleyball, ping-pong, cards, and dominoes. Every barracks was equipped with a radio. We had newspapers, movies, books, even concerts. With the scrip that we were given we bought Gillette razor blades and Brilliantine at the PX canteen. We could even buy wine and beer.

"When not taking classes in English or American History at the Educational Center, or playing sports, cards, or chess, I made that chessboard we've been playing on. It took me two months to make. I spent another month carving the pieces you see in front of you from sections of a sliced broom handle.

"Work details were voluntary and paid 80 cents per day. Every morning our employers would pick us up: four prisoners and a guard. I enjoyed the work. We moved a farmer's barn, damned a river, and built a stone foundation for a house.

"As far as I knew there'd been no escape attempts from our camp. Why escape when we had it so good?—better than when we had been soldiers? As for missing home, from the newspaper articles I read, and the serials we were shown, I gathered that the country I'd left behind no longer existed. From my aunt and uncle, I heard nothing. No Red Cross letters or packages came for me. Maybe they'd been killed in an air raid. Or maybe they wanted nothing more to do with me; they'd washed their hands of me, their 'monster.' It was best for me not to think about them, to not think about the past at all, to cut it off like a festering limb, to dispose of it like a used tea ball.

"Only with the war's end, when we saw the newsreels of the concentration camps being liberated, the corpses stacked like cordwood, the skeletal survivors in striped pajamas gaping at their saviors, did morale among us prisoners decline swiftly, as did conditions at the camp. The orchestra and theater were disbanded. The library was closed. No more razors or beer or tobacco for sale at the canteen. No more fruit salad and ice cream sandwiches. We were fed cabbage soup five days a week.

"But what distressed me more than any of that was the prospect of repatriation. The lucky ones among us would be reunited in their homelands with friends and family; some would be turned over to the British or the French to help with the reconstruction. As for me, I faced far grimmer prospects, my homeland having fallen under Soviet rule. I'd be shipped off to a labor camp, or worse.

"And so, once again, Hoff, I escaped.

"As first I considered making a folding kayak from powdered milk tins and rubber raincoats or sealing myself away in a trash drum to be carted off with the rest of the refuse, or simply walking away from my work detail. In the end I chose the most reasonable and reliable plan. After midnight, taking advantage of a blind spot that the camp's searchlight beam didn't reach, between a walkway and the shadow cast by the warehouse, I would slip through the compound fence. This plan, too, had its risks, chief among them a trigger-happy tower guard whom we prisoners dubbed 'Buffalo Bill.' If he saw me in the so-called 'kill zone,' he'd shoot me dead. But I timed the searchlight beam and planned my escape to coincide with the full moon that would cast a shadow deep enough to hide my own. As for the camp's guard dogs, the howls of local coyotes would often set them to barking; most likely they'd be ignored. Whatever sounds I made that their barks and the coyotes' howls didn't mask, the rasps of crickets would cover.

"I packed my canvas rucksack with bread, two tins of beans, the gravity knife you've seen that I'd inherited from a paratrooper in exchange for cigarettes, my escape clothes, a cap with a long visor, sunglasses, a road map stolen from the glove box of a farmer's truck, two books of matches, tobacco, a pipe, two pairs socks and underwear, a raincoat, an extra pair of laces for my boots, a compass, and the chessboard with hand-carved figures that, however unnecessary, I couldn't part with.

"At 9:10 p.m., ten minutes after lights out, I crept to the darkened corner of the warehouse and waited for the searchlight beam. After the third sweep I dashed through the kill zone, climbed the first fence, and lay between the two fences in the shadow of the warehouse wall cast by the full moon. After three more searchlight sweeps I scaled the second fence. From there less than a dozen yards separated me from the woods. Once deep inside the woods, I lit a match to illuminate my compass, which guided me to the river that would carry me downstream to the trestle over which—according to the whistle I'd taken note of for the past two weeks—a freight train passed every night at ten-thirty-five. I wore my prison fatigues inside-out, so if seen exiting the woods I wouldn't be identified immediately by the large yellow PWs sewn onto their back and sleeves.

"Once in the river, with my rucksack held high over my head, I waded out to where the current was strong. The moon and stars were bright. I heard the howl of a coyote and smelled chimney smoke. I gave myself to the current that carried me toward the trestle that loomed ahead, black against the indigo sky. As I drew close to it I tried to slow myself down, only the current was too strong; it swept me past the trestle. I grabbed onto rocks, overhanging limbs—anything to slow my progress. Eventually I made my way into the shallows, where the current was less strong, and from where I was able to clamber up the embankment. By then the trestle was far behind me. I heard the train whistle. To get back to the trestle I had to bushwhack my way through a thicket along the riverbank. There was no other way. I used my knife. Meanwhile the train whistle sounded louder and louder. If I missed the train all would be lost.

"I was cutting through the brambles when I saw what looked like a path or a clearing. I raced toward it, following the sound of the whistle which grew louder. I was running along that path when suddenly a beam of light broke through the darkness in front of me, so bright it blinded me. At first I thought it was a car or truck full of soldiers come to capture me. I felt gravel under my shoes. To my left something gleamed in the moonlight. A rock? A scrap of metal? A bottle? Then I realized: it was the railroad. The beam of light was that of a freight train bearing down on me.

"I spent the next three days in a boxcar stuffed with bags of fertilizer. The fertilizer stuck to my skin. It burned my eyes and my nostrils. By then I'd eaten all of my food and drunk all my water. All I had left was a rock-hard heel of bread. Every now and then the train would pull into a siding where the railroad bulls would inspect its cars for hoboes. Knowing this, soon as the train slowed down I'd jump out and wait in the shadows as the bulls did their job, then jump back into a car that they'd already inspected. The third freight car I jumped was packed with big burlap bags of sugar. I sliced one of them open with my knife and stuffed handfuls of the sugar into my mouth. According to my compass the freight train was headed northwest.

"The sugar made me very thirsty. But something other than thirst was preoccupying me. If someone asked me my name, what would I answer? Could he pass myself off as something other than German—as Yugoslavian, or Norwegian? What would a good Norwegian name be? Anders? Knut? Knut Anders? As the train clacked on I struggled to arrive at a good name.

"Knut Eriksen. Erik Knudsen... *clickety-clack, clickety-clack...*

"Then I remembered the stories of Kasper Hauser and Peter the Wild Boy that so fascinated me as a boy. Kasper, the waif found staggering through the streets of Nuremberg: speechless, half-starved, carrying a letter saying only that he had been baptized Catholic, and nothing more. His captors concluded that he wasn't an imposter or an idiot but someone totally unfamiliar with civilization. Presented with a candle flame, he'd thrust his fingers into it, burning them. According to one theory he was the actual prince of Baden, who had been kidnapped and hidden away on orders from Countess von Hochberg, who sought the title for her own progeny. Another theory had it that he'd been raised by wolves...

"Peter the Wild Boy was found living in a cave in the outskirts of Hamelin, the same town the Pied Piper supposedly delivered of its children, surviving on squirrels and nuts. Like Kasper, he didn't speak... Could I pretend to be mute like them? I wondered. I remembered Günter's—my swimming coach's—advice. 'Make the smallest splash possible.' The simplest plan was always best. I'd choose an ordinary, American-sounding name. But what?

"Part of the answer was there in front of my nose, stamped on a hundred-pound bag of Jack Frost sugar: Jack, a name as far removed from Johann as the Elbe from the Mississippi. Jack-knife. Jackpot. Jack-in-the-Box. Jack in the Beanstalk. Jack sprat....

"*Clickety-clack, clickety-clack...*

"All I needed then was a surname. The train was passing through an intersection when I saw a truck stopped at the crossing, a delivery truck for something called 'English muffins.' There, in old English-style letters on an orange field next to a silhouetted carriage pulled by a team of silhouetted horses, was my new surname.

"The train brought me to Seattle, Washington, where I worked as a dishwasher and lived in a boardinghouse by the docks. I bought a new set of clothes and a cardboard suitcase.

But I knew I had to keep moving. For a while I worked as a fruit-picker in Oregon, picking cherries off twenty-foot-tall trees. When cherry season ended I took a job topping trees at a lumber camp. I wore a leather harness and climbing boots with spikes attached to them. While sawing the top off a hundred-foot spruce one morning my harness broke. I fell thirty-three feet. My femur burst clear through my leg. While in the hospital recovering, in a newspaper the nurse gave me I saw an FBI notice with my mugshot. On crutches that very same day I hobbled to the bus station and got on the first departing bus—which, it so happened, was bound for Chicago.

"For the next four years I worked at various menial jobs," Jack said, "stacking boxes of cereal in a warehouse, skinning hams in a slaughterhouse, that sort of thing. All the while I kept on the move, never staying anywhere for more than three months. Eventually I made my way east to New England. I had heard the autumns here were beautiful. While hitchhiking in New York State the driver of a car that picked me up told me of a resort in the Adirondacks called The Birches, saying he knew the owner and would put in a good word for me if I wanted a job, and so I went there. At first the owner, whose name was Budd, put me to work washing dishes and doing other odd jobs, but seeing I was a good swimmer, he had me give swimming lessons to guests and eventually made me head lifeguard.

"Budd called me 'Fritz,' since I'd told him I was Swiss.

"I'd been working at The Birches for two years when I met the woman who gave me the book about swimming—well, she didn't give it to me, not exactly. Her name was Margaret. She owned an antiquarian bookstore in a town about eight miles from the resort. I had a bicycle that Budd had given me and would ride it there. Budd also gave me a car—an old Bantam convertible held together mostly by rust, but as I had no driver's license, I was reluctant to use it. Anyway, one rainy morning I rode my bicycle to the bookstore as I'd done once or twice before. The bookstore was in an old wood and stone barn.

Three black cats had the run of the place. At the center of the main floor was a rococo desk with a green-shaded lamp and a plaster bust of Voltaire. I recall how that day, thanks to the rain, my shoes made squelching sounds on the wooden floorboards. I had taken a book about lakes down off a shelf to examine it when the women seated behind the desk spoke to me.

"'Are you a student of natural philosophy, by any chance?' she said. Her reading glasses made her sharp nose look even sharper. 'We have a great many books on that subject.'

"Her accent was British. I told her I liked lakes. When she stood from her desk, she was very tall. 'In that case,' she said, 'you've come to a good corner of the world.'

"She asked me if I was German; I said, 'No, Swiss.' When she learned that I worked as a lifeguard at The Birches, she showed me the book about swimming. She took it from a locked cabinet and, with great care at her desk, turned its pages, explaining that it was nearly three hundred years old.

"After that we saw each other often. She had a seven-year-old son, Avery. He and I swam and built a sailboat together. Margaret had a gift for not judging people. She looked to them as though they were books: some had been splayed opened so often their spines were broken; others never had their pages cut. She never pried into my past, which may have been the main reason why I married her.

"We built a house on the lake.

"The one time my past became an issue for Margaret was when she wanted us to go to England for our honeymoon. I told her I didn't fly. She said we could take a ship. I told her I was afraid of ships as well. She wondered how on earth I'd gotten here, if not by osmosis. I couldn't tell her the truth, that I had no passport, and couldn't get one without a birth certificate. We honeymooned at Niagara Falls.

"The one other time I felt the past catching up with me was one morning at The Birches, when, wanting a canoe for his children, a square-shouldered, paunchy man approached me at the boathouse.

"'Don't I know you?' the man asked. He had a German accent. 'I've seen you before,' he said. 'I'm sure I have.'

"I said, 'I don't see how.'

"'During the war, maybe? Did you serve in the artillery?'

"I said I had no idea what he was talking about.

"'The German artillery.'

"When I said I was Swiss, not German, the man laughed. 'Of course you're German!' he said. 'You think I can't tell? You're as German as me!'

"'Here are your life vests,' I said. But the man wasn't through. 'The 3rd Heavy Artillery,' he said. 'Crimea. In the Siege of Sevastopol. Yes, I'm sure of it! Don't tell me you've forgotten that!'

"I told him I'd never set foot in Crimea—or anywhere else in Germany, for that matter. 'Now, if you'll excuse me,' I said, 'I have things to do.'

"Through the rest of his stay I managed to avoid this fellow, and felt safe again until two more years later, when, one afternoon while I was lying in a hammock I'd strung near the boathouse, Budd's shadow fell over me.

"'Johann Verhoff?' he said, handing me a circular. 'Is that your real name?'

"I shook my head. I wasn't lying. By then the man in the black-and-white photo was a complete stranger to me. Budd spoke quietly. I was to pack my things and leave by noon the next day. 'As far as I'm concerned,' he said, 'you were never here. You don't exist.'

"I said, 'What about Margaret, my wife? And Avery? He's like a son to me!'

"'Sorry, Fritz,' he said, 'but you brought on this situation, not me.'

"'I would say many things brought it on,' I said.

"That same night, while Margaret and Avery slept, I packed the few belongings that I needed into the Bantam and drove off. Maybe I shouldn't have. Maybe I should have stayed and let myself be caught and fought the deportation. Margaret would have helped me. If it had come to that, Budd might have helped me, too. But I wasn't just running from the FBI. I was trying to escape from myself, Hoff, from the monster my aunt had declared me to be. My marriage to Margaret was a sham and I knew it. She must have known—or felt it—too. I was doing her and her son a favor. That's what I told myself.

"The most impressive—and the scariest—thing about human beings is how, excepting death, we adapt to almost anything. This's why I admire water so much, why I identified with it. It is the most adaptable of substances. But there's such a thing as *too much* adaptation, Hoff, as being so used to changing not only one's attitude toward things, but one's personality, one's nature, even one's shape and form, to where one no longer knows who one is anymore. It had become that way for me. I'd gotten so used to adapting I no longer knew who I was. I couldn't trust myself.

"I say all this to try and make you understand why it was that I left my wife. No, Hoff, now that I think of it, it was more like those moments when you're saying goodbye to someone you love who has just boarded a conveyance, a bus or a train. Have you had such a moment in your life, Hoff? The train hasn't left the station, and you're on the platform looking up through the dirty window, waving and blowing kisses, saying things your loved one can't hear because the window is closed and the train is chuffing and hissing and the echoes of other passengers under the domed terminal are like the thunder preceding a storm. You keep waving and blowing kisses. Yet the train doesn't move; there's something wrong, some delay. You start to feel awkward, worse than awkward: you start feeling impatient, angry, even, your anger tinged with guilt, since by now you're wishing the bloody train would move, cursing its stubbornness, wanting nothing more than to be able to stop blowing kisses and saying things no one can hear and get on with the rest of your life. That's how my marriage to Margaret had come to feel—like a train that wouldn't—could never—leave the station. Oh, I wanted to love Margaret. I *did* love her, very much, as much as I'd ever loved anyone. But to feel that love, to really *feel* it, I needed to get away from her. That doesn't make sense to you, I know. How can it make sense to you? It *shouldn't* make sense. Not to you; not at your age. I hope it never makes sense to you, Hoff. That Budd had uncovered my identity and asked me to leave, though it horrified me at first, when the horror wore off, what I felt more than anything was relief, as though finally I'd come up out of a pool where I'd been holding my breath the whole time. I could breathe free again. Anyway, when I left Margaret that night, more than anything else I felt relieved.

"Before heading off through the night I needed one thing. I stopped at the bookstore. Without switching on the store lights, with a flashlight, I found the key to the rare book cabinet where Margaret kept it hidden in a holder under her desk drawer. With the swimming book under my arm, I returned to the car. It was all I kept from those happy years, a kind of severance package.

"I'd driven as far as New Haven when the Bantam's engine gave out. Amid a cloud of smoke I left it on the highway. With my suitcase and rucksack, I walked to the nearest exit.

"For a time I lived in the wharf district. More menial jobs, more hand-to-mouth existing, more inexpensive rented rooms. To get and keep jobs grew increasingly difficult. I was unpleasant. I argued with co-workers and bosses. I was sick of merely surviving.

"I'd been fired from a job and was homeless, spending my days and nights in an all-night café by the university, playing chess by myself and sometimes with students on the board I had made and that I'd taken with me. One day, seeing my destitute state, a student who played chess with me told me of an opportunity to make some money, a psychological experiment in need of volunteers. The following morning I gave myself a sponge bath in the café men's room, and, dressed in my best shirt, presented myself to the professor in charge of the experiment, a sturdy-looking man with a beard and cornflower blue eyes. He wore a white smock. With a paternal hand on my shoulder the professor sat me down before a console covered with meters, dials, switches, and colored lights. A number below each switch indicated the level of voltage, from slight—15 volts—to severe (450). At the far end of this scale the word DANGER was stenciled in red.

"The professor assured me that the experiment was harmless, that with each increase in voltage the amperage was stepped down proportionately to prevent any serious discomfort. To assure me further the professor had me sample a 45-volt shock. I felt a mild tingling sensation, nothing more.

"The subject—a white-haired man wearing suspenders—sat in an adjoining room with a glass window. As instructed I asked him a series of questions. With each incorrect answer I administered a shock, increasing the voltage each time. At 15 volts, when the subject cried out, I called the professor, who, smiling, reassured me that the procedure was entirely harmless. 'Please continue,' he said. With each step-up in voltage the subject's cries intensified until I again called for the professor, who again offered his assurances, his cornflower-blue eyes gleaming.

"'But the man seems to be suffering!' I said.

"'It's a reflex response,' said the professor. 'Now please continue. It's absolutely essential to the experiment that you continue.'

"I think it's safe to say that at that moment, Hoff, for me the man with the cornflower eyes was no longer just a professor conducting an experiment. He was my father, the one I'd lost as a child, the one who used to chase away my nightmares with a fire poker. He was Uncle Ernst with his plum stone kisses and marzipan treats. He was Günter, my swimming instructor. He was the *Hauptcaptain* whose boots I'd polished and whose car I chauffeured over bombed-out roads. He was all the fathers I'd had and lost or would never have.

"At the maximum voltage—250 volts—the subject's cries faded to soft mewls, and there the experiment ended. Only then was it revealed to me by the professor that I, not the suspender-wearing man, had been the experiment's true subject. The man was an actor; the console an elaborate functionless prop. The electrical current existed only in my mind.

"An hour after entering it, with a twenty-dollar bill folded into my shirt pocket I stumbled out of the research building into a bright winter day. I felt myself back in one of the rivers I'd escape into, back in their current again, being borne downstream by it, carried off in its watery arms. To what end? For what purpose? I had no idea. Nor did I care. I didn't exist enough to care. I'd forgotten completely my identity. Like Kasper Hauser or Peter the Wild Boy. That's how I felt as I staggered out across the university quadrangle, like a man who had been living in a cave in the woods somewhere. As I stumbled past mounds of snow and under icicles hanging from the parapets a queer odor of nightshade filled the air. I heard church bells chiming, playing a familiar melody, a lullaby. *Schlaf, Kindlein, Schlaf.* Sleep, baby, sleep. It was one my mother used to sing me to sleep with. But how could that be? I asked myself. They can't be possibly playing *that*! But I *heard* it, Hoff; I'm sure of it. Who was it that said, 'What a mother sings to the cradle goes down with the coffin'?

"After that I'm not quite sure what happened. I must have collapsed. The next thing I recall is waking up in a hospital bed. A nurse stood at its foot. The sun was in my eyes. She lowered the blinds. I wanted to thank her for doing so, but when I opened my mouth to speak no words came out. I had the thought but I couldn't say it. Something in me refused to let me speak. It was the same with a series of doctors who visited me. One by one the doctors came with all kinds of questions, and one by one they left, frustrated, since I refused to speak. I had nothing to say, for one thing, nothing that *needed* saying. But there was more to it. I felt as if I were naked, that nothing but my silence stood between the world and my nakedness, as if my silence protected me. Oh, they looked for causes. Vocal cords, physical or psychic trauma—or both. They couldn't accept that there was nothing wrong with me, that I just didn't *feel* like talking. Eventually I was taken to another facility, to a place called Silver Hills. You may have heard of it. How long I spent there I'm not sure. But the entire time I said nothing. By then I had gotten very good at not speaking!

"The one time I spoke was when a man came to visit me. He carried a briefcase and wore a hat with a red feather in its band. He wasn't a G-man, as I first assumed. But he knew who I was. He said he was my wife's—Margaret's—solicitor. How he'd found me I have no idea. She must have put a detective on my trail. This explained the sensation I'd had over the past several months of being followed. He took off his hat, sat down by my bed, and opened his briefcase, from which he removed a folder with some documents, one of which, he explained, was an Affidavit of Defendant. I don't suppose you know what that is, Hoff?"

I shook my head.

"On the grounds of abandonment Margaret had sued me for divorce. I signed it. Another item in the folder was a letter she'd written to me. The solicitor asked me if I cared to have him read it to me. I nodded. In the letter she explained that Budd had told her everything, how she wished that I'd done so myself, how she would have helped me, gotten me a good lawyer, and so forth. She was writing from Manchester, England, where she'd gone to visit her father, who was ill. The letter went on to say that she'd sold the bookstore along with the house that we'd built, which Budd bought from her and turned into another lodging for the resort. Out of the proceeds she'd instructed her solicitor to cut me a check in the amount of $5,000 dollars. This, her letter went on to say, along with the swimming book that I'd stolen, would constitute my share of the proceeds from the house sale along with the equity I had earned through helping her at the store and with other things.

"Margaret ended her letter by wishing me luck. 'May you find some peace,' she wrote. To her letter the solicitor added a footnote, explaining that, a week after she'd written it, while still in England, Margaret and Avery had both been killed in a car accident. They were headed north on the Hardknott Pass to Cumbria, to visit the Stone Circle at Castlerigg, when a lorry collided with the Humber Super Snipe Margaret had been driving. They both died instantly.

"The next day I discharged myself from Silver Hills. They couldn't keep me against my will. It was a lovely, breezy spring morning. With my rucksack slung over my shoulder, I started walking. I had no idea where I was going. I walked and walked until I came to this town whose brick chimneys reminded me of the town where I grew up and which had been known as 'The Town of a Hundred Chimneys.' In the window of a hardware store I happened to see a notice poorly typed on a sheet of yellow paper. One-room cabin for rent by lake, it said. Wood stove. No running water.

"That's how I wound up here, Hoff, here in the woods where I've come to worship the God of things unknown and unknowable; here where, until you and I met, I spoke not a word to anyone. Let them think me mute—like Caspar Hauser and Peter the Wild Boy. Let them think me mad! My conspicuity would be my cover; my silence would be my shield.

"But then you came along…

"There you have it, Hoff. My war story. Does it explain things? What is explainable, finally? Nothing—or very little. We can never know each other, Hoff, any more than you can ever know the universe, or God, if you like. Or yourself. And what we don't know we can't—shouldn't—judge. Agreed?"

Part 9

The Strike

Christmas was anything but jolly that year. For one thing I missed Jack, whom I hadn't seen since that last visit. But I was far from alone in having a less-than-merry Christmas that year. As if Kennedy's assassination hadn't been enough bad news, on December 17, 1963, all 234 employees of Hattertown's only surviving hat factory, the Caxton-Dumont Hat Works, went on strike. The headline in the *Hattertown Gazette* read:

Thanks a Lot, Santa!

The headline in the *Danville News Times* shouted:

BLACK CHRISTMAS

The strike started at the Dunlop Hat Manufacturing Company, in Norwalk, after its owners rejected a new job security clause that the workers' union tried to insert into their latest contract, one that would have prevented management from shipping unfinished hats down to a finishing plant in Winchester, Tennessee. In a statement to the press, William S. Tuttle, the Dunlop factory's attorney, defended his client's position using a vegetable simile:

"Management," Tuttle wrote, "refuses to submit to any agreement that tries to fix us like a cabbage in a garden patch. We are a free enterprise company, not a cabbage!"

Frank Baerd, spokesman for the United Hatters, Cap, and Millinery Workers Union, replied, "If plant operations are moved to Winchester, Dunlop Hats will be signing its own death warrant!" To which Mr. Tuttle responded: "We assert that this insistence on a bald act of protectionism is entirely foreign and contrary to the notion of free enterprise!"

"Call it protectionism and call us foreigners," countered Mr. Baerd, "it's no way to do business in the United States of America!"

When he first learned about the strike my stepfather concluded that the union had to be bluffing. "They're all foam and no beer, if you will," he said, then went on to predict that the strike wouldn't last more than a few days. When the strike entered its second week, he swore it wouldn't last through the New Year. When it lasted through the New Year, he averred that it would be settled by mid-January at the latest. When the strike dragged on into February, with violence breaking out at the Dunlop plant and other parts of Norwalk, my stepfather vouchsafed that—though Norwalkers had resorted to bats and bricks—Hattertown's citizenry would settle their differences by civilized means. When Hattertown's citizenry took to smashing store windows and slashing car tires, Walter Waple insisted that such were the acts of "a lamentable subset of hooligans."

"Can't judge the tree by one or two rotten apples, if you will," my stepfather reasoned.

As the strike entered its seventh week one factory worker who had crossed the picket line returned home the same evening to find his garden shed broken into and rakes, hoes, and shovels scattered across his snowy front yard. Another scabby was awakened by sirens to find his garage in flames. The manager of the Caxton-Dumont factory woke up in Danville Hospital after someone cut the brake lines of his Plymouth, which crashed into a lamppost at the north end of the Grand Union parking lot.

Hattertonians of all persuasions—Lowlanders and Highlanders, grade schoolers and senior citizens—exchanged looks, taunts, threats, even blows. In school hallways fights broke out between the sons and daughters of workers and managers. In the Grand Union produce section, armed with a celery bunch, one Back Shop worker's devoted spouse assaulted the equally loyal wife of her husband's shop foreman.

"Hooligans," my stepfather repeated, snapping the newspaper with a manicured finger, having read of the latest violent act in its pages.

"I wish you wouldn't call them that," my mother said.

"It's what all these strikers are, Gladys. There's no better word for it."

My stepfather lit his briarwood pipe. My mother fired up her own tobacco product. On a tray next to the sofa, the remains of a bowl of Campbell's cream of celery soup sat congealing. Gordon and I stretched out in front of the TV watching *Petticoat Junction,* a show that interested me only insofar as it featured a steam locomotive.

"What do you say, sport?" my stepfather asked. "Are the strikers hooligans?"

"Don't drag him into this, Walter!"

"Why not? He's entitled to an opinion."

"He's thir*teen.* He doesn't *have* an opinion."

"Well, sport?"

I looked back over my shoulder to see my stepfather looking at me from his chair, his right eyebrow pointedly raised. Only Vincent Price could raise a better eyebrow. With a shrug for an answer, I returned to *Petticoat Junction.*

"See? He doesn't care."

"How about your friends? What's their take on all this?"

"First you ask for his opinion, now you want to know what his *friends* think?"

"Shhh! Let him answer, dear."

"They're on the strikers' side, mainly, I guess," I answered, not taking my eyes off the TV screen on which Uncle Joe tore the Shady Rest Hotel apart searching for a winning raffle ticket he'd lost.

"Is that so? And I suppose you share their sentiments? I suppose you think it's perfectly fine for grown men to go around acting like a bunch of juvenile delinquents, slashing car tires, smashing windows, like—like—"

"Don't say it, Walter."

"—like a bunch of hooligans? Is that what you and your friends think?"

"They're just *boys,* Walter!"

"The strikers put themselves out of a job, as it were. For that they've no one else to blame but themselves."

"In other words, they should do whatever their bosses say, like good little slaves?" I said without taking my eyes off the TV.

"Will you listen to this, Gladys! A regular Bolshevik, this kid you've raised! A died-in-the-wool fellow traveler, if you will!"

"You asked his opinion, Walter."

"And I sure as Shinola got it!"

My stepfather snapped his newspaper again, more emphatically this time, then went on reading it, or pretending to.

My stepfather didn't stay angry for very long. That year my birthday, the fifth of March, fell on a Thursday. I woke up to find my stepfather's birthday present waiting on the breakfast nook table. Outdoors, a blizzard raged. Schools were closed. With my nose pressed to the window I watched snowflakes drifting and swirling. As I did my stepfather's reflection appeared in the glass behind mine. I turned to see him standing there in his pajamas, puffing his brier pipe.

"Morning, sport!"

He pointed his pipe at the cylindrical box on the table.

"Go on, sport. Open it!"

On the box's lid embossed golden letters spelled CAXTON-DUMONT. Attached to the box by a red-and-gold satin string was a card bearing a sketch of a square-jawed man in a business suit strutting down an urban sidewalk, his shirtsleeves rolled, his sport coat flipped jauntily over one shoulder, his striped necktie streaming over the other. In the background a policeman and a pair of female shoppers cast the man admiring looks. The man wore a fedora that, presumably, was manufactured by the Caxton-Dumont Hat Manufacturing Corporation.

"Read what the card says!"

Reluctantly, I did.

> *Congratulations! You are now the proud owner of a Caxton-Dumont Suburban Commuter, made of the finest quality pure rabbit fur, the finest hat money can buy. Follow the simple care instructions on the back of this card, and your Caxton-Dumont is 100% guaranteed to give you a lifetime of hat-wearing pleasure!*

"Happy birthday, sport!"

Over the box lid's embossed surface I spread both of my palms, examining it as though I were a phrenologist examining the lumps in a skull. I wondered what sort of hat was inside. Not that it mattered. I hated all hats. Hats were death; they spelled doom. While grazing my fingers over the embossed letters I wondered how I might defuse the wool felt time-bomb ticking away inside.

"Go on! It won't bite you!"

I shook the lid loose. My eyes were met by the crown of a tan fedora surrounded by crumpled red tissue paper.

"I know, I know," my stepfather said, "you were hoping for that minibike you saw in Cummins Lawn and Tractor Supply. But, sport, a minibike would give you two, maybe three years' worth of satisfaction, and possibly break your neck to boot. Whereas, assuming that you take good care of it, a hat of this quality will stand you in good stead, if you will, for the rest of your earthly days."

Having let that terrifying fact sink in my stepfather added: "Besides, you're fourteen—a man, practically. And a man ought to have a hat! Here, allow me!"

Pipe in mouth, my stepfather freed the fedora from its red tissue fortress, and—like a waiter serving a gourmet dish—presented it to me. I jammed the thing on my head—jammed, I say, since that's how my stepfather would have characterized the graceless way in which I crowned myself with his offering.

"For Pete's sake, that's no way to treat a hat!" said my stepfather taking it back. "This is a Caxton-Dumont quadruple-X 100 percent pure rabbit fur fedora, and there's a right and a wrong way to wear it!"

He demonstrated, putting the hat on his own head first, showing me how to hold and position it, one of three ways: first, by the front pinch; second, cradled in the palm; and finally, with the first three fingers curled gently over the underside of the brim and the thumb serving as an anchor, with only the faintest pressure applied from above. Using the first method, sighting the hat like a telescope—his head tilted forward as though in deference to a defeated Japanese emperor, the fedora gripped firmly (but *not* forcefully) by the dents in its crown—my stepfather brought it to his scalp. Still holding the fedora, his unshaven chin raised, his gray eyes focused dead ahead, my stepfather adjusted its tilt and pitch.

"There. Now you try it."

I did. Never before had I seen such a grin break the waters of my stepfather's normally placid face. Like the ripples of a stone tossed into a pond his laugh-lines radiated clear up to his hairline. The fedora covered my ears. It was at least a size too large.

"I factored in some leeway in case you decide to let your hair grow out as seems to be the fashion these days."

Taking the hat from me again, my stepfather folded and tucked three strips of the morning paper under the brim.

"That ought to do the trick!"

He replaced the hat on my head.

"Go on, have a gander at yourself, as it were!"

With my stepfather watching from behind, in the downstairs bathroom mirror I scrutinized myself. The face that returned my gaze was the face of a fool—a pimple-faced fool wearing, or lurking under, a tan fedora, a hat that had nothing whatsoever to do with the person wearing it. Some people just aren't meant to wear hats. The thing sat on my head like some science fiction creature out of *The Twilight Zone* that sucks brains out of human skulls.

Though outdoors a blizzard blew from below the hat's rim a bead of sweat trickled down my forehead. I was about to wipe it away with a finger when I noticed the business card tucked into the fedora's hatband. I plucked it and read:

Waple & Son Hats
Since 1898

"What's up, sport?" my stepfather's reflection said, grinning.

"I dunno," I replied hopelessly.

"Gas prices are up, taxes are up, unemployment is up—and hats are up!" He gave my shoulder a slap. "Come on! We'll have us a celebratory breakfast at the Doughboy Diner. My treat!" He went to the closet for his camel hair coat. This was the moment of truth, I thought. I had to speak then or forever hold my peace.

"Sorry, but I can't have breakfast with you," I said.

His coat still on its hanger, my stepfather stood there.

"I have other plans."

Though he stood five foot ten, just then my stepfather seemed much shorter. His lips moved but no sound escaped from them. I reached past him into the closet, the door to which was still open, and grabbed my own winter coat from it.

"See you later," I said.

I was about to step hatless out into the blizzard when, seeing the stricken look on my stepfather's face, I relented. "Oh—almost forgot!" I ran back into the kitchen to retrieve the fedora. "Thanks for—for the hat!"

With my stepfather's gift on my head I stepped out into the snowstorm.

There were very few people outdoors, most of them digging their plowed-in cars out with snow shovels. My boots pushed through mounds of snow. Stiff gusts of wind blew in every direction. I had to hold the fedora down with one hand. I let my aimlessness carry me into town where, across Felt Street, Christmas decorations were strung as if by giant yuletide spiders from pole to pole, alternating bells and six-pointed stars.

Soon I found myself walking past the Caxton-Dumont plant. One side of the factory's chimney was furry with snow. In front of the main gate, despite the blizzard, a handful of strikers marched back and forth on the sidewalk. They wore wool caps and earmuffs. Some had scarves wound over their faces. Their boots stomped the snow into slush and mud. A black cat wove its way between them. Flurries danced in the frozen air. Above their scarves and under their hats, the strikers' eyes were round and bleary with sleep.

Though I'd never met any of the strikers, I felt as if I knew them all. I hadn't forgotten my Back Shop worker dad. Through a scrim of swirling snowflakes I watched them trudge back and forth along the sidewalk in unison, as if connected by wires, their flimsy signs bent by the icy wind. If I crossed the street to shake hands with one of them, I knew I'd feel the same callused fingers that thickened my father's grip. If I looked into their eyes, I'd see the same blurry dark pupils floating in bloodshot whites. Nuzzled by one of them, I'd have felt the same prickly stubble and smelled the same half-metabolized alcohol oozing from their pores. Had I whispered to any one of them the words *I love you*, I'd have seen the same embarrassed proud look as on my father's face, accompanied by moist eyes and a quivering lower lip.

With my ears burning from the cold (the fedora failed to shield them), I turned and headed back the way I'd come.

I was recrossing the green iron bridge when a wayward gust yanked the fedora off my head to send it sailing between green girders into the frozen river. Amid jagged ice floes my stepfather's birthday present floated downstream.

During the strike's eighth week both display windows at my stepfather's store were smashed, including the one with the elf tableau, which still hadn't been taken down, destroying it and the flashing neon sign of which my stepfather had been so proud.

With that Walter Waple's heretofore unwavering faith in humanity did more than waver: it collapsed. "Upon my word," he proclaimed the next morning over his Melba toast and tea. "This world of ours has gone to hell in a hatbox, if you will."

To illustrate his point, he showed me a photograph in that day's newspaper of four young men with unusually long hair descending the gangway of a British passenger plane. The evening before, with Gordon, my mother, and me among seventy-three million other people watching, to the roar of an audience of mostly teenaged girls, the same four men performed their music live on *The Ed Sullivan Show.*

"Six million years of evolution," said my stepfather, "and what have we got to show for it?" He snapped his finger into the photo. "Four British mop-heads who never heard the words 'hat' or 'haircut.' Upon my word, if this is the future I want no part of it!"

My stepfather looked up from his rant to see Gordon and me standing there in our winter coats. Soon I was pedaling us furiously across the bridge, headed for Skunky's house for an emergency meeting of the Back Shop Boys, our first gathering since Zag's return from the boy's reformatory in Cheshire.

Zag had grown something like a goatee. He wore a checkered black-and-white hunter's jacket with his father's Knights of Columbus pin on the lapel. By his side a taciturn Zippo wagged his tail. We had been relegated to the Bledsoe's garage by Skunky's upholsterer dad, Skunky having set off one too many explosions in the downstairs rumpus room.

In that gasoline-and-lawnmower-clipping-scented Siberia of dangling fan belts and garden hoses, shivering in winter coats around a ping-pong table, we planned our mission: to sabotage the Caxton-Dumont Hat Factory Works' truck fleet. Our purpose: to prevent said trucks from carrying their cargoes of capelines under cover of darkness to that sinister plant in Tennessee. Zag learned of the plan from his father, who got wind of it from a friend, who overheard it being discussed by management in the booth next to his in the Doughboy Diner while having breakfast one morning.

"According to my intelligence," Zag explained, "they plan to load the trucks at midnight and have them on the road by three a.m. We've got to stop them. Unless they can ship those hats south, they'll have no choice but to give in to the strikers."

"What if they catch us?" Victor wondered.

"A battleship may be safer in the harbor," Zag opined, "but that's not what battleships are for."

"Even if we aren't caught," I said, "what's to stop them from repairing the trucks and rescheduling the deliveries?"

"If they repair them, we'll just have to sabotage them again. And keep on sabotaging them," Zag said. "Long as they keep trying to ship those hats, we'll keep stopping them. Every day that we delay them costs management money. When they realize it's costing them more to defy the strikers than to give in to them, that's when the strikers win. Anyway, we're their best bet, their *only* bet. The workers' fates are in our hands!"

Having put to rest any doubts about our mission, we advanced to tactical and technical considerations. Skunky was the Back Shop Boys' explosives expert. He'd taught us how to make magnesium flares and how to dump potassium permanganate into toilets to make them flush purple. Plopped into the same toilets, chunks of sodium hydroxide exploded into white clouds of hydrogen. From Skunky we learned all the ways of wreaking havoc using common household products like vinegar and baking soda (which, combined in a soda bottle and thrown from several stories onto pavement, produced a most satisfactory explosion). It was thanks to one of his finer explosions that Skunky got his nickname, along with the streak of white hair that shot up from his widow's peak. It had grown back that way after the original hairs were scorched off in the process of making gunpowder from the tips of a hundred wooden matches. The resulting explosion produced a five-foot flame. It shot up to the rumpus room's ceiling, scorching the acoustical tiles there and setting Skunky's—or rather Wade's, as he was still known then—hair on fire. Luckily Victor was there to douse the flames with a can of Yoo-hoo he'd been drinking.

On the dark green ping-pong table's surface, with a stubby piece of chalk Skunky diagrammed our plan. He drew a crude representation of the Caxton-Dumont truck yard. To one side the yard was enclosed by a loading dock with three bays. The two other sides were each enclosed by brick walls ascending in height from four to six feet, the walls' lower sections augmented by chain-link fences topped with ghastly coils of razor wire. The gate was on the fourth side—cast iron, spiked, electronic, eighteen feet tall, and controlled by a watchman from inside a kiosk located in front of and to its right.

Though the yard looked impregnable, Skunky assured us that it could be breached.

"There's just one problem," he noted, tapping the kiosk he'd drawn on the table. "Ever since the strike started they've posted a night watchman there twenty-four-seven. Getting past the night watchman, that's our big problem."

"Maybe one of us can give him a karate chop?" Victor proposed. "Like the one Cagney gives the Jap police chief in *Blood in the Sun*?"

Victor's idea having met with scant enthusiasm, other solutions—from setting a decoy fire to a rag soaked in chloroform—were put forth and rejected. The night shift watchman, we'd learned, was none other than Coach Reardon, the recently retired middle school phys-ed instructor. Reardon was known for persecuting non-jocks, using them as targets in dodge ball, making them hang five on the climbing rope that, thanks to my partially missing middle finger, I never could climb. He'd snap towels at our naked butts as we headed for the showers. Is it any wonder we nicknamed him "Coach Hardon"?

According to Skunky's reconnaissance, in his guard shack Reardon kept a thermos bottle of something from which he'd sip at regular intervals. Knowing this, I arrived at what seemed to me an obvious solution. "We'll slip him a Zippo!" I said, earning perplexed looks from Victory and Skunky, though Zag knew what I meant. For a retired phys-ed coach of Reardon's height and weight we calculated that seven Benadryl tablets would do the trick.

The means of entry having been arrived at, Skunky distributed our instrument of sabotage: a pint of Fuller's Earth, a clay-like substance used by hat factory workers to suck grease and other impurities out of raw felt. He filled three Coca-Cola bottles halfway with the stuff, a tablespoon of which was all it took to foul the average diesel engine. In case the Fuller's Earth didn't do the trick, he outfitted each of us with a matchbox containing two three-inch roofing nails. The final item in our sabotage kit was a sheet of typewriter paper.

Before we set out on our mission Skunky reacquainted us with the Ten Basic Rules of Sabotage:

1. Use readily available tools of a household nature
2. Only attack familiar or properly researched targets
3. Work for specifically stated gains
4. Give yourself a wide margin of error

5. Never attack targets beyond the capacity of your means
6. Destroy only things known to be of use to the enemy
7. Use long fuses whenever possible
8. Avoid capture and detention at all costs
9. Resist any temptation to loiter
10. Remember: anything can be sabotaged!

Shortly after sundown, our faces blackened with charred bottle corks, humming the jungle-humping theme from *The Bridge on the River Kwai*, we set out. The evening was unusually warm. A bright moon followed us to our objective, its light soothing and companionable. We dodged the headlight beams of passing cars. Whenever possible we cut through yards, lurching from shadow to shadow.

Across the street from the factory gate a Volkswagen bus was parked. Hidden behind it we waited for Coach Hardon to emerge from his kiosk and go off on his rounds. While waiting Victor told us his latest lie about the time his father blew up a Nazi ammunition dump. He was halfway through the story when the door to the kiosk squeaked open and Coach Hardon exited it with his flashlight. We heard a series of owl-hoots: Skunky's signal for Victor to proceed with Stage One: spiking Coach Hardon's thermos bottle. It wasn't long before Victor returned with both thumbs raised.

Twenty minutes later we watched as Coach Hardon's head bobbed a few times before slumping forward. Crouching, with Zag carrying a pair of wire cutters, we made our way to the lowest section of the yard's wall. Victor and Skunky stayed behind, posted at strategic lookout points, prepared to finger-whistle us at any sign of danger. Using the clippers Zag snipped an opening into the chain-link fence through which he and I climbed. Once on the other side we crept to where the trucks slept in their bays and advanced to Stage Two.

The trucks were war surplus Bedford models with flat armadillo noses and canvas-covered backs. Curious, I drew back one of the canvas covers to discover—not boxes of unfinished hats, but a cone-shaped object of shiny, pale-bluish material, with a brim-like flange almost as wide as the truck itself: yes, the Mysterious Object we'd seen along Bum's Trail, or the spit-and-shine of it. Zag crept up behind me.

"What are you doing?" he asked.

"It's here!" I said.

"What?"

"The thing—whatever it is!"

"Stop wasting time!" said Zag.

He tugged my arm. I let the canvas drop.

We rolled the typing paper sheets into funnels and slid them into the truck's fuel pipes, then emptied the Fuller's Earth from our Coke bottles into them. Before leaving we placed a matchbox under the rear tire of each truck.

We were about to climb back through the fence when the nearby fire station siren went off. As it wailed deafeningly Zag and I looked at each other. We'd been caught red-handed. We'd be packed off to reform school, both of us this time. Or worse: to prison. As though by the wave of a magician's wand our young happy lives had miraculously turned to shit. Surrender and throw ourselves at the mercy of the juvenile judge, that was our best option, our only option, under the circumstances. No point trying to make a run for it.

We ran. We climbed through the fence and jumped off the wall and ran and kept running, splitting up as we'd agreed in advance to do if anything went wrong. Through a kaleidoscope of shadows I ran till my legs turned into sandbags and flames clawed at my lungs and my heart seized like a diesel engine clogged with Fuller's Earth.

I ran all the way to Cheese Hill where we had agreed to meet up. In a wheezing heap I collapsed next to Zag, who'd gotten there so far ahead of me he was no longer even breathing hard. A few minutes later Skunky arrived. At least a dozen more minutes passed before gasping Victor brought up the rear.

That siren, we learned the next day, had nothing to do with us. While we were busy sabotaging trucks, the hay barn at the feed and supply depot—the one where Virgil Zeno's legs were crushed by a stack of peat moss bags—burned down. In the past we Back Shop Boys had used that barn as our secret smoking lounge. I know: a barn filled with hay would not appear to be an intuitive choice for said purpose, but you have to factor in the secrecy provided by all those bales of hay, which could be configured into mazes such as King Midas himself would have envied. As far as I knew, though, none of us Back Shop Boys had been in the barn for months.

The burning of the hay barn along with our act of vandalism occasioned an address by the Right Reverend Wallace Stumpf, pastor at the Congregational church and President of the Committee of Citizens for Peace and Prosperity. The address took place on a snowy Saturday (a blizzard had been forecast) in the old Veterans of Foreign War Meeting House, two blocks from the train station. Though the veteran's hall had a maximum occupancy of one hundred, at least twice as many were in attendance.

Zag's father sat in the first row. Next to him, holding his father's crutches, sat Zag. A row behind him Victor Szentgyorgyi sat between his mother and father. Skunky and his parents sat behind them. Across the aisle Belinda Dalton sat with her mother and her little brother. Behind them, between Gordon in his Boy's Club cap and my mother wearing her navy pillbox hat, sat my stepfather in his camel hair coat and matching camel homburg.

I stood in back by the main doors, the better to make my exit in case the proceedings got too boring. I wore my winter jacket and a wool cap. In that drafty old building everyone kept their coats on, along with their scarves, gloves, and, needless to say, their hats.

As Reverend Stumpf approached the lectern set up at the center of the stage, the hubbub died. Reverend Stumpf was the sort of person who seems never to have been anything but old, as much a fixture in Hattertown as the trees lining Felt Street. As if by centrifugal force his beady eyes were drawn toward the hub of his round ruddy face. A fringe of yellow-white hair ringed his bald head, giving him a monkish appearance that the blush of his cheeks heightened. Flakes of dandruff, visible even from where I stood at the very back of the hall, speckled the shoulders of the black suit that he wore in place of his cassock. He scanned the audience, his dark beady eyes darting in all directions at once, so that, no matter which way they looked, they seemed to be both avoiding and looking at you. He cleared his throat ostentatiously.

"Thank you all for coming," he said and waited for the crowd to settle further. Then, gripping both sides of the lectern, he launched into his speech.

"Good citizens of Hattertown, friends and neighbors of our community, those of you who are members of my congregation are accustomed to seeing me wearing a surplice and speaking from the pulpit. However, this morning I speak to you not as a clergyman, but as a fellow citizen, a deeply disturbed and concerned fellow citizen.

"No mystery surrounds our purpose. We meet here this morning as citizens of a town beseiged. That's right: besieged. For on this February morning, we find ourselves in much the same position as did our forefathers on the terrible eve of April the 16th, 1777, the day British troops marched down these very same streets of ours, burning everything in their path.

"Listen," said Reverend Stumpf, cupping his hand theatrically behind his ear. "Do you hear that sound? It is the sound of angry footsteps marching past these doors. Those shadows that you see dancing behind the windows? They are shadows cast by the torch flames of suspicion and hatred. And where were those torches lit? Twenty-three miles from here—in Norwalk, Connecticut!"

Murmurs and sober nods from many in the audience.

"And who lit those torches? Outsiders! People you and I have never met, who've never set foot on the sidewalks of our town! Who don't patronize our businesses, or work in our stores and factories, or send their children to our schools, or pray in our churches, or attend the Volunteer Fire Department's annual summer picnic, or our parades and carnivals and fireworks displays. People, in short, who have nothing, absolutely nothing whatsoever, to do with us!"

Murmurs of consensus. Reverend Stumpf thrust his palms out for silence.

"No doubt, most of you here have heard of the acts of vandalism that have taken place as recently as two nights ago here in our town. Deliberate acts of vandalism. A witness to one of last night's activities claims she saw a group of boys fleeing the Caxton factory, the truck fleet of which was sabotaged! Our own spirited youth incited to violence by the corrosive influence of outsiders!"

Boos, jeers, and other sounds of disapprobation.

"However we are not here to cast aspersions on our neighbors in Norwalk. No, ladies and gentlemen. For they and we are on the same side; we share the same concerns. To be sure we have our differences, but those differences are nothing next to what we have in common.

"Once upon a time, ours was a great town, a mighty and prosperous town, 'The Town that Crowned America'! Together with our next-door neighbor Danville we produced enough hats per year to cover the head of every grown man living in New York City today. Over *five million* hats!"

Applause. Cheers. Cries of *Hear, hear!*

"Alas, ladies and gentlemen, those days are gone. Our town is no longer advancing; it is *retrograding*. The reason for that precipitous decline? It can be summed up in precisely two words: *outside interference*. Strangers who have come here to harm us."

More shouts from the audience:

"Let's rout 'em out!"

"Send 'em to hell!"

"Send 'em back to Norwalk!"

"Same difference!"

Just then the big oak entryway doors behind me swung open, blinding all who turned to see who'd opened them. Haloed in winter sunlight and falling snow, Al Jenson, editor of the *Hattertown Gazette,* stood wearing a raggedy Pendleton coat with a fleece collar.

"Begging your pardon, Pastor," Jenson said, his smile exposing a set of jagged, tobacco-stained teeth.

He stepped aside, making way for his two strapping teenaged sons, each carrying one side of a wheelchair in which, wearing his freshly pressed, spanking-white carpenter's coveralls, looking like an Indian emperor upon his palanquin, sat (rode?) Virgil Zeno.

"That's right," Virgil said as the Jensen boys settled him and his wheelchair among the hall's last row of chairs. "Forgive us, for we know what we do!"

Snorts and sniggers.

"Not at all, Mr. Zeno, not at all," said Reverend Stumpf indulgently. "We're pleased that you're able to join us!"

"Wouldn't miss it for the world!"

"Which one?" some wise-guy in the audience yelled, igniting a fresh burst of laughter in which Virgil Zeno himself partook.

"What've I missed?" Virgil asked.

"We have been discussing outsiders," the reverend answered, daubing sweat from his brow despite the cold.

"Now *that's* something I know a thing or two about!" Virgil, remarked, igniting more laughter.

"I'm afraid the outsiders we're concerned with exist far closer to home than those in your purview, Mr. Zeno."

"Don't bet on it, Reverend!"

More laughter.

Once again, Reverend Stumpf bowed his fringed head, but the ruckus persisted. He had to clear his throat again loudly several times before he could resume.

"Many of you here, I'm sure, are aware of the story of the Amalekites, that pestilential nation of desert nomads who for centuries raped, murdered, mutilated, sodomized, and by various other means ravaged the people of Egypt. They burned their crops, salted their soil, killed their livestock, urinated on their stored grains… They preyed on the weak and the vulnerable in particular, on women and children, on the feeble, the hungry, and the infirm. Such a terror were the Amalekites, of their leader Jehovah himself said, *He shall be the first in hell!*

"Citizens of Hattertown, we here now have our own Amalekites to contend with, our own pestilential outsiders who've come here to destroy our cherished way of life. Just as the bark beetle threatens the lovely elms lining our main street, these outsiders threaten to decimate us. We must identify, isolate, and exterminate this blight! We must rout out the invasive aliens among us and cast them forth forever from our midst!"

From the furthest row of the audience a voice recited: "'For I was hungry and you gave me food, I was thirsty and you gave me drink, I was a stranger and you welcomed me.'"

All turned to face Virgil in his wheelchair.

"That's Matthew 25," Virgil said. "In case you've forgotten."

"I am familiar with the passage," Reverent Stumpf responded with a tight little smile.

"How about the Parable of the Stranger? Or the Book of Exodus, wherein God commands the Israelites to not oppress the alien? 'For you yourselves know what it feels like to be an alien, for you were once yourselves aliens in Egypt.'"

"Souse it, Virgil!"

"Let Reverend Stumpf speak!"

"Go turn a chair leg!"

"Go fly your flying saucer!"

Amid the ensuing chorus of hisses Reverend Stumpf made

a supplicatory gesture. "With due respect, Mr. Zeno," he submitted when the ruckus had died, "in equating Amalek with our Savior, you make a considerable error."

"I drew no such comparison, Father. That's your doing. I only meant to say that when a stranger asks to drink from your well you should think twice before turning him away."

Murmurs, boos, hisses.

"In this instance I'm afraid the stranger may have already poisoned our well. Thanks to him, we may all soon die of thirst, if we don't all murder each other first!"

"Hear, hear, Father!"

"You said it!"

"Damn Amalekites!"

"Damn outsiders!"

"I have one more story to tell, if I may," said Virgil.

"Stow it, Virgil!"

"The story of Korah, son of Ithar, who rebelled against Moses and the Commandments only to have the earth split open and swallow him and all who rebelled against him. That's it; that's my story."

Virgil signaled the Jenson boys. To a chorus of jeers, they lofted and carried Virgil in his wheelchair back outdoors into the by then heavily falling snow.

"Poor man," Pastor Stumpf said, watching Virgil depart. "He has suffered many a terrible loss."

"Yeah," someone yelled. "Including most of his marbles!"

"What should we do, Reverend?"

"Yeah, what do we do?"

As if on cue Reverend Stumpf removed the black suit jacket he wore and held up his right arm, revealing a band of dark ribbon worn over the sleeve of his white shirt.

"See this ribbon?" he said. "A strip of hatband cloth. It's the heart of Hattertown that I'm wearing on my sleeve. True, we have our differences, chief among them the conflicting desires of workers and management. But let us not forget that at the end of the day we are all, all of us here, Hattertonians. Either we stand together or we fall apart!"

"Hear, hear!"

"Hence, following this address, the Citizens for Peace and Prosperity intend to meet in this same venue to weigh solutions to our dilemma, a symposium to which all of you here are cordially invited. Meanwhile let us all wear our hearts upon our sleeves as you see me wearing mine—sewn, by the way, along with two hundred others, by my beloved wife Nancy and our beloved friends Judith Carmichael, Lois Kellog, and Dorothy Bristol. In wearing these ribbons on our sleeves, we declare our solidarity. We'll show each other, as well as any outsiders watching, that we are united in opposing those pernicious forces that wish to tear us asunder! Whosoever wears a hatband over his or her sleeve is a friend, a brother, a sister, a mother or father, a son, or a daughter. And whosoever doesn't is an outsider—to be feared and scorned!"

As the Right Reverend Stumpf uttered these last words of his address, a cardboard box filled with hatband armbands made its way through the crowded hall.

After the meeting the Back Shop Boys converged on Cheese Hill. As always Zag arrived ahead of us. He sat on the cliff's edge overlooking the town, smoking a cigarette, his view obscured by swirling snowflakes. The forecasted blizzard was underway.

"Look!" Skunky said. "My armband matches my coat!"

"Mine doesn't fit," said Victor, struggling to work his over an obese arm.

Zag gazed abstractedly out at the swirling snow.

"Well?" Skunky asked him.

"You heard Reverend Stumpf," said Victor.

"We must cast the Amalekite from our midst!" said Skunky. "We must rout him out!"

"Exactly," said Zag. He turned to me. "Well?"

"Who are you talking about?"

"Uhn haah dah," said Gordon.

"You know who."

The blizzard blew harder.

"The strike started in Norwalk. Jack had nothing to do with it!"

Zag stared at me, his eyes shifting back and forth, as if he were examining my pupils one by one like an optometrist. "What's happened to you, Half? You've lost your bearings. You've been fraternizing with the enemy so long you've forgotten whose side you're on."

"I'm not on Jack's side. It's not a matter of sides! It's just that I don't happen to believe in condemning someone without a shred of evidence against them!"

Zag shook his head and went back to watching the view. After two more drags of his cigarette, he spoke again, quietly. "Listen to you," he said. "You trust a complete stranger more than you trust me, your best friend."

"Jack's my friend too."

"Jack Thomas isn't your friend. He's your enemy; he's *all* our enemies. He's an enemy of the United States of America!"

From the inner pocket of his coat Zag withdrew a folded tattered sheet of paper. He unfolded it and held it under my nose. It was the same FBI notice I'd seen at the Hattertown post office, or one just like it, with the three black-and-white photos taken from different angles of "Johann Verhoff," otherwise known as Jack Thomas.

"Look familiar?" Zag asked. "Guess where I got it?"

"The post office!" Skunky guessed.

"Shut up. I'm not asking you. I was asking him." Zag turned to me. I could see he was angry now. He drew back his upper lip against his teeth. He clenched and unclenched his gloved fists.

"I have no idea," I said.

"Skunky's right. The post office. Not this one, the Danville Post Office. I rode there before the meeting this morning, after going to our post office to pick up a package for my dad. I was headed out the door when this notice on the bulletin board catches my eye, an FBI notice just like this one. I thought: *What if . . . ?* So I looked at all the notices, there had to be at least a dozen of them. While looking at them I noticed someone had taken one down. They must've been in a hurry, since they left behind a torn corner of paper. That made me curious. That's when I decided to go to Danville, to the post office there. Guess what I find on the bulletin board there? This. Hmmm, I wonder who tore that notice down. Any idea?"

"Uhn haah dah," said Gordon.

"Jack hasn't done anything!"

"He's an escaped German POW."

"So what?" I said.

"So what?" said Zag.

"Yeah, so what? Who cares!"

"The FBI, that's who!"

"It's been eighteen years! The war's over; we won. Why the hell don't they leave him alone?"

I must have said this a little too loudly. The others all stared at me—even Gordon.

"It's not like he committed war crimes or anything. He was one of millions of Germans who fought for their country. They weren't all evil. They were just about to release him when he escaped."

"So why did he escape, then?" Skunky wanted to know.

"Because. He had no choice. They were going to send him home."

This answer satisfied no one.

"He'd have ended up in a Communist country, in a work-camp in Siberia, or something like that!"

"How do you know all this?" Victor wondered.

"Jack. He told me."

"And you believe him?" Zag snorted.

"Why shouldn't I?"

Zag grabbed me by my coat collar and yanked my face close to his. "Do you have any idea what the hell you've done?" Our faces were so close together the condensed water vapor of Zag's breath clouded my vision. "Aiding and abetting a fugitive. That's a crime, a serious crime. It makes no difference if he's innocent or guilty. Anyway, it's not up to you or me or anyone else but the United States government to decide. You could go to jail! We could all go in jail! Jesus, Half, I just got out of the goddamn boy's reformatory. Thanks to you I may end up right back there again!"

Zag let go of me. I rubbed the back of my neck where my coat collar had chafed it. The snow fell harder. Already two inches had settled on the corrugated roof of the Caxton-Dumont factory's reject shed.

"Are you going to report him?" I asked helplessly.

Zag shook his head.

"No," he said. "You are."

He refolded the FBI notice.

"The number to call is here," he said, tucking it into my pocket.

I looked up at him.

"Say you'll do it, Half. Otherwise, I'll have to."

I nodded. What choice did I have?

Zag put a gloved hand on my shoulder.

"This is your last chance to redeem yourself. Don't blow it."

Part 10

Missing

I didn't phone the FBI. I went straight to Fern Cottage. I took Gordon with me. I had no choice. I had to warn him.

By then the roads were too snowy for bicycles. I ditched my bike in town and we hoofed it the rest of the way, trudging down streets and roads that had yet to be plowed, with more snow coming down, the flakes falling heavy and fat as the temperature rose to just below freezing. The snow chains of the few rare vehicles on the roads threw up tattered sprays of wet snow.

By then the lake had frozen over completely. To save time we walked across it, past the island with the miniature stone lighthouse, over the same stretch of water Jack and I had swum across together dozens of times. By cutting across the lake we shortened the distance to Fern Cottage by almost a mile.

Walked on, Lost Lake seemed a lot smaller, as if the humiliation of being reduced to a footpath under our boots had caused it to shrink. Unless you're Jesus, to walk on water is to insult it. I didn't know that, yet.

When we arrived at Fern Cottage wisps of umber smoke rose from its chimney. I knocked; Jack answered. He didn't seem all that surprised to see us. As if we hadn't been AWOL for over a month, Jack nodded us inside. I was still stomping snow from my boots when he said: "Care for some tea?"

I nodded. As he filled the kettle, I said: "They know."

He looked up from the stove. "They?"

"My friends."

"What do they know?"

"About you."

I handed him the folded FBI notice from my pocket. He unfolded, studied it, nodded slowly, and handed it back to me.

"What are you going to do?"

He smiled. "What can I do?"

"Leave."

"And go where?"

"Anywhere. You can't stay here! They'll find you!"

"Yes, I suppose they will."

"You're not giving up, are you?"

"Why not?"

"Because—you can't!"

He smiled again. The kettle whistled. He filled our mugs. "Here's your tea," he said, handing me mine. "Sit down. I have something for you."

With Gordon and me sitting, Jack got something from his cabinet. He came back to the table and handed it to me. Though it was wrapped in brown paper from a shopping bag, from the shape it was obviously a book of some kind.

"Happy birthday," Jack said.

"My birthday was in March."

"Yes, I know. But I'm giving it to you now."

"Should I open it?"

"Why not?"

I did. It was the old book about swimming.

"You can't give me this!"

"Why not?"

"It's the most valuable thing you own. You said so yourself."

"I've no use for it now, except to give it to someone I like. That someone happens to be you."

As I flipped absently through its pages a card fell out, a handmade one. On the front was a crude drawing of someone swimming. Under it Jack's handwriting said, *For Hoff.* I was about to open the card when something occurred to me. I closed the book and asked:

"If they do catch you, what will they do?"

"I've no idea."

"Will they really send you to Russia, or whatever?"

"Quite possibly."

"Uhn haah dah."

"They wouldn't…?"

"Execute me?" Jack smiled. "I don't think so, Hoff. More likely they'll send me to a labor camp. Shall we play a game?" He set up the chess board.

"Won't you at least try to escape?"

"I've had eighteen years of escaping and hiding, Hoff. Twice as many, if you count the years I spent escaping from myself, or trying to. Don't you understand, Hoff? It's not the FBI I've been eluding. Or the German army. Or a fortress of brick walls and barbed wire. It's my own self, Hoff. It's the boy who fell in love watching those boys diving off the high-board one summer's day. It's him I've been hiding and running away from. But one can't escape or hide from oneself, Hoff, not in the long run. In the long run we're bound to catch up with ourselves. So, to answer your question: no. I won't try to escape. Not this time."

"If they arrest you, I may never see you again."

"One never knows, Hoff."

"I'll miss you."

"I'll miss you too. I'll miss swimming with you. I'll miss our chess games and working on the monument with you and Gordon. Perhaps you and Gordon will carry on without me. I hope so. Perhaps you'll find a way to lift that stone."

My throat tightened. Tears blurred my vision. I turned away so Jack wouldn't see them. Through the window I saw the branches of a nearby tree sagging under the weight of snow. I looked down at the swimming book. Jack put his hand on my shoulder.

"Come. Let's play a game."

I shoved his hand off me.

"You can keep your lousy book!" I said, standing.

"Hoff!"

I grabbed mine and Gordon's coats.

"Hoff, what are you—?"

"Quitter! Coward!"

"You don't understand."

"You're right; I don't!"

"Hoff, please—"

"Fucking Nazi faggot!"

"Hoff!"

With tears streaming down my face and Gordon trailing me, I stormed out of Fern Cottage.

By the time we left the sky had already grown dark. Wet, heavy drifts of snow lay everywhere. Sounds of dripping water engulfed us. I wiped my coat sleeve over my eyes. In the dimming light the woods looked sketchy, like a smeared charcoal drawing.

A blanket of heavy snow had spread itself across Lost Lake. I saw the softened footprints where Gordon and I had crossed it earlier. As we made our way across again, the ice grumbled. With each grumble Gordon stopped to look up at me with a questioning look.

"It's safe," I said. "Come on!"

We were two-thirds of the way to the main road when Gordon realized he'd left his Boy's Club cap in Jack's cottage. He stopped and stood there, lips trembling, pointing to his bare head.

"Christ," I said. "Can't you keep track of *anything?* Do I have to think of *everything* for you?" Gordon started crying then. I kept walking, hoping he'd follow. My stepbrother refused to move.

"We are *not* going back there!" I said. "We'll get it some other time." Even in the dimming light I caught the glimmer of reflected light in his tears. Until that stupid cap was back on his head, I knew my stepbrother wouldn't stop crying.

"God*damn* it!"

With a huff I turned and started back across the lake in the direction we'd come from.

Though molecularly identical, ice and water have little in common. Ice is a *mineral;* it floats on water. Of the four earthy elements, water is the most protean. Still, in its liquid form at least, with water you have some idea of what you're dealing with.

Ice, on the other hand, is an illusion. It looks solid and can be incredibly strong. Two inches of ice can support the average person. Four inches will support a man on horseback; ten will support about a thousand pounds per square-foot, or roughly the weight of a Patton tank. That evening by my estimate the ice covering Lost Lake was at least two and a half inches thick.

But ice is also extremely fickle. Of all the materials that make up vast parts of our planet, ice is the least predictable. It's also the most unreliable and treacherous. In moderate climates it exists only provisionally.

As for a frozen lake, at best it's a contradiction in terms. Though it's a well-known fact that black ice spells danger, how many people know that a lake covered in snow is ten times as dangerous as a frozen lake with no snow on it? Snow is an insulator. Like a blanket, it protects the ice underneath it from the cold, weakening and ultimately destroying it.

All afternoon the temperature had been climbing. Now, with the sun close to setting, it fell sharply again. Like a medieval torturer stretching his victim on a rack, the cooling air caused the degenerate ice covering Lost Lake to expand.

We had gone a third of the way back across the lake again when we heard the first thunder-like boom. A dozen steps later another boom. Each boom echoed across the lake. Lost Lake was talking to us, trying to tell us something, saying, *Get the hell off me!* With an animal's frightened instinct, the way a horse knows when a hurdle's too high or a dog knows when it's being taken to the vet, my stepbrother knew the danger. He stopped and stood there as another boom sounded.

"Damn it, Gordon," I said. "It's safe! Now *come on!*"

But Gordon refused to budge. He stood there, his twilit features gleaming with snot and tears.

"I'm telling you it's *safe!* There's *nothing* to be afraid of!"

To demonstrate—also out of frustration—I stomped my booted foot on the ice.

"See?" I said. "See? *See?*"

Remember the story that Virgil told at the VFW hall, the one about the world opening up under Korah's feet to swallow him? Lost Lake opened up under our four feet to swallow Gordon and me. The jagged crack ran right between our two pairs of winter boots, exposing a lightning-shaped river of blackness. Behind his thick glasses, Gordon's eyes burst open.

Then down he went on an invisible elevator.

I shouted his name. As I did down I went in my own elevator.

For a second or two I managed to cling to the ice shelf before slipping into frozen blackness. A screeching filled my skull. Tracer-like sparks ricocheted from the edges of my vision. Like a medley of frozen fists, the icy water pummeled my face. It was like swimming in broken glass. Somehow, I managed to grab hold of another ice shelf, but it broke. I kept grabbing at hunks of ice, my legs kicking blindly in the frozen inky water, my arms reaching up toward the blurry light that I guessed was the sky, though I couldn't be sure. My brain lit up like a pinball machine. More tracers flew. A tortured violin sound faded into a chorus of silver bells, like the bells that tinkled whenever customers entered my stepfather's store, but louder. As my lungs begged for one last gruesome breath my hands found another mantle of ice, a thicker one that held me enough to haul myself up and out.

I stood there then, bent in half, clutching both knees, coughing and gasping. With my breath half caught I looked around, expecting to see Gordon standing there, picking his nose where I'd last seen him. All I saw was a frozen lake with a black gash in it.

Minutes later I stood soaked and shivering at the front door of Jack's cottage. He was wearing his plaid robe.

"Where is your stepbrother?" he asked, scanning the darkness over my wet shoulder. I stood there, shivering.

"Good God," said Jack *(Gut got).*

❧

With his coat flung over his robe, using a pickaxe as his walking stick, Jack followed me out onto the lake, to the place where

Gordy had fallen through the ice. Using the pickaxe, over an area the size of my bed, he broke the ice up into hatbox-sized chunks. Then, dropping the pickaxe, he held his nose and plunged feet-first into the jagged black hole. Three times Jack came up and three times he plunged back under again.

But it was no use. Gordon was gone.

"Missing. Gordon's missing."

That's what I told them.

I got home just after seven o'clock. By then it was snowing again. The shoulders of my jacket were flaked with snow. Though Jack had spread it out to dry on the tiled apron in front of his stove the jacket was still moist.

I'd stepped into the parlor. My mother and stepfather had already eaten dinner. *The Outer Limits* was on. On the screen a futuristic spacecraft enshrouded in fog glided across an alien-looking landscape. The voiceover said: "*In the vast immensities of cosmic space bold adventurers streak their way to do battle with strange enemies on strange worlds...*" My stepfather smoked his corncob pipe and read the newspaper. My mother was spread out per usual on the sofa, her hair rolled up in pink curlers, the *TV Guide* splayed open on her lap. She turned and looked at me standing there behind the beaded curtain, alone.

"Leo! Where on earth—!"

I shivered. My teeth were chattering.

"Where's Gordon?" she asked.

I licked my lips. *Missing,* I thought.

"Leo, where is your stepbrother?"

A look of horror spread over my mother's face. My stepfather looked up.

"Missing," I said.

On TV a scientist mutated by rainfall on an alien world held his colleagues hostage, demanding a return to earth.

"Missing," I repeated. "Gordon's missing."

Missing: an oddly appropriate word. "To miss (verb): to fail to hit, reach, or contact. To discover or feel the absence. To fail to obtain, escape, or avoid. To leave out; to omit. To fail to comprehend, sense, or experience. To fail to perform or attend an event." *To fail.* "Miss (noun): disadvantage or regret resulting from loss."

"Missing. Gordon's missing…"

My mouth went dry, my lips contorted with the lie, my eyes welled. Shivers filled my body again, as if Jack's stove hadn't melted them away an hour ago.

"Missing…"

Why didn't I tell the truth? To this day I'm not sure. To cover up one inexcusable deed with another, even worse one. Because it's one thing to lose your stepbrother in the woods, another to cause him to drown by forcing him to walk across a supposedly frozen lake that isn't frozen enough?

Anyway I did it; I lied.

I sat there, in the parlor, but I wasn't really there. My mother and my stepfather were standing by then, too, saying things to me. Gesturing, asking questions. How did it happen? Where did you last see him? What were you doing?

We'd gone up to the Dalton Estate, into the woods near the lake to hike there. It was mid-afternoon. We were walking along this path when I turned and suddenly Gordon wasn't behind me anymore. I called his name. No answer. I kept calling. One minute he was there, the next he was gone. *Missing.* Just like that. *Missing.* I searched the woods, I said. The sun was going down. I searched till it got too dark to search anymore.

That's what I said.

In the fireplace the fire snapped and crackled; next to it the Zenith glowed and murmured. I didn't see any of it, or I did, but the way you see things in a dream, as if they don't really matter, since they aren't real. I saw my mother's head covered with curlers, saw the beads of the room divider falling like a blizzard of amber and ivory snowflakes, saw my stepfather's pipe curving down from his lips like a wooden question mark. Nothing seemed real. Even I didn't seem real to myself just then, at that moment. Except as a mechanism for telling lies, I didn't exist.

There's a word for it: *denial.*

While my stepfather phoned the police I climbed the stairs up to my bedroom, threw myself onto my bed, buried my face in my pillow.

❧

Search parties were organized. Half the town turned out to help. Along with citizens, local and state police and volunteer firemen combed the woods of the former Dalton Estate, their lanterns, flares, and flashlights flickering like fireflies as more snow fell in fat slow flakes. Cries of *Gordon!* and *Gordy!* punctuated the dark snowy night. Between forays into the forest, the searchers warmed themselves at a bonfire they'd built and that blazed in a clearing alongside the gravel road to Fern Cottage. They sipped from thermos bottles of coffee, hot cocoa, and bouillon.

Through the night the searchers combed the woods. I searched alongside my mother and my stepfather, the three of us trudging through ice and snow. My stepfather carried a red storm lantern. It swayed on its hinged handle. He and I both wore galoshes over our shoes. Mom wore rubber boots with metal fasteners. We were told to keep the other search teams' torches in view at all times to keep from getting lost ourselves. Now and then a search team leader blew a whistle, and everyone converged on some scrap of evidence: a snapped twig, a footprint, a torn piece of fabric…

With morning more volunteers joined the effort. Zag, Skunky, and Victor arrived with their families. Unable to search by foot, Mr. Lengyl drove the surrounding roads in his Dodge Dart. Sergeant Pomeroy brought a pair of search and rescue dogs. Mr. Kirby, owner of the hardware store, arrived with a contingent of freckle-faced Catholic teenagers. I recognized a few teachers past and present, including Miss Delvecchio, Mr. Oates, and Mr. Blum. Principal Laurelton was there; so was Miss Stanhope, who brought six boxes of doughnuts and a silver samovar filled with spiced hot cider. Even Virgil Zeno did his part. From the trunk of his DeSoto he distributed nine pairs of snowshoes, the old-fashioned kind with leather laces. Reverend Stumpf joined the effort, too, wearing a hat ribbon over the sleeve of his winter coat. Over their coat sleeves everyone wore symbolic black hatbands.

One search team carried its torches and lanterns to the lake, where they came upon the gash in the ice. By then snow had obscured most of the footsteps we'd left. Questioned by one of the searchers, I answered:

Yes, we'd crossed the lake that afternoon.

No, the ice didn't break, not while we were crossing it.

"Did you cross in both directions—coming and going?"

"Yeah," I answered. "We did, but on the way back, halfway across we heard the ice boom, so we turned around and headed back the way we'd come. I guess the ice must have broken right after that," I lied—though by then it no longer felt like a lie to me; by then I'd come to believe that my stepbrother really had gotten lost in the woods somehow, that no imperfectly frozen lake had swallowed Gordon whole, that the ice breaking and him falling in was all part of a bad dream I'd had.

By then everyone must have started realizing there was little if any chance of Gordon having survived the night, not with the temperature below freezing, unless he'd built a fire, something even someone without his severe limitations would have been hard pressed to do in the dark snowy woods without matches or dry kindling. (But Gordy's not in the woods, I reminded myself. He's at the bottom of Lost Lake somewhere, down there with Benedict Dalton's skeletal ghost and The Water Master, where even the greatest arsonist in the world couldn't build a fire.)

By then my lies had set me on a course from which there was no turning back. Even if I'd come out with the truth, if somehow instead of the woods those search teams had been able to comb the depths of Lost Lake with their lanterns and flashlights, what difference would it have made? By then nothing would have brought Gordon back to life.

Nothing would save him. Or, for that matter, me.

❧

After two days of searching I could read the hopelessness on the volunteers' faces. They were tired. They were hungry. They wanted to go home—to their homes, to their beds, to their own problems. One by one they hung their storm lanterns back up in their garages. They tucked their flashlights back in drawers. They were sorry. *We're sorry,* they said. *So sorry.* Everyone was sorry. For my stepfather, for my mother, for Gordon, who they knew mostly as the kid who followed me everywhere wearing a red Boy's Club cap.

And sorry for me, too, since I missed Gordon more than anyone. It was like losing my own shadow. I missed his plaid shirts and his thick glasses and how his hair and his ears stuck out from under his red Boy's Club cap. I missed him gawping at his fingertips and having to smack him to keep him from chomping down on them. I regretted all of the cruel names I'd called him and all the times I swatted him a little too hard. I missed his big wet sloppy smile whenever I'd buy him a Bonomo Turkish taffy or let him borrow my yo-yo or tousle his hair or knuckle him in the forehead. I missed taking him everywhere with me on the back of my shitty Royce Union. I missed him looking up to and depending on me for just about everything, like I was some sort of god.

As much as I missed Gordon, I know he must have missed me too. So many things my stepbrother must have missed, starting with his magical hot dog. But there were lots of other things he missed, too, I'm sure, like waking up in his bedroom, in his bed, and eating his favorite foods (Campbell's beans and franks; creamed corn; Chef Boyardee canned ravioli…). I bet he missed *Fireball XL-5* and wearing his argyle socks and having me tie his sneaker laces for him. I bet he missed smelling his dirty feet. I bet he missed playing with my Duncan Midnight Special yo-yo, the string of which I must have repaired for him at least a hundred times. I bet he missed riding the yellow bus to school and the alarm between classes and earning gold stars from Mrs. Lundenberg, his special ed teacher. I bet he missed all sixty-four colors in his Crayola Crayon box. I bet he missed hot lunch pizza and rubbery Jell-O and pollywogs and bulrushes. I bet he missed the nozzle on the garden hose, the smell of bacon frying, the sound the eggshells made when my mother cracked them against the Formica counter. I bet he missed Post Sugar Smacks. I bet he missed picking his nose and sampling the snot. I bet he missed mixing mustard and ketchup on his hot dogs. I bet he missed the sharp smell of gasoline and the spinach soufflé-like clods of grass clippings clinging to the bottom of the lawnmower. I bet he missed popsicles wrapped in thin frosty paper and the mealy dull taste of the flat wooden stick. I bet he missed every single one of his internal organs. I bet he missed walking and running and chewing and tasting and swallowing and spitting and pissing and shitting and burping and farting and all his other bodily functions.

Especially breathing. I bet he missed breathing most of all.

On the fourth day of the search, at around five o'clock in the afternoon, the shrill cries of a whistle pierced the dimming atmosphere. The rest of the Back Shop Boys and I joined the other search teams as they climbed through the breach in the chain-link fence and through the copse of pine trees to converge around the flooded drift of the abandoned mica mine. They stood there, more than two dozen volunteer searchers, their mouths gaping, their eyes blinking, their breaths condensing in the cold, twilit air, their faces frozen with a mixture of wonder and bafflement as they took in the Thing in the Woods, its junk figures dripping snowmelt.

"What the — ?" said Zag.

"Hot dribbling spit," said Skunky.

They were still staring when another whistle sounded.

To this day what happened after that remains a questionable blur. Did we follow the whistle to Fern Cottage? Had other search parties already gathered there? Was it dark by the time we got there? Did some searchers carry flaming torches? Did it start to rain? Was the rain frozen? Did the frozen rain sizzle when it touched the torch flames?

Were two Hattertown police cars parked there, on the gravel road, engines rumbling, tailpipes fuming, their gumball lights spinning, turning everyone's faces into ghoulish masks? Did a CB radio crackle? Was a cop sitting in the driver's seat of one of the cruisers? Did Zag knock on his window and ask what was going on? Did he ignore Zag? Did the door to Fern Cottage open? Did Jack step out accompanied by two police officers? Was the second officer Police Chief Leffert? Did he wear a yellow parka? Did the other cop hold Jack's arms behind his back? Did I stand there, a few yards away, holding my breath, caught like a fly in a web?

Was my heart beating like mad?

Did someone switch a floodlight on in one of the cars, setting the frozen raindrops on fire, blinding Jack, his glasses throwing back the reflections of the spotlight and the torches? Did the look on his face reveal nothing: not fear or even surprise, just resignation and maybe even relief, as if he'd expected this moment, as if he was prepared for it, as if he was glad to have it done and over with? As they escorted him to the car, did Leffert wave a flashlight at the crowd and say, *Mind giving us some more room here, folks?*—or something like that? In the hand not holding the flashlight, did he hold a pouch of some kind? Did the frozen rain make pinging sounds as it bounced off the car's hood and trunk? Did the car's red taillights turn the rain into blood? Did its tires make crunching sounds as it backed up into the gravel road with Jack in the rear seat? As it did, did I yell: *What are you arresting him for? It's not his fault! He didn't do anything!*—or words to that effect? Hearing me yell, did Chief Leffert step toward me, still holding the plastic pouch? Did he call me by my proper name, then by my nickname, saying: *Half—that what they call you?*

Did I nod? Did frozen rain bounce off the visor of the chief's cap? Did Zag nudge me in the ribs while I stared, not sure what to say? Did Chief Leffert extract something red and soft from the plastic pouch? Was the soft red object Gordon's Boy's Club cap?

Did Chief Leffert say: *Recognize this cap, Half?* Did I look down at it and say nothing? Did Chief Leffert repeat the question? *Is this your brother's baseball cap, son?* Did I correct him and say: *My stepbrother?* Did he say: *Was he wearing this when you last saw him?* Did I say nothing again? Did he say, *Answer me, son.*

Did I nod again? Did Chief Leffert wave to the car with Jack inside it? Did the car's windshield wipers go on? Did it drive off? Did I start blubbering? Seeing me blubber, did Chief Leffert put his hand on my shoulder? Did he say: *It's okay, son… It's okay…*

Was I already gone by then, swimming with Jack across Lost Lake, out to the island with the miniature stone lighthouse? Did I lay stretched out next to him on the smooth rock at its base, a blend of breeze and sunshine kissing the water droplets from my skin?

They kept Jack in a holding cell at the police station. He was allowed no visitors, whether to protect him from others or to protect others from him, I don't know. Both, probably.

To anyone who would listen I defended Jack. I told Chief Leffert we were friends, that Gordon and I had visited him regularly, that we'd all worked on the Thing in the Woods together. I told the police everything other than the two things that would have mattered most to them: 1) that Jack Thomas was an escaped German POW wanted by the FBI, and 2) that the body of Gordon Waple, my stepbrother, was somewhere at the bottom of Lost Lake.

Meanwhile I fended off accusations and insinuations by others. In the cafeteria line at school one day, I overheard Ronnie and Ricky Hermann, twin redheaded sophomores, referring to Jack as a murdering pervert—terms I myself might have applied to him back before I got to know him—saying that he should get the death sentence, that they should "fry his homo ass," better still, they should cut off a certain part of his anatomy and feed it to him for lunch.

"With or without mayonnaise?" Ricky Hermann wondered.

"Mustard," said Ronnie. "Definitely mustard!"

The Hermann twins were giggling when I brought my plastic lunch tray down hard, one by one, onto each of their red heads. For my trouble I got a black eye, a bloody nose, and three days' suspension, shortened to two by Principal Laurelton, who took pity on me, claiming I was still overcome with grief and therefore not in my right mind. Which is true, but probably not for the reasons he had in mind.

Three days after Jack's arrest, while hiking in the Dalton Estate, a father and his six-year-old son discovered Gordon's body jammed into the sluiceway at Lost Lake. When Chief Leffert phoned to inform my mother and stepfather, neither of them was home. When I asked him why he was calling, at first Leffert refused to say.

"If it has to do with Gordon," I said, "I wish you'd please tell me."

The police chief relented. "The town coroner has ruled it death by misadventure."

"Misadventure? What does that mean?"

"It means your stepbrother's death was an accident. He must have fallen through the ice."

"You mean Mr. Thomas is innocent?"

"That's all I'm free to say, son. Have your mom or your stepfather get hold of me as quickly as possible. Okay?"

Another person I defended Jack to was Belinda. She'd recently been cast as Guinevere in the Thespian Society's production of the then new musical *Camelot* and asked me to run her lines with her. Out at the football field we wiped snow off one of the bleachers and sat there, reading one of her scenes, with me doing King Arthur. We'd done the scene once and were about to do it again when she blurted:

"Your stepbrother's death was no accident, Leo."

"What do you mean? It was so an accident!" I shot back a little too forcefully. "That's not just my opinion. That's according to the police." I tried to sound matter-of-fact but couldn't hide the panicked defensiveness in my voice.

"I guess it's just a coincidence," Belinda said sarcastically.

"What?"

"That Jack Thomas happens to be insane."

"Says who?"

"He was a patient at Silver Hills. Did you know that?"

I shook my head, though by then I knew that and much more.

"A friend of my mom's told her, a psychiatric nurse who

works up there. She saw his picture in the paper and recognized him. She said he was there for over a month and the whole time he never said a word to anyone. If she'd known that, my mother wouldn't have rented the cottage to him. Not that it matters anymore. Soon the cottage won't be hers to rent anyway."

"What do you mean?"

"Uncle Baxter. He sold it."

"Sold? To who?"

"Some guy who wants to build a development up there."

"On Lost Lake? A development?"

"This developer guy's been trying to buy that property along with the rest of the old Dalton Estate for years. He finally offered Uncle Baxter enough so he gave in. Yeah, it sort of stinks, I know, but Mom got a nice piece of change out of the deal, enough to put me through college, so I guess I can't complain."

Just then I wasn't thinking about Fern Cottage. I was thinking about Jack, about what had happened to him mainly because of me.

"Jack's not crazy," I said quietly.

"Right," Belinda said. "And you're not a fool for thinking so."

Was it Belinda calling me a fool, or her calling Jack crazy? Or was it the thought of Lost Lake being destroyed by some developer? Or was it my own defensive rage—or a combination of all of those things? Anyway, my rage burst out of me:

"Your uncle's a greedy shithead, your mother's a witch, and you're a class-A bitch!"

We attacked each other, wrestling over the side of the bleachers and into a snowbank, where, by a clump of her flame-colored hair, I yanked Belinda's head back, exposing her snowy throat to the cloudy sky. She screamed. As I kept yanking and she kept screaming, both of us rolled across the frozen ground, until we found ourselves underneath the bleachers, with me on top of her. Before I knew it we were kissing each other, and doing much, much more, enough so that, when we emerged from under those bleachers a half hour or so later, neither of us was the same person, quite. Anyway I wasn't.

As we headed back toward the school where we'd left our bikes I made a feeble attempt to hold Belinda's hand.

"Please," she sneered, shaking me off like something sticky and wet.

❧

The next day after school I went to Fern Cottage. It had snowed again the night before. The roads were too icy to ride my bike so I walked. By the time I got there it was a quarter to five. There were fresh car tracks in the few patches of snow that remained along the gravel road. The cottage sat dark against the sky. No smoke rose from the chimney. I knocked on the green door. Did I really expect anyone to answer? I knocked again just in case. I tried the door then and found it locked. With my Swiss Army knife I jimmied it open.

"Jack?" I said, stepping inside, as if by some miracle he might be there. The echoes of my own voice answered me. I found the lamp with the long sooty snout and lit it.

It was no warmer inside the cottage than out. My breath made clouds in front of me. Otherwise, everything was pretty much as I'd last seen it. The table was there with the chess set on it and all the pieces set up for a game. Jack's bed was still tucked in the corner. The cabinet too was still there, the one with the drawer that held the book about swimming. Except for three pin insulators the bookshelves were empty. Jack's few books lay scattered all over, strewn across the stormy floorboards. I shivered. The stove was ice cold. I searched through the scattered books in search of the book about swimming. Could he have taken it with him? I didn't think so. He hadn't been carrying it when …

Then I saw it. On the counter by the sink. The card with the crude drawing of a man swimming jutted out of it. *For Hoff.* I pulled it out, opened the card, and read:

Remember: the deepest water you'll ever drown in is yourself.

I sat on the floor with the lamp burning, the blue floorboards turned to dusky waves. A lump formed and grew steadily in my throat. Tears tugged at the corners of my eyes. I didn't cry when my father died, or when Gordon died. Not really, not actual tears. But I did now. The tears broke loose and slid cool down my cheeks.

Were the tears for Jack? For Gordon? For me?

❧

When I next looked out the window, beyond the black silhouettes of tree trunks and branches an especially colorful sunset burned.

With the swimming book tucked under one arm, I left Fern Cottage and started down the gravel road. I'd taken less than twenty steps when I turned to see the cottage looking darker than ever, its green front door looking more black than green, its windowpanes aglow with the sunset's garish reflection.

What came over me then I'm not sure. I bent down, picked up a fistful of gravel and snow, and flung it, hard as I could, at the cottage's windows, smashing a pane. It felt good, so I did it again. For every windowpane I smashed, I cursed. I kept smashing windowpanes and cursing until there were no more windowpanes left to smash.

I'd started back down the gravel road again when a sudden camera-bulb-like flash lit up the twilit air. An explosion followed soon afterward. It in turn was followed by a thunder-like rumble rolling across the sky, an upside-down version of the rumbles that sounded before the ice broke on Lost Lake.

Weird, I said to myself as I kept walking toward those garish colors, this heat storm at the end of March. I assumed the colors were either an unusually show-offy sunset or the latest hat factory fire. They painted the whole Eastern sky in oranges and reds.

❧

It wasn't a sunset or a hat factory fire. It was Virgil Zeno's carpentry shed burning.

By the time I got there a dozen fire trucks had already converged on the scene. The flames had already consumed most of the building's upper half, including the large billboard with the extraterrestrial greeting on the roof and the colossal white cross next to it. As it settled into the conflagration like the stern flag of a sinking ship the cross's many floodlights kept burning.

By the time the last flames were extinguished dawn had broken. Among the smoldering ruins no trace remained of Virgil's secret back room or the wooden flying saucer that occupied it. As for Virgil Zeno, he was never seen or heard from again.

The date was March 29th, 1964.

Easter Sunday.

Part 11

The Flood

Gordon's funeral was on a Wednesday, a cherry pipe day, according to my stepfather's pipe-smoking schedule, though he didn't smoke at the funeral. That morning it poured. As Reverend Stumpf delivered the homily my stepfather held my hand, the one not holding an umbrella. As the reverend went on speaking his grip grew stronger and stronger, until I thought he'd crush my hand. Still, I didn't pull my hand away or cry out. I'd have let my stepfather break every bone in it if it had come to that. It was the least I deserved.

Through the whole funeral I didn't shed a tear. Afterward, though, with my umbrella folded, as I climbed into my stepfather's Buick, feeling his hand as he placed it gently on my shoulder, I suddenly lost it and collapsed in a bawling heap into a puddle next to the car. My mother nodded to my stepfather, who let me sit up front. As he drove us home, with me still sobbing, Walter Waple did something he'd never done before: he steered his Buick with one hand only, the other hand stroking my shoulder.

The next morning, April 7, 1964, the following story appeared on the front page of the *Danville News-Times*:

ESCAPED POW CAPTURED

HATTERTOWN (AP). The man who called himself Jack Thomas, and who several weeks ago was arrested and questioned in the disappearance of Gordon Waple, the mentally retarded son of a local hat merchant, who went missing and was later discovered to have drowned, turns out to have been German army soldier Johann Verhoff, sought by the FBI for more than 18 years.

Verhoff, 42, escaped in August of 1945 from POW Camp Henderson in Bernadotte, Illinois, where, for 23 months—from October of 1943, when he'd been captured in North Africa while part of a Panzer division on its retreat to Tunisia—he had been POW# 81G-9385.

Verhoff's escape coincided with the end of the war and with his imminent release from the camp. It is conjectured that the motive for his escape was to avoid repatriation to his homeland. A champion swimmer and high-diver, Verhoff had been training for the 1940 Summer Olympics in Tokyo when the war erupted.

Verhoff's escape route took him across the country, from the Pacific Northwest, where he worked as a lumberjack, and where he broke his leg in a fall while topping a tree, to Chicago, where he was employed by a slaughterhouse as a "ham-skinner," and then to the Northeast, where he worked as head lifeguard at a resort lodge in the Adirondacks, and where he met and married antiquarian book dealer Margaret Chapel.

After suspicions caught up with him at the lodge, Verhoff fled to New Haven, Connecticut, and from there to Hattertown by way of Newbury, where he was briefly a patient at the Silver Hills State Psychiatric Hospital.

It remains unclear whether the statute of limitations may have run out on prosecution for Verhoff's case, or whether it applies to escaped POWs. Since he was properly admitted into the United States as a POW, Verhoff cannot be charged with illegal entry. When questioned, a spokesman for the FBI would say only that Verhoff had been turned over to the Immigration and Naturalization Service.

As a POW, Verhoff made 80¢ a day working for local farmers, money that would eventually help him in his escape. According to the FBI spokesman, he arrived at his pseudonym, Jack Thomas, after hopping a freight boxcar packed with bags of Jack Frost sugar. His last name, Thomas, he took from the well-known baker of English muffins.

❧

In the days, weeks, and months following Gordon's funeral, my stepfather never said a word about his lost son. He went on about his routine, eating his breakfast of Melba toast and tea, reading the paper, working at his failing hat store, as though nothing out of the ordinary had happened, let alone a personal tragedy of enormous magnitude, let alone losing his one and only child. I wondered if he'd behaved similarly after his first wife committed suicide.

Every so often, though, in the middle of the night, I would wake up to creaking sounds coming from somewhere downstairs. One rainy night I investigated to find my stepfather sitting in his rocking chair in the dark parlor, the faint orange glow from the bowl of his pipe when he puffed it the only light in the room.

"Is everything okay?" I asked him.

"Sure, sport. Fine, just fine. Just sitting here listening to the rain. Always relaxes me, the sound of raindrops falling. I wonder why that is? Unruffles the feathers, as it were."

"I'm getting a glass of water. Would you like one?"

"Sure. Wet the ol' whistle. Make mine a double!"

It was the closest thing my stepfather and I had ever had to an intimate conversation.

Of all the dumb ideas religions have come up with, hell is by far the dumbest. Who needs a pitchfork-wielding devil slaving over subterranean ovens in which the damned are roasted perpetually when hell can be had right here on earth, its fires fueled by evil deeds, fanned by winds of guilt, remorse, and regret? For three months I lived in that earthly purgatory.

Then something broke in me.

My mother was in the parlor watching TV. The latest episode of *The Twilight Zone* was on, about a hit-and-run driver haunted by his Ford Fairlane—the car he committed his crime in. The car wakes him up in the middle of the night, its headlights flashing, its horn blaring, pushing him deeper and deeper into his guilt, until finally it drives him to the police station to turn himself in. With the episode over, while the credits rolled, with tears in my eyes I threw myself at my mother on her couch, blubbering:

"I killed Gordy! It was all my fault!"

"What? Don't be silly, Leo!"

"I'm not! It's true!"

"You have no reason to blame yourself, Leo," she said, stroking my head. "None at all. It was an accident."

"But it wasn't!"

"Leo, please. Stop talking that way!"

I wanted to say more, to confess everything, to explain to my mother and the world how in the space of less than a week I'd lost the two most important people in my life, and that it had all or mostly been my fault, that I was an irresponsible foolish worthless selfish liar who didn't deserve to partake of even the most ordinary, earthbound things, let alone something of the infinite. All I managed to say was:

"It wasn't! It wasn't!"

"Oh, Leo…" my mother said and went on stroking my head.

The second Wednesday in April the strike at the Caxton-Dumont Hat Works finally came to an end—not with a new contract for the workers, but with the announcement that the factory would be terminating operations and shutting its doors for good.

Winter was over. All but a few stubborn clumps of snow had melted. May showers would finish the job.

We call our planet Earth, but if we'd had our wits about us we would have named her Water. We're a planet of water: a molten spinning globe slathered with heaving, swaying, crashing, rolling, sloshing oceans, streaked with rivers, splotched with alligator-infested bayous, daubed with mosquito-dazzled swamps, smeared with muddy marshes, basted with brackish bogs, bays, and tidal basins, to say nothing of canals, ponds, puddles, reservoirs, lagoons, creeks, and lakes. Since the first mammals shed their gills, eons have elapsed. Yet some part of us never left the water, or it never left us. To remind us of this fact, every so often the earth's waters gather for their version of a family reunion. We call those gatherings *floods*.

The Flood of '64 was the worst to visit The Nutmeg State since the fabled Hurricane of '38, bad enough to make some wonder if, like the Flood of Genesis, it was an act of divine retribution.

I was sitting alone on Cheese Hill, idly tossing cheese bombs down at the reject shed roof of the newly defunct Caxton-Dumont plant, when a black mountain-like cloud loomed up in the southeastern sky. As the mountain rolled closer a stiff breeze kicked up, exposing the pale undersides of the leaves of a nearby elm tree and making me shiver. Except for the sound of the wind, things went suddenly, eerily quiet then. The air around me turned a queer blue-gray shade, like those wide floor planks in Fern Cottage. I smelled the tangy odor of ozone, a short circuit smell. That's when I ran for it.

❧

The first of the two storm systems drew its strength from the waters off Long Island Sound, sucking schools of bass, sturgeon, and cod from shallows, carrying them southwest past the beaches at Mystic and Lordship before veering sharply inland between Stanford and Cos Cob.

The winds ripped off store awnings. They rattled shop windows, blew the lids off garbage cans, knocked street signs off their posts, uprooted shrubbery, privet hedges, and picket fences. For twenty-four hours there was only the wind.

Then the rain came, falling at five inches per hour. It took less than six hours for the Brim River to breach its banks, turning Felt Street into a muddy torrent navigated by perplexed-looking drivers, their Fords, Chevys, and Plymouths turned into amphibious launches. Children frolicked in mud-puddles, ignoring their parents' frantic pleas to remove to higher ground. The same parents and children arrived home later that day to find frogs swimming in milk boxes, snakes curled up in flowerpots, and lily pads clinging to the soles of their shoes and sneakers.

The second of the two storm systems had yet to arrive.

Like those of most Highlanders, my stepfather's Crown Boulevard house perched high above the floodplain, threatened only by high winds and lightning. Given that, reason dictated that along with the rest of us Walter J. Waple should stay there until the storm blew over.

But when it came to hats Walter Waple was anything but reasonable. As the floodwaters rose, my stepfather donned his yellow Mackintosh and galoshes. With a plastic bonnet stretched over his fedora he stepped out into the watery world.

Gone to store, said the handwritten note he left behind for us on the breakfast nook table. As my mother studied it with a dully abstracted look on her face, I sat at the end of the bench, tugging on my own galoshes.

"And just where do you think *you're* going?" my mother asked.

"To help Mr. Waple!"

"You pick now of all times to be a decent stepson?"

I flipped the rain parka's hood over my head.

"You are *not* going out in this crazy weather, Leo Napoli. Do you hear me? You are staying right here inside this house with your mother. Understood?"

I yanked up my zipper.

"Take off that raincoat this instant!" she ordered.

But I was already headed out the door.

❧

Roads, houses, trees, sky, and clouds, all had merged into a swirling wet mass of gray and brown, as if seen through a waterlogged kaleidoscope. The wind smelled of dead fish. I pedaled my bicycle into town, the gusts so strong at times I had trouble steering. By then the police had barricaded the flooded downtown streets. To get to my stepfather's hat store I had to cut through the alleyway between the movie theater and Kirby's hardware store. Muddy torrents threatened to drag the wheels of my bicycle out from under me. When the water rose to my calves I gave up and ditched the bike in the alley.

By the time I got to my stepfather's store, water was lapping at the bricks under both display windows. I found my stepfather, his rolled trouser-bottoms soaked, sucking the cold stem of his brier pipe—his Thursday pipe, though it was a Friday—shifting inventory to higher shelves. By then the store's basement storage room was completely submerged. Rainbow-tinged water covered the maroon carpeting on which my stepfather had arranged boxed hats in staggered, staggering piles.

Working side by side, my stepfather and I unboxed hats and jamming them onto higher shelves. Meanwhile the oil-stained bog at our feet deepened steadily, licking the tops of our galoshes. It wasn't long before it had climbed to the glass knobs of the lower display cabinets. By then the higher shelves were jam-packed with hats, with dozens of boxed refugees still awaiting rescue on the floor down below. Those on the bottom were already partly submerged in flood-gunk, the hats inside them undoubtedly destroyed.

I heard a sharp tapping noise and turned to see Mr. Mortimer, owner of Mortimer Jewelers four stores down, rapping on the window with a coin. Through the rain-streaked glass I saw his distraught mouth form the words *Get the hell out of there!* before he turned and sloshed away in hip-waders.

I faced my stepfather who stood on an aluminum stepladder, its lowest rung now mere inches above the rising water. As he held a swaying pile of boxed hats, for which he had found no space on the shelves, his eyes bore the look of a chess champion who, though intellectually he grasps that his king is doomed, has yet to grasp it emotionally. In the greasy reflecting pool that had been the carpeted floor, a medley of hats nosed and thumped each other.

"We've got to get out of here!" I said to him. "Don't you see? It's hopeless! There's nothing more to be done!"

Just then the overloaded shelf we had been piling stock onto gave way, sending a dozen Silver Beaver XXX homburgs (priced at $10.99 each—$83.72 in today's money) cascading down into the muck. My stepfather stood frozen on the stepladder, balancing a totem pole of stacked hats, gazing down at the disaster.

"Go on ahead, sport," he said. "I'll be done in a jiff, if you will."

"But it's *hopeless!*" I said. (Jack: *"Nussing iss owblez."*)

"Just as soon as I get these last few hats shelved…"

"Will you forget the damn hats?"

"Sport, these are triple-X beaver. Too good to drown, as it were. If I can make just a bit more room for them up here…if I can just…make a bit more…just a bit…"

A vacant look took hold of my stepfather's face. His unlit pipe fell from his lips to land with a *plonk* in the murky water below, which by then lapped at the ladder's third lowest rung. As if only just realizing his predicament, he took one cautious step down the ladder, then another. Then, as if answering a call, with the stacked hats still balanced in the crook of his arm, he aimed his gaze through the right-hand display window, out at the flooded street, though his pupils seemed to be focused on something farther away.

"Upon my word…" he said.

As he kept staring, between ladder rungs the toe of my stepfather's left galosh groped blindly for a few moments. Then stepladder, stepfather, and hats all tumbled down. I cried:

"Dad!"

I'd never called him that before, ever.

"Dad! Dad!"

I said it again and again, as if along with all his unwanted gifts I'd stored away all those "dads" in some dark closet.

"Dad! Dad!"

I put an arm under and turned him over. His top front tooth was chipped, his upper lip split and bleeding. A trickle of bright red blood fanned out into the muddy water.

"Dad!"

While stroking my stepfather's head I looked helplessly around. Through the display window, whose broken neon sign proclaimed a partnership that was never to be, I watched a cop in a yellow rain slicker yell at a truck driver who'd breached the barricades.

With my stepfather's head propped onto a hatbox, I stood up. Against the weight of rushing water I managed to heave the front door open and staggered out into what had been the town's main thoroughfare but was now a muddy canal. Through brown, murky, knee-high waves I splashed toward the cop, crying:

"My dad! Something's happened to my dad!"

By rescue boat my stepfather was taken to the Methodist church, which occupied a rise at the edge of the flood plain. On the front steps of the church I sat beside him, stroking his hatless head, listening to his shallow breaths as I waited for one of two army helicopters that were making the rounds to see us and fly him to Danville Hospital. Finally—in a monsoon of rotor wash—a helicopter arrived. Through a megaphone the guardsman straddling its opened doorway informed me and everyone else in earshot that Governor Rubicoff had declared a state of emergency. Martial law had been imposed. The flood area was now officially off-limits to all. Looters would be shot on sight.

"Get yourself to high ground, son," the guardsman yelled down after raising my stepfather by harness up into the chopper.

"Can't I come with you?" I yelled back.

The guardsman shook his head. "No room. Your dad will be fine. Now shag your ass out of here!"

I watched the helicopter flutter away, a black hornet buzzing high above the church steeple.

By then the floodwaters were lapping at the church's lowest steps. I was about to obey the guardsman's orders when—out from behind the rectory—a skiff appeared, manned not by national guardsmen or by a fire & rescue team, but by the Back Shop Boys.

The skiff's aluminum hull was badly dinged and battered. Using a plank as a tiller, Zag steered the craft, while Skunky and Victor manned one oar each. The bilge was piled with cases of Pepsi-Cola and Seven-Up, loaves of Wonder bread, and gallon-jugs filled with what I guessed was water. All the skiff's crewmembers wore bright paper party hats. In the forepeak, next to the car battery that apparently powered it, a Citizen's Band radio spluttered.

Victor blew a party blowout.

"Ahoy, matey!" he said.

"What's all this?" I asked.

"A rescue party," said Skunky. "What does it look like?"

"Who have you rescued?"

"No one yet," said Victor. "But the day is still young!"

"Martial law's been declared," I informed them.

"We heard." Zag pointed to the radio.

"Martial Dillon! *Gunsmoke!*" Victor said. Drawing imaginary six-shooters, in the half-swamped skiff he and Skunky shot each other dead.

"What brings you to these cheery surroundings?" Zag asked.

I filled him in about my stepfather.

Zag nodded. "Need a lift?"

"You can be our first rescue victim!" said Skunky, bailing.

"Climb aboard!" Victor said.

"Thanks, but I'll take my chances on not-so-dry land."

Another helicopter fluttered overhead. A loudspeaker blared: "Clear the area! Clear the area!" Through the CB radio a panicked, scratchy voice reported that the reservoir dam had been breached.

"The dogs!" said Zag.

By the time we got to the pound the floodwaters were already raging over the dam. A dozen men stood atop a rise overlooking it. Nearby a hook and ladder and a national guard truck were parked. Judging by the anxiety engraved on the men's faces, we guessed that the dam wouldn't hold for much longer.

In the pound we found Sergeant Pomeroy slumped over his desk on which a Wild Turkey fifth rolled, toppled and empty. Water licked the toes of his orange brogans. A red comet of blood streaked across the top of his desk. I lifted the sergeant's head, exposing a gash on his brow. He must have sliced it open on the desk's edge when he passed out.

Shouting, "Every dog for himself!" Zap opened all forty kennel cages. Two-dozen canine POWs yapped and howled their way into the flooded world. Meanwhile I tried to rouse the sergeant, shouting into his ear, slapping his ham-shank cheeks, splashing paper cups of ice water from the Crystal Rock dispenser on his face. Having failed to revive him, we dragged him out to the canine van only to find that it wouldn't start. We had to get him to higher ground.

The pound phone was dead. We tried the CB.

"Mayday! Mayday! *Help!*"

A flurry of static answered.

We ran up the hill to the nearest house, a yellow Cape Cod with a Volkswagen Beetle parked under a lean-to alongside it. We knocked. A girl of five or six answered. She gazed at us, her round blue eyes deepening with confusion as we explained our predicament to her, or tried to. Soon her mother appeared, frazzled and ready to defend herself and her daughter to the death in a chiffon housecoat and fluffy pink slippers. We asked if we could borrow her car.

She looked at us like we were crazy.

"How old are you?" she wanted to know.

"Fourteen," Zag answered for us. "But I know how to drive!"

"And I know how to say you are out of your minds!"

"It's an emergency!" Skunky told her.

"Sergeant Pomeroy's passed out!" Victor explained.

"What else is new?" the woman asked.

"Any minute now, lady, the dam's gonna burst," Zag said. "We all need to get out of here, pronto!"

"Sure," said the woman, rolling her eyes.

By the sleeve of her housecoat Zag yanked her onto her stoop and pointed up at the cluster of emergency vehicles gathered on the rise next to the dam. "You and your daughter and everyone else here need to get to higher ground, now!"

With the little girl on Victor's lap in the passenger seat, her mother (an oilskin flung over her housecoat) at the wheel, and Pomeroy jammed into the back seat between Skunky and me, we rode in the Volkswagen to the same hospital where they'd taken my stepfather. While Zag checked Sergeant Pomeroy in, I went off to look for him. I found him stretched out on a gurney in a corridor outside the emergency room. My mother sat in a chair near to him.

"I swear," she said when she saw me, "I'd beat the daylights out of you, only I don't want to give these poor doctors more work to do."

I leaned over my stepfather. He looked like he was sleeping. His face was white. They had stitched together his upper lip. Against his pale skin the sutures looked extra black. I held his hand.

"Do they know what's wrong with him?" I asked.

"The doctor says he had a stroke. That's when the blood—"

"I know what a stroke is, Mom."

"Do you, now, smartypants? Answer me this, Mr. Einstein: how is it that a complete fool like you who doesn't even know to keep out of a hurricane knows so darn much?"

Before I could answer she pulled me into a hug so fierce I couldn't breathe.

At two o'clock in the morning the dam gave way. The resulting deluge tore the green iron bridge from its moorings and swept it two hundred yards downstream, where it lodged at a bend in the river. Six tons of flotsam, including two cars, a sofa, and a refrigerator, joined the bridge, forming an impromptu dam that National Guardsmen, in cooperation with the Highway Department, blew up.

The army flew in two more helicopters to pluck stragglers from rooftops. By then the middle and high school gymnasiums, which had been converted into emergency shelters, were both filled to capacity. The Red Cross provided food, medicine, and first aid.

Seven days after the rains had begun, the floodwaters subsided. As the pressure from the water eased off, a gas main between the Doughboy Diner and the bridge's moorings exploded. The fire burned all through the night and into the dawn, when fire crews managed to extinguish it. The same morning a three-member task force—a National Guardsman, a police officer, and an army corpsman—were assessing the damage to another exposed gas main in a fifteen-foot motorboat, when the vibrations from the boat's outboard engine blew out its stern, casting all three task force members into the floodwaters. The police officer and the guardsman both drowned.

Later that same day a mother of four was crushed to death when a hat factory smokestack collapsed, the ground supporting it having been weakened by all the rain. Six more deaths—including that of Mr. Kirby, owner of Hattertown

Hardware, who suffered a heart attack—brought the final death toll to nine.

In the weeks following the flood, acting under the advice of the U.S. Army Corps of Engineers, as a precautionary measure, the town selectman ordered all ten remaining hat factory chimneys imploded. Over as many days the sole remnants of Hattertown's once-glorious past, each rigged with a quarter ton of dynamite, were imploded.

Along with others who gathered to witness the spectacle, I watched them settle one by one into clouds of ruddy dust.

Part 12

The Last of the Back Shop Boys

The summer after the flood the gypsy moths came. Actually they had been there all along, incubating in their ugly brown cocoons. Since late spring I had noticed their lampshade-like tents clinging to the branches just as the trees were starting to bud. As the temperature rose the tents burst open, releasing hundreds of tiny inchworms no larger than the plastic things on the ends of shoelaces (which, as any trivia-minded person knows, are called *aglets).* The worms quickly grew into hairy caterpillars, eating their way from tree to tree, turning green hills gray and summer itself into a muggy, snowless winter. On clear nights without a cloud in the sky the worms' droppings made a sound like falling rain.

My stepfather's stroke had left most of his left side paralyzed, including the muscles on that side of his face, which drooped from his jaw and cheekbones like mozzarella from a slice of pizza. When he did speak, it was with great effort and a pronounced slur. Needless to say he had to give up the store. Mostly he sat in his rocking chair in the parlor, puffing his unlit pipe, staring off into space, or at the television set.

Over time more strokes did more damage. When my stepfather couldn't feed himself anymore, that task fell mostly to me. I'd put a bib on him, pull up a chair, and spoon-feed him mashed potatoes, mushroom soup, and tapioca pudding. Between spoonfuls I would wipe his pale lips from which the following four utterances alone escaped: "If you will… As it were… So to speak… Upon my word…"

I was glad to feed my stepfather, glad to be able to do anything to atone, if only slightly, for the miserable way I'd treated him.

The way a stroke victim's blood vessels seal themselves off to prevent further damage, I sealed myself off from people around me. When school started again that September, I kept to myself as much as possible with one exception: I signed up for the swim team. Swimming, that least social of all sports. Even if I'd wanted to, it would have been hard to socialize with my face in the water.

When not half under water, I swam in a deep ice-cold lake of my own aloofness. On rare occasions when other people's eyes met mine, the look in mine said, "Back off!" or something to that effect. Questioned on different occasions by worried parents, teachers, and my guidance counselor as to my "withdrawn" behavior, I shrugged off their concerns and said I was fine.

The one time I got together with the Back Shop Boys we squabbled. Using a pair of old boxing gloves that, according to Victor, his father had worn when he pounded Rocky Graziano (or was it Marciano?) to a ninth-round technical knockout, we sparred in the Szentgyorgyi garage, the same one under which Mr. Szentgyorgyi supposedly built a fallout shelter, and that also housed his father's XKE Jaguar—which, as usual, was in the shop for repairs (the car parked in the Szentgyorgyi driveway was a Corvair).

The boxing gloves hung by their laces from a rusty nail driven into a rafter. Victor being too fat to climb ladders, I got them down for us. Zag and I put on one glove apiece and sparred there in the Szentgyorgyi garage, amid dust motes and oil stains, with Skunky timing the rounds on his cereal box premium Huckleberry Hound wristwatch. Like a pair of fencers, while jabbing each other above the waist and below the neck, we kept our ungloved hands tucked behind our backs. The parched decrepit gloves lacerated our forearms.

We'd been boxing for less than two minutes when a stray uppercut of mine grazed Zag's jaw. Off went Zag's one glove, out came bare knuckles. As Zag turned my head into a punching bag Victor laughed; he couldn't help it. *You fat tub of shit,* I thought as Zag punched me. *You goddamn fat miserable tub!*

When Zag had finished with me I got up, grabbed both of our boxing gloves, ran outside and across the yard to the

Szentgyorgyi's open septic pond, and tossed them in. Then I stood there, panting, watching them float among turds and toilet paper.

❧

After that the Back Shop Boys and I got together one last time. I needed a favor from them.

We rode our bikes to the Dalton Estate, where I led the others to the Thing in the Woods. By then the junk sculptures had been thoroughly vandalized, their rusty arms and chain conveyor spines broken, their hat-block heads split open. Others had been knocked over and heaved into the flooded drift. To every one of the hundreds of glass insulators lining the mine's walls, someone had taken a hammer or something equally destructive.

The gantry was still where we'd left it. Though they had rotted a bit, the ropes still held. It took some doing, but with Victor—who'd lost a lot of weight recently but still weighed more than any of us—tailing on and the rest of us hauling, we lifted the obelisk out of the flooded drift and onto the pedestal.

As we stood admiring our handiwork, wiping sweat from our brows, Skunky said:

"I still don't get it. What's the point?"

"Things unknown and unknowable," I said under my breath.

"Huh?" said Victor.

"There is no point," said Zag. "That's the point."

Skunky spat into the drift.

That was the last time we all got together.

❧

But that still wasn't the real end of the Back Shop Boys. The real end came toward the end of senior year, when Victor told me that his father had been an engineer on the Hartford & New Haven Line. This was presumably after singlehandedly winning World War II and knocking out Rocky Graziano/Marciano.

"Dad engineered the last of the old steam locomotives," he explained proudly. "The day his foreman told him they were switching to diesel, he took off his striped engineer's cap, spit a wad of tobacco juice into the ballast, and said, 'In that case, Mr. Railroad Foreman, I quit!'"

Before quitting, however, according to Victor, Mr. Szentgyorgyi absconded with *seven* locomotives. One by one under cover of darkness he made off with them to a secret location in the hills of Southern Vermont. Having learned of Mr. Szentgyorgyi's courageous deed, other engineers in all forty-nine contingent states appropriated their own condemned locomotives and drove them surreptitiously to the same secret Vermont location.

"All Dad had to do then was wait seven years for the statute of limitations to run out," Victor explained. "Which it has. Now he's free and clear to line up investors and raise capital. Soon as he does, he'll announce the opening of the greatest railroad museum in the whole world. 'Steamtown, USA,' is what he's gonna call it."

When he told this latest lie, Victor and I were standing side by side before a bank of urinals in a high school lavatory, emptying our bladders between classes. On the tiled white wall in front of us, in black Magic marker someone had scrawled a horizontal line. Above the line they had written, *If you can piss above this line, the Hattertown volunteer fire dept. wants you.*

"Can I ask you something, Victor?" I said, peeing.

He looked at me.

"Why are you such a goddamn liar?"

In my peripheral vision, I saw Victor's face drop. Right away I regretted my remark. I waited for him to say something—anything—to try and wriggle out of the question I'd thrown over him like a net over a butterfly, or just lie to me more and make me feel a little less cruel, a little less heartless. Instead he stood there looking down into the urinal, licking his lips, holding his dick. And that's where I left him.

The next day while I was at my school locker Zag walked up to me.

"What did you say to Victor?" He clenched and unclenched

his fists. His lips drew back up against his teeth.

"I called him a liar," I said.

"Why did you do that? You shouldn't have done that. You of all fucking people." The way he said it, it was like I'd wiped out a sandcastle we'd spent our whole lives building together. Zag didn't even wait for an answer. He didn't even bother to punch me, he was so disgusted. He walked away, shaking his head.

That was the real end of the Back Shop Boys.

On the third anniversary of President Kennedy's assassination, my stepfather died, a coincidence that, had he been alive to experience it, would have appalled Walter Waple. A pine casket was all that my mother could afford, her second husband having left her in debt to the tune of over $25,000 dollars. We buried him in the cemetery at Gravity Hill, the one where Dwight Riddell bashed open his skull.

The Comformator—my stepfather's invention that was supposed to revolutionize the hatting industry while making him and us, his family, rich—ruined us. Having already taken him to the cleaners for thousands of dollars, Harvey Gilmore, my stepfather's business partner and patent attorney, fleeced him further by filing a claim for patent infringement against the American Totalizer Corporation, the firm to which he'd leased the rights to the invention, so he claimed. According to the complaint, ATC underhanded the Comformator's "unique, patented technology" to another firm, which underhanded it to a third company. A court order was issued; a private investigator was put on retainer. In the end nothing was proven—at a cost of $10,000 dollars in legal and detective fees. Guess who the detective turned out to be? Harvey Gilmore, dba Allied Investigation Services, LTD. (Last reports had Mr. Gilmore in Venezuela by way of Las Vegas and Tijuana.)

The bank having finally foreclosed on the Crown Heights house, we moved into a one-bedroom apartment over the Top Hat Bakery, a few doors down from what used to be Waple & Son Hats. For the next six months, my mother and I were greeted each morning by the heady odor of baking pumpernickel bread wafting up through the floorboards. The smell triggered my mother's migraines; it didn't sit well with me, either. After that, Mom found us an even smaller apartment, this one over a beauty parlor. The smell of scorched hair was no big improvement over that of baking pumpernickel, but by then my mother and I were too worn out to care.

Half the male graduating class of '68 were drafted and sent overseas. Victor received his order for induction soon after he graduated, by which time he and his family had relocated to Bellows Falls, Vermont. By then Zag had already enlisted in the Marine Corps. Skunky joined the army, where (big surprise) he trained as a demolitions expert. Since he was a quaker, Dwight Riddell applied for and was granted conscientious objector status.

As for Belinda Dalton, it would take me the next decade to discover that more often than not the people you expect most from in high school turn out to be the biggest under-achievers. I had her pegged as a famous poet or actress, or maybe a top-notch magazine or newspaper editor. She'd go to Harvard or Yale or maybe Princeton. Inexplicably, she never went to college; she never left Hattertown. Having spent most of junior and senior year abusing sex first, then alcohol, and finally various drugs, Belinda turned to the biggest and most addictive drug of all: religion. She became a Jehovah's Witness and married…not Dwight Riddell (who wound up marrying a florist ten years older than he), but Wesley Conklin, the accordion player, whom she succeeded in converting.

Thanks to my missing middle finger, I was permanently 4-F ("unqualified for military service"), which didn't stop me from putting myself at the mercy of Uncle Sam.

It is said that among certain primitive tribes the first-born male is removed from his parents at birth and taken up into the mountains where he's put in the care of a shaman. For the next eighteen years his experience of the world is limited to the inside of the shaman's hut, veiled in darkness, lit only by the stars or the moon. On the dawn of his eighteenth birthday the shaman throws open the hut door. Sunlight spills in, blinding the boy. Leading him by the hand, the shaman guides him through the jungle to a clearing where he turns to the boy and says, "The time has come for you to see the world."

On the dawn of my eighteenth birthday the door to my shaman's hut burst open. In the blinding daze that followed, I struck upon the monumentally dumb idea of enlisting in the United States Air Force. I did so on the assumption that it would put me on the quickest path to my dream of becoming an astronaut. Little did I know that the same missing finger that had spared me from the draft meant that I could perform only limited military duties, and only in times of war. The war presented no problem; we had one of those. As for "limited duties," roughly translated it meant: *don't even dream about flying.*

Zag had been in Vietnam for ninety-six days when the sergeant leading his platoon through a jungle patrol was blown into the air by a homemade mine detonated by a Vietcong soldier lying in wait. The sergeant was killed instantly. The soldier in front of him got shrapnel in his thighs. Zag's left foot—the same foot his father lost to a combination of gangrene and #4 lead shot—was blown off at the top of his boot and had to be amputated. A month later, at the Battle of Hill 723, Victor's number came up. He was awarded a posthumous Bronze Star.

The Air Force having granted my request for a bereavement leave (the army denied Skunky's request for a similar leave), in my mother's Rambler American, with Zag riding in the passenger seat next to me, I drove us to Victor's wake, which took place at the Presbyterian Church in Bellows Falls. And though Mr. Szentgyorgyi was there for his son's graveside sermon, afterward, at the reception held in the Szentgyorgyi home, among mourners and cold cuts, Mr. Szentgyorgyi was nowhere to be seen.

"Bet I know where he is," Zag said to me with a sly look.

Back in my mother's Rambler, Zag directed me down a series of increasingly small roads to a tree-lined curve along an embankment, where he had me pull over. I got out and stood there. All I saw was a bunch of scraggly pine trees overlooking a gulley.

"What am I looking at? There's nothing here!"

"Ye of little faith..." said Zag.

He indicated that I should step through the trees.

With a sigh, shaking my head, I made my way between pine trees and scrambled down the steep embankment. That's when I saw them, soaking in the bright sunlight of a cloudless October day: five, six, eight, a dozen—more—broad-chested steam locomotives, all cinnamon-dusted with rust. Like a desert nomad intent on a mirage, tripping over rails and ties, I hurried toward them. Soon I found myself alone among those engines, a sole human interloper among rusting dinosaurs.

Or so I thought until I noticed a pair of pinstriped legs jutting out from under a set of locomotive wheels. Wearing old-fashioned railroad overalls and holding a long-stemmed oilcan, Mr. Szentgyorgyi emerged.

"Hello, Leo," he said, wiping himself.

"What are you doing?"

"Oh." Mr. Szentgyorgyi shrugged. "I couldn't take any more condolences."

"No, I meant—?" I pointed to the oilcan.

"Oh, *this?*" He held the oilcan up. "Heck, it's all I can do to keep these babies from rusting solid."

I underwent basic training at Chanute Air Force Base, near Rantoul, Illinois, a two-and-a-half-hour drive from where Jack had been a POW. From there I was transferred to Tyndall AFB in Florida. On my arrival my sergeant presented me with the weapon with which I was to defend my country against all enemies foreign and domestic: a paintbrush, three-inch square trim. The "ammunition," a can of gray latex paint, was in the supply hut next to the ladder.

Despite having my wings clipped, I still managed to defy gravity. My space capsule was the twelfth-floor balcony of the high-rise apartment building that was our air force dorm. On the July 20th, 1969 at 4:17 p.m. Eastern Standard Time, at a moon landing party there, by a combination of nine fingers, as many fingers of bourbon, and pure dumb luck, I dangled from that balcony. You never saw a party clear out so fast. The following morning, having puked my guts along a mile-long stretch of white sand beach, as I lay throbbing in my barracks, an inner voice that might have been God's (though it sounded a lot like my dad), said, "Do that again, son, and you'll have your answers."

It was in that jungle of beaches and strip malls that I met my future wife, Bernadette Gomek, a twenty-five-year-old drug rehab nurse from Greta Falls, Montana. In May of '75 she and I made it legal. Three years after we married, I resigned my Air Force commission. A year later Bernie gave birth to our first and only child, a boy. Guess what we named him?

Though as you know by now I've never been a religious person, still, I think Jesus had a few very good suggestions, chief among them: when someone slaps your cheek "turn the other one to him also." It's called forgiveness and it applies equally when you've slapped your own cheek.

When a person does something wrong in life they have a choice: they can live with it, or they can not live at all. Having made the first choice you learn to forgive yourself, since you can't go on otherwise. You live with your shame and guilt the way other people live with psoriasis and tinnitus and ulcers and other ailments invisible to others. Meanwhile you keep a sharp eye out for redemptive opportunities: tipping generously, smiling at waiters and shop clerks, helping blind people across streets, performing other random acts of kindness. To the cashier who hands you your receipt at the supermarket and the high school senior bagging groceries there, say, "Have a nice day," and mean it. Understand that others have their own reasons for feeling remorseful or guilty, their own sorrows and secrets and sins burrowing like scabies under their skins. Forgive them, one and all. It may be a cliché, but it also happens to be true: forgiveness begins at home.

Over time the guilt that I'd harbored over my role in Gordon's death and Jack's capture dissolved, as did my sense of disappointment: in my life and with myself. Eventually the future started looking bright again. By then, of course, it was more my son's future than my own, but still, it would do.

As for Jack, the day would soon dawn when there would be no one left to remember World War II, let alone that there had been over 400,000 German POWs in the United States, let alone that a handful of them managed to escape for more than just a few days or weeks. By the time I met Jack, the rest of that handful of prisoners had long since been captured and sent back to wherever they were from. Which, I guessed, is what happened to Jack. He'd been sent back to what had been his country but was now locked away behind the Iron Curtain and may as well have been the dark side of the moon.

Still, I did my best to learn what happened to him. I wrote the FBI, who referred me to the State Department, whose offices informed me that they only investigated missing persons cases involving US citizens and suggested that I contact what was then called Immigration and Naturalization Services. This I did, only to discover that in early May of 1963 one Johann Verhoff, also known as "Jack Thomas," was deported to the German Democratic Republic, to Berlin in the Soviet Zone. No further information was available.

Since the United States government didn't recognize the GDR, we had no embassy there. Instead there was something called the "U.S. Mission Berlin" (USBER). They directed me to the Wehrmacht Information Office for War Losses and Prisoners of War (WASt) which, since its creation in 1939, has kept records on every German soldier during World War II, but they were only able to trace Jack's whereabouts as far as East Berlin. Thanks to the Cold War it was impossible to get any more information from behind the Iron Curtain.

I considered writing the KGB, then thought better of it, realizing a letter from a citizen of the USSR's archrival could only get Jack in worse trouble than might already have found him. I pictured him in the equivalent of a Soviet gulag (the penal camp system having been officially dismantled by 1960), pushing a wheelbarrow like the one I'd seen him push in the woods behind Fern Cottage, but much steeper, with no trees anywhere, just piles of mud and rock, one of an army of exhausted men, digging and hauling, driving pickaxes into the frozen earth, freezing, sweating, and starving to death in a Sisyphean Soviet moonscape.

Or maybe not: maybe Jack had found happiness. He was alive and well. He lived in a cozy neat apartment, had a good job. He'd met someone—a man, a woman, whatever—had fallen in love. Maybe he'd had, or adopted, a child—or two, or three. He could have been anywhere, on a Greek Island, living on the French or the Italian Riviera. I liked to think of him swimming every day in a lake, river, or a pool—or in a sea, the Baltic, the Aegean, the Mediterranean (though had it been up to me, it would have been a lake).

Assuming that he was alive somewhere, did Jack Thomas ever think about me? If he thought about me, did he think well of me? Or did he resent me for getting him caught and delivering him to whatever fate was his? Did he hate my guts?

As the years went by, when I remembered Jack at all, it was like remembering a dream. Our time together seemed that unreal to me. It was too happy to be real. And too sad.

Then, six years ago, something happened that convinced me that the dream had been real after all. My son was born with a condition called polycystic kidney disease. He inherited it from his mother, who had inherited it from her father, who died of it. Seven years ago, Gordon lost the second of his kidneys to it. That he's alive today I owe to POW # 81G-9385, aka Jack Thomas, the Man in Blue.

We were broke, our health insurance maxed out, desperate to come up with the money for Gordon's kidney transplant. Already I was working two jobs, moonlighting as a carpet steamer. Then, one night, I remembered the book Jack had given me, the old one about swimming. The next morning I phoned a bunch of antiquarian book dealers. Though several expressed interest, they all insisted on examining the item in person.

On a rainy Saturday, with the book wrapped in brown paper riding next to me in the passenger seat of my Honda Civic, I made the eight-and-a-half-hour journey to Asheville, North Carolina, in the Blue Ridge Mountains.

The used bookstore reminded me of the one Jack had described in the Adirondacks, a barn with a stone foundation. The sign out front said, *Whitaker's Antiquarian Book Barn.*

The antiquarian bookseller was a woman in her seventies, with wire glasses, a small nose, and short-cropped silver hair. Before examining the specimen she pulled on a pair of sheer white gloves. So slowly did she flip through the book's pages I felt myself aging in the process. Finished, she took off her glasses (they left angry red hollows on the sides of her nose), looked up at me, and said in a faint Irish brogue:

"I can do one of two things, Mr.— I beg your pardon. What is your surname?"

"Napoli."

"Mr. Napoli. I can give you thirty percent of the appraised price, or I can broker the sale for you, in which case I'll take a thirty percent commission."

"Thirty percent of what?"

"Of the final sale price minus the house's commission, which will be twenty percent. That's if we go with Swann."

"Swann?"

"The auction house in New York."

"I see," I said, nodding.

With her glasses back on, the woman looked at me as if I

were a book she'd been asked to appraise. After a moment she said:

"You don't know much about this business, do you?"

How had she arrived at that conclusion?

"Mr. Napoli, I'm a businessperson. Like most business people, my first priority is to look out for myself. In any business, you'll find various levels of—" she paused "—of scrupulosity. I'm afraid this is no less true of the antiquarian book trade, where often values aren't readily known or apparent. Which is to say that occasionally—not often, but occasionally—even a relatively honest dealer like myself is tempted to take advantage of someone. This is one of those occasions." Her eyes narrowed to slits under her bifocals. "Mr. Napoli, have you any idea how much this little book that you've brought me is worth?"

"I know it's worth something," I said.

"It is the first book in English about swimming, one of only three copies known to exist in the world. The plates are hand-colored woodcuts. One of the other copies is housed in the Beinecke Rare Book & Manuscript Library at Yale University, the other in the Rare Books Division of the National Library of Australia. At auction this book should fetch no less than thirty thousand dollars."

It fetched thirty-five thousand dollars from a collector in Lisbon, leaving me twenty-eight thousand dollars after commissions and taxes, roughly the cost of a kidney transplant.

Though he couldn't save one Gordon, Jack saved another.

Epilogue:

Cape Canaveral, Florida, 2020

My wife and I live in the River Palms RV and Mobile Home Park. Our home: a so-called deluxe doublewide, with vinyl shutters, a fiberglass deck, and a broken Jacuzzi. Two lemon trees, five barrel cacti, and a century plant grow in what we are pleased to think of as our yard.

We live on the barrier island called Cape Canaveral, between the Banana River and the Atlantic Ocean, fifteen miles south of the Kennedy Space Center. Yes, I worked for NASA. No, I am not and have never been an astronaut. I was a "fuel technologies specialist": I drove fat green tanker trucks filled with liquid nitrogen for the space shuttle. Which, like me, is now retired.

It is August. During the past six months Bernie and I have hardly seen another human soul. We have our groceries and other necessities delivered. Though Governor DeSantis recently re-opened restaurants, bars, and other businesses, we don't partake.

But we still go clamming and crabbing. When the breakers are low I don my bright yellow swim cap and goggles and take to the open water. And I walk. Seven days a week, mornings, Mr. McDog and I walk each other up and down the Space Coast.

Immediately after McDog and I found the Mysterious Object that had washed onto the shore, I phoned my former employers. They dispatched a team of experts, wearing face masks and carrying Geiger counters, to investigate. But even NASA's crack ufologists had no idea what the thing was. Two days later a storm blew the thing out to sea.

When I'd asked him if he believed in God, Jack answered: "Some people embrace the god of things unknown and unknowable. I embrace things unknown and unknowable." So much I'll never know about Jack Thomas, so many questions I'll never have answers for. *Why insist on answers when the questions are so beautiful?* I remember Jack's love of water, its ambiguous, unpredictable, enigmatic nature, how its identity is defined by circumstances. Like water, Jack could never stand still for very long; he had to keep moving or turn into a bog and die.

That Mysterious Object that washed up on that Florida beach and its identical twin that turned up on Bum's Trail one bright sunny May morning in 1963? I think I know what they were, now. They're the Thing Unknown and Unknowable, the thing that frightens and intrigues us, that fills us with a sense of awe and wonder, that makes us ask: *Who are we? Where did we come from? What are we doing here?*—the thing that reminds us of how small and clueless we are, and at the same time how lucky to be alive in the presence of so great a mystery.

Call it God, if you like.

Two days ago I returned here, to Connecticut, where my mother, now ninety-three, still lives. Thirty years ago she quit smoking. Apart from her Type-2 diabetes and partial blindness owing to macular degeneration she's doing well.

Though she no longer drinks or suffers migraines, Mom still likes to dance. Nor has she lost her taste for nuptials. Two years after Walter Waple died, she married husband #3, Lloyd Stevens, the optometrist for whom she had worked for years. Together they bought a house on Lake Candlewood, where they lived until Lloyd's Parkinsonism forced my mother to put him into a nursing home.

Now my mother has sold the lake house and will be moving to a condominium in a retirement village in Newbury, next to Silver Hills State Hospital. Thanks to President Reagan and deinstitutionalization, most of that hospital's buildings are boarded up; only a few dozen patients are still in residence there. Coincidentally or by design it and the retirement community next door share the same brick Georgian architecture, making me wonder if retirement and insanity have other things in common.

For the past week I've been helping my mother sort through her worldly possessions, deciding what to keep and what to throw out, debating the value of threadbare rugs, stained linen tablecloths, frayed tartans, a torn hassock, and countless stacks of *Good Housekeeping* and *Prevention* magazine. On the verge of committing myself to the institution next door to her future home, the other day I got in my rental car and took a drive.

I drove to Hattertown, passing shopping centers and developments where, fifty years ago, woods, fields, and swamps flourished. A year after the terrible Flood of '64, authorities had the Brim River incarcerated between concrete walls. As for Hattertown itself, it survived the flood only to confront a worse disaster: the opening of the Hat City Mall, Baxter Dalton's brainchild, to the decimation of downtown businesses. From that debacle my hometown arose yet again as a quaint cluster of antique shops, vintage clothing boutiques, used bookstores, and cafés, most of them closed now due to the pandemic, many possibly for good.

As for the hat factories, the last of them—the Caxton-Dumont Hat Works—was demolished in July of 1969, the same week Neil Armstrong walked on the moon. A Safeway occupies its site. What was once Waple & Son Hats is now a Verizon store. Next door to it is a Starbucks with a sign on the door requiring all patrons, Republicans and Democrats alike, to wear face masks.

Having toured the town, I drove to the former Dalton estate, a section of which is now Dalton State Park.

The Thing in the Woods has vanished completely along with the abandoned mica mine. Apart from the land that was given to the state, the woods themselves are mostly gone now, too, replaced by a twenty-four-acre condominium complex named—with no intended irony—"Barclay Woods." The gravel road that once led to Fern Cottage has been paved over. It now leads to the parking lot for the park, one presided over by a recently commissioned statue of Barclay Moses Dalton, this one of him plugging a hole in his boot with a scrap of rabbit fur. That's where I parked.

Mid-afternoon, the temperature in the mid-nineties. I stand before what used to be Fern Cottage. Where it stood a patch of ostrich ferns grows. Carrying my Speedo and a towel, I wade through the ferns, their jagged fronds stroking my thighs. In the midst of that choppy green lake, I lie on my back looking up at the sky, at clouds sailing by, remembering, thinking:

The deepest water you'll ever drown in is yourself.

No, I never made it to the moon. I never touched the stars. I never partook of anything of the infinite.

Or did I?

The following books informed my research into German POWs in the U.S. during WWII: *Nazi Prisoners of War in America*, by Arnold Krammer, *Stalag Wisconsin: Inside WWII Prisoner of War Camps*, by Betty Cowley, *Stark Decency: German Prisoners of War in a New England Village*, by Allen V. Koop, *Nebraska POW Camps: A History of WWII Prisoners in the Heartland*, by Melissa Amateis Marsh, *The Enemy Among Us: POWs in Missouri During WWII*, by David Winston Fiedler. I am particularly indebted to *Hitler's Last Soldier in America*, by Georg Gaertner, the last escaped German POW to be captured. Gaertner surrendered to authorities in 1985 after forty years in hiding.